I'LL BE MARRIED FOR CHRISTMAS

CLAIRE CAIN

Cover design by Jess Mastorakos - Jess@jessmastorakos.com

EBOOK: 978-1-954005-46-4

PRINT: 978-1-954005-48-8

To those brave enough to make a change.

And to the NSYNC Home for Christmas album, without which we would tragically never have been blessed with confusingly creepy and delightful "Under My Tree."

M.O.M NETWORK

Mothers Of Military Network Message board:

JusticeLVR: They're finally meeting to discuss everything today! Ah! This is it, ladies!

SCLDG: Are you sure she's right for him? You said she's leaving her profession. Doesn't this indicate some amount of... shall we say *inconstancy*?

Vic: No, @SCLDG, we shouldn't say that. It's not a word anyone says unless they're silver-spoon-fed ivy league fancy pants. So no.

CoolyKay: She's only double-checking. I think it's nice. @JusticeLVR seems pretty darn certain, though.

JusticeLVR: I've known this young woman all my life. The fact that I found out from her mother two weeks ago she was both out of a job *and* house was too perfect. Sounds terrible but you know what I mean. I used to dream of this.

Vic: Yes.

CoolyKay: Of course.

SCLDG: Naturally.

CoolyKay: And he's willingly showing up to this meeting? He's agreed to the marriage?

Vic: @JusticeLVR? Did he agree?

JusticeLVR: I wouldn't say he has the full scope of understanding just yet. But it'll be fine. My son won't stand by and let a woman falter. And @SCLDG arranged things to put a little pressure on him from the military side, which I know has helped.

Vic: I don't think the military academy imagined their Moms of the Military group for moms of cadets while they're in college would end up becoming a message board of old biddies trying to get their sons married off decades later.

SCLDG: Offensive. I've never been nor shall I ever be an *old biddy*.

CoolyKay: The military academy wants our soldiers to succeed. They know sometimes parents step in.

JusticeLVR: Exactly. There is no love fiercer than a mother's... except that of a mother whose child has joined the Army. *Eye roll emoji*

Vic: Careful now. They'll get stuck like that.

CHAPTER ONE

Grace

Here I am at a coffee shop in Alexandria, Virginia, sitting at a table, waiting for a man who is now a veritable stranger and who also happens to be my fiancé.

Okay, fine. Let's back up a tick.

Long story short, I'm getting married. To my childhood neighbor and sometimes protector against bullies. To a man who's seen me at all stages of life, including the bucktoothed pre-braces me, the brutal middle school years, and more than once when I had a crush on him and he was completely clueless.

As I was saying...

I've only seen official military photos of grown-up JJ—Justin, sorry. I grew up calling him JJ, though I guess "JJ Justice" doesn't sound all that professional. Maybe neither does Justin Justice, but the poor man has been saddled with this curse by his own parents, so what can I do? Call him by his given name, I guess.

Also side note, I've always fantasized that his middle name starts with J too, but they wouldn't have done that to him, would they? No. *No.* His parents are lovely people.

So anyway, those photos—his official Army ones? They're... severe. No smiles. Very specific bearing in those hazel eyes. Shaved face and stern jaw and generally, completely... well, completely, devastatingly hot. Like, light-my-pants-on-fire hot. I'm not really into the clean-cut war-hero type—I know, do I even have a pulse?—and even then, I find myself... not entirely unhappy to be getting hitched to Lieutenant Colonel Justice.

Does his name sound like a superhero alias? *Yes.* Am I entirely too broken to be an adorable superhero love interest? *Sadly, also yes.*

Did I mention it's a fake marriage? No? *Well, details.*

The circumstances leading to my willingness to enter into such a loveless alliance may indeed be somewhat distressing, but I've decided to accept the situation. I've spent years—yes, multiple years—wishing things were different. Wishing *I* was different. But I'm me, a little pile of ash with only a lone tendril of smoke curling above it to show just how recently I burned up to a crumbly crisp.

I've extended myself so far beyond what I have to give that I'm just now coming up for air. Scratch that—I'm just now *trying* to breathe, and it still feels like my lungs are brand new.

Lieutenant Colonel Justice will likely not be impressed by how my lifeless brown hair hangs around my face and shoulders in need of a cut, or the way my nails haven't been anything more than scrubbed clean and trimmed short in years. Lieutenant Colonel Justice will see the miserable heap of exhaustion and dead ends sitting across from him, but maybe, just maybe, he'll see the potential.

"Holly Jolly Christmas" earworms its way into my head as I tear at the edges of the napkin under my coffee mug and wonder if I have time to write in my journal for a minute. Maybe I can tune out the Christmas music, which I'm already sick of even though it's only mid-November. Probably not. At least it's not Mariah Carey gifting me a splitting headache blaring about all she wants for Christmas as it so happens in every single mall in London come October. He's not late yet, but Justice better not stand me up.

Aaaaand yes. We can circle back to Justin's last name: Justice. So whatever his rank, he then is *Insert Rank Here* Justice. Right now, he's a lieutenant colonel, and as his mother explained to me, when one says the rank aloud, one should skip the lieutenant part.

As of course one does.

This might not sound important, but actually, it's precisely the information I need. We're getting married, and part of the deal is to be Justin's date to all of his official functions. Apparently, being a lawyer in the Army stationed in Washington, D. C. means he does a lot of social stuff at Christmas, and I'm now going to be his plus one.

Am I nervous? Glad you asked.

I'm pretty low-key. I like to go with the flow—barring the burning dumpster fire that is my career path, of course. In other aspects of life, though, I don't mind seeing how things turn out.

I haven't been nervous about a date or meeting a guy in... well, like most things in my life, in years. So I don't really even remember if I get nervous for dates. Not that this is one, but it's the closest scenario available for comparison. Professionally, I don't get nervous for interviews, and that's because as an experienced registered nurse, I'm in demand. Here in the US, back in the UK where I just spent a couple of years, and anywhere I care to roam. The shame is, I can't summon any enthusiasm for my career since, at least in my experience, summoning anything from a pile of ash is quite impossible. Well, maybe not if you have a magic wand handy. Sadly, I'm fresh out.

And yet, I'm sitting here realizing I'm cotton ball-in-mouth-style, *did I even put on deodorant?* level nervous today.

Because here's the thing. I tried to make a connection. His mom basically brokered this whole situation based off some magical only-child spellcasting she did, and I'm in a position to say yes. Or maybe the better way to say it is, I'm in no position *not* to and highly incentivized by the opportunity and the reality that it meets a bunch of needs I can't see my way into meeting for myself anytime soon. A roof over my head, a place where I can seek shelter and safety, an environment conducive to rebuilding myself—how did it get so bad? Great question and I'd love to tell you, but for now, back to this deal-brokering with Mrs. Justice.

So, when I texted Justin to break the ice after not seeing or speaking to him in at least a decade, it went... differently than I expected.

Silly me, being all foolish hope. You'd think I'd learn, but no. I reminded myself like a new mantra: I'll be getting a relocation out of this, saving myself from homelessness and launching a fresh start without my former life haunting me, and a chance to... help.

In reality, I need this. But because I hate my reality—the fact that I've burned out as a nurse so hard in the last few years that the thought of putting on scrubs makes me nauseated just thinking about it—I have to focus on the helping. I am, by nature, a helper. Yet I could literally no longer stomach doing the thing I've always done to help. So helping Justin, doing something that yes, gets me what I need, and also helps him?

That's the real reason I said yes.

So, once I agreed, I shot off a text to the number Marcy Justice had given me.

Me: *Hi Justin. This is Grace. Just wanted to connect before we meet up next week. I'm really glad we're doing this. I'd love to catch up.*

I sounded all kinds of nonchalant, primarily because I curated those last three sentences to within inches of my sanity—not much of a feat considering my current state. Still, I waited until, hours later, he responded.

Justin: *Hello, Grace. Thank you for contacting me. I look forward to talking.*

And that was it. Just that. I'd been kind of stunned into not knowing how to respond, so I wussed out and simply sent, "*See you soon.*"

I had a whole list of questions for him, but his formal response had thrown me. It felt a little bit like he'd responded to a request for an interview or a professional networking event instead of my softball text suggesting we get to know each other a bit before getting hitched.

It also cleared up a bit of the confusion on the whole him-not-being-married thing because, frankly, his texting skills were lacking. If you couldn't make a decent impression when you had time and space to think through your response, what hope did a woman have in person? Granted, he's handsome, though he's also striking me as severely... well, severe. Serious.

AKA a super fun guy to get fake married to.

It makes more and more sense why his mom reached

out to me rather than him. Would I have considered this whole mess if I'd been met with the brick wall of communication that was Lieutenant Colonel Justin Justice?

Honestly? Hard to say. Because I do know him... or I did. And he was sweet. Nice. *Kind.* Though it all seems to be missing now.

And the whole discussion would've taken a lot of words which he, thus far, seems rather reluctant to share with me.

No such luck on the ice-breaking front in the end, obviously enough, and now a week later, here I sit waiting to see him in person with no more information than I had a couple weeks ago when we made everything official.

Well, okay, we aren't actually married yet. It'll happen soon, from what I'm told. And while I appreciate the plan to get to know each other in person, it feels a little old-timey, doesn't it? I mean, these days, with online dating, I usually have a solid sense of a man, at least who he presents himself to be, before I ever swipe on his profile.

Or I did in my past life, where I wasn't too exhausted and browbeaten to even consider attempting to go out with someone.

Fine. I'm going for honesty with myself, so maybe I should admit I have never actually swiped on someone. I signed up one celebratory weekend years ago at a friend's urging, though I never managed to commit enough to browse, let alone swipe.

Anyway, with Justin, I have no idea who he is. I'm six years younger and my impressions of him way back when, beyond thinking he was simultaneously dreamy and nerdy, are fairly limited. He disappeared from town, and aside from one fateful Christmas when he came back to visit his family and I was borderline awestruck by the sight of him in uniform but only seventeen and entirely unable to summon the guts to talk to him, I don't know the man.

I read the bio his mom gave me—yes, his professional, official military bio. He has more than one bronze star, which sounds like a big deal, and a few more medals I figure probably mean something, and has been in a lot of different military units and has a lot of fancy degrees. The man is highly educated, super smart, very successful... I don't get it.

It's got to be his communication skills. He never was a real chatty fellow, but I was younger and I kind of loved that he was shy. Now the picture might just be coming into focus, and said focus is—

"Grace? I apologize for being late."

The deep timbre of his voice shakes me from my thoughts, and I glance up to find a ridiculously handsome man in a crisp gray suit, white shirt, and black tie standing next to the table, looking at me.

A thrill races through me as I stand. "Hi, Justin. Great to see—"

My words cut off because while I go in hard and fast for a hug, he extends an arm and ends up lightly punching me when his long fingers get forced into a fist by my over-eager move launching his hand straight into my diaphragm.

"I'm so sorry." He takes me by the shoulders. Concerned eyes dip to mine, then he releases me when I offer a tight smile.

"No problem, not your fault," I scrape out, sucking in a full breath.

"I was going for a handshake," he explains, his voice sounding completely dismayed and like I might actually believe he meant to punch me in the stomach as a greeting.

"And I was aiming for a hug. Sorry." Cue the blush because my whole approach is clearly too familiar.

"It's fine. My fault entirely."

"No, no." I shake my head, furiously wondering how we've gotten off to *this* bad of a start. What does that spell for us, for our future? "Do you want to sit?"

He nods, then slips into the wooden seat across from me and swallows. "I'm truly so sorry."

I sigh, wishing I had a little more circumspection in my bones since if I did, I wouldn't have tried to hug a man I hadn't seen in a decade. Call it a truly odd nervous tic that has never before manifested until this moment.

"Seriously, it's fine. I'm fine, see?" I gesture to myself in a weirdly timed *ta-da!* motion.

His eyes follow the movement, slipping down over my T-shirt, then bouncing back to meet my gaze again with a stark blink. "Okay."

Erm. Okay. "So."

He blinks back at me, a stillness to him that makes me twisty. My knee bounces under the table as I will him to say something. Anything.

Nope. He's silent, and the holly jolliness of Christmas seems wildly aggressive through the speakers all of a sudden. I want to run home and snuggle up on the couch with some cocoa and a Christmas movie and be far away from this man I used to know.

Then I remember I have no home, part of why I'm here. All stops on the fun journey I've taken to get to this increasingly rocky rock bottom.

So. Onward. "We're doing this? You're up for it?"

I don't know why I frame it as a question for him, like he isn't the one who needs me in this whole scenario, but I do. Granted, I need a place to live and the sooner the better, but worst case, I could find a studio or rent a room or... something. Airbnb could come to the rescue temporarily, maybe.

Not ideal, though. This is preferable, even if unconventional.

Justin blinks again and does actually speak this time. "I am. It should be fine."

Fine. Fair enough, though part of me also shouts, "Don't get too excited, man, you might pull something!" because his generally closed-up, unreadable black hole of energy thing he's got going on is throwing me. I know it's not a love connection, but could he act any more blasé? He's not picking out hand soap at the grocery store. This is a *marriage.*

"Good. And... your mom talked you through what I'll need?"

I've been over the details with her since she'd set all of this up, but I want to confirm I'll have my own room. He seems about as likely to make a move on me as he does to summon the Iron Man suit and shoot off into space, but one never knows. The reality here is that I don't know Justin, and though I assume he hasn't turned into a total weirdo who would decide this fake marriage was an excuse to—

"Yes, I believe she did. Everything should be in order."

"Great. And then, day to day, you'll be at work and I'll..."

His brows notch low like I've spoken in Elvish or Groot and when he speaks, it's slowly, like I'm new to the English language and he thinks slowing down will help me translate.

"Presumably, if you get the job, you'll also be at work."

Wait, what? I rear back a touch. If I get *the job*? Marcy made it abundantly clear I'll be doing Justin, and therefore her, a favor—a massive one. Yes, I'll get an apartment in a fantastic Alexandria neighborhood for no rent out of the bargain, but *if you get the job* sure sounds like this is some kind of interview. With numerous candidates lined up. No wonder he's acting so calm—for him, I'm on a shelf and he's picking out his discount bride.

I'm here because there's been no haggling. His mom set everything up, gave me the answer to my own problem in the form of a solution for her son's. And *that* is the appeal here. I recognize the delicately lacy piece of wool I'm pulling over my own eyes on this, though focusing on helping Justin is what makes this even remotely palatable.

"Sorry, *if?* I sort of thought it was decided." Did I completely misunderstand everything Marcy said?

Impossibly, that brow drops lower, his face such a stern, somber thing, I want to pinch his cheek, though I would never.

"If you want the job, you'll have to apply and interview like anyone else, Grace. I can get you the introduction, provide the contact information, but they won't hire you based on my recommendation alone. Add to it, I hardly know you and wouldn't feel right about something like that anyway, so the usual process will need to take place."

A few thoughts fire off as he speaks, but the only thing that comes out of my mouth is, "The usual process?"

Justin's ice-cold demeanor shifts with the slightest edge to his expression. It's irritation, and I feel oddly triumphant at eliciting *something* from him, even if his words and that condescending tone are making me want to kick his shins under the table. Right now, he sounds as unsufferable as Tony Stark himself. Honestly, I can get behind Ironman, but this guy?

No.

Apparently, being around my childhood neighbor turns me back into a child. Super.

"Yes. The usual process. Application. Interview. Etcetera."

It's the way he pedantically annunciates *etcetera* that pushes me from polite and maybe a little overeager to offended and more than a little ticked off. "Oh. *Oh*. It must be the *etcetera* I wasn't getting."

His expression changeth not.

I continue. "Because see, here I was thinking I'm doing you a bit of a favor by agreeing to marry you and take care of this pesky problem of singlehood you seem to be having, but now I see I need to *apply* and *interview* and *etcetera*. Silly me! Why didn't I realize there was due process for things like a fake marriage? I—"

"Wait, wait. You—"

Fed up, I wave him off. He's got a new look now, at least. Something like fish-out-of-water—his lips open a touch and his wide hazel eyes make him seem shocked to find I can actually speak for myself. I have no interest in analyzing the utter surprise radiating off him, so I shoot to my feet and plow ahead.

"You know what? No. I'm good here. I'm really not a snap-judgment kind of person, but I'm realizing maybe I should be. I reached out last week, and I got this formal, weird response. It's all adding up now, though, because you were just as sterile then. And idiot me, I thought it felt like you were responding to a work colleague, not the woman your own mother has rustled up to hit the courthouse with you and move into your place, so you seem less like an overworked robot."

He blinks and his mouth drops open for a beat before his hand shoots out and grips my wrist. "Marriage?"

Impatience coils through me, a spring about to jack-in-the-box into his face. But instead of standing here feeling like the world's biggest idiot, I've got things to deal with. An apartment to find. And I'm done.

"Justin, I don't know what your deal is, but you should probably have a chat with mommy dearest since y'all are on different pages. You used to be a nice guy. I don't understand why you'd meet me here or why she'd—whatever. Best of luck to you on your journey to the next promotion or... wherever you're heading."

I yank my arm away from him, and he drops it at the same time, evidently only just now realizing he was touching me.

"Grace, will you please wait?" he asks, standing. A garland of snowflakes is dipping low enough to brush his stupid-tall head.

I'm already blazing a trail out of this little coffee shop, already on the sidewalk and wishing I'd mastered parallel parking so my car would be right here instead of in a lot around the corner. Footsteps pat-pat behind me, and it's only when Justin's winded voice reaches me that I stop.

Well, maybe it's the words, too.

Because they're stop-worthy.

He repeats himself as I turn around.

"I'm sorry, Grace, but I have no idea what you're talking about."

CHAPTER TWO

Justin

My mother's hug is warm and familiar, as is the little gleam in her eye telling me she's up to something.

As if I didn't already know that.

"Why have you been lying to me, Mom?"

Her brows arch high before they plummet into a perturbed frown. "I never lie to my children."

I sigh, the sensation of my very cells aging more by the minute gripping me. "I'm your only child."

One shoulder lifts a fraction of an inch. "Well, there you have it. I don't lie to you."

I'm not giving in on this one. "You and I are both fully aware that omitting massive swaths of information is a form of lying."

"I object. Falsifying evidence."

"That's not—*Mom*."

Her twinkly little grin has likely charmed my father a

thousand times, but it won't work on me. Neither will her attempt to distract me by using wildly irrelevant legal terms in completely erroneous contexts.

"What's all this about? Just tell me since you're bound and determined."

She waves a hand, then dumps a half cup of pumpkin spice creamer into her coffee. She hasn't shifted to peppermint mocha, which is how I know it's not *actually* Christmas and we've yet to hit Thanksgiving, though the décor around this town says differently.

My patience has been slowly unraveling since Grace's "Maybe you should chat with your mom and figure it out" two hours ago.

I gawped at her like a dunce for a few seconds before she huffed out an irritated, "Call me if you ever do that." Then my mind ran through the entire encounter over and over, on repeat, as I messaged my mom to find out if she was home, then drove the two hours to her house in my childhood hometown, and here we are.

I level her with a look that tells her I'm not laughing, and she sobers a touch.

"I just saw Grace Murphy."

Her brows rise high again, and she sticks out her chin a bit. "Did you?"

"You know I did. You set it up. But what I thought was me putting her in touch with a State Department contact for a possible job was definitely *not* what she had been told."

Her lips pinch. "Well. Sounds like a miscommunication to me. Nothing another meeting can't patch up in a jiff."

I pull on every patience-generating habit I've ever developed and inhale slowly. Calmly. I may not feel calm at all, though having been to war a handful of times, I can handle my mother's schemes.

I can.

I can do this becomes an internal mantra as I speak. "I'm attempting to do that now, as it seems the primary miscommunication is not between Grace and me, but rather between me and you. Or possibly you and Grace, and I suspect—"

"Oh, settle yourself, JJ. I knew you wouldn't go if I told you the whole situation, although I hoped you'd at least have some discussion prior to meeting or stick around long enough to break the ice and get this sorted out so you can benefit from it."

My jaw clenches. I ratchet it open to squeeze out a few words. "Benefit from *what?* Please spell it out so I don't end up believing you've created as big of a mess as I'm afraid you have."

Her nostrils flare slightly, and this tells me I've toed the line and might be about to cross it. I don't want to do this. I love and respect my mother. But I've also been on one too many accidental setups thanks to her sneaky machinations, and I'm furious with myself for not guessing that meeting with Grace was one of them.

That said, Grace is a family friend. I may not have seen her in years, but Mom has lived right next to her parents all this time and therefore kept up with her in some ways. I'll always have a soft spot for the little girl the kids in the neighborhood used to pester mercilessly. She was always sweet and tenderhearted.

She's certainly grown a backbone since then. And *wow*, has she grown into a beautiful woman. But that doesn't really matter, does it?

"You were just telling us how you're being pressured.

How there's a stigma about single men at this rank and how your boss has hinted you'd be a shoo-in for Colonel if you were married. How you end up working all the longer hours and taking the crap jobs because you don't have a family, and everyone knows it. How many holiday events you have and how it'd be nice to take someone you can trust."

A familiar cocktail of shame and embarrassment hits and sours my stomach. I work to avoid those feelings quite persistently, and I'm not going to sink into them now, especially since I know she doesn't mean to dredge up anything other than my acquiescence to her plan. "I did tell you that. So your solution was to... hire Grace to be my date?"

For some reason, I start here, even though the word Grace threw at me won't stop slicing through my head, a piping hot brick of fruit cake burning through snow. *Marriage.*

Mom squints.

I cringe. Because I know it's worse.

"Not *hire* her, per se. And not date, even."

"Please just tell me."

Something in my voice must say I need it laid out. She knows me well enough to know this is a stretch—whatever *this* is—and her tiptoeing around it isn't helping.

A sigh slips out as she pumps some pumpkin spice lotion into her hands—one, two. The action is so familiar, such a signal of home to me, but I'm waiting for her to spill the truth so I can hardly enjoy it.

"I happened to learn Grace is going to be out of her home at short notice. In a matter of days. She's back from an overseas humanitarian something or other and had planned to live with her parents until she gets settled, but they've sold their house. It's fabulous, actually. The sweet Murphys are off on an around-the-world cruise! Did I tell you this? They're starting in—"

"Mother. Please."

Her lips thin and she huffs. "The girl is down on her luck with nowhere to go. I would've gladly offered her your room to put a roof over her head, but she needs to find a job, and the hospital is the only option around here. The town's sleepy at best, and she can't start over here."

She's running away with her words again. And she was going to give Grace *my* room? "Mom..."

She shrugs. "Anyway, I was thinking about how kind Grace is, how sweet she's always been. We should help her. *You* could, and I just thought..."

My chest squeezes, but I grit my teeth against the cloying sensation. "You thought she could rescue me."

Her mouth drops open, and she gapes for a moment before rushing me, arms outstretched and unavoidable. Her hug comes with impact and the scent of pumpkin spice and coffee, and her words rush out.

"No. You don't need rescuing."

She clutches me with the ferocity she so often embodies, and I hug her back, welcoming the comfort.

"It's okay if you think so, Mom. I know this isn't..." I clear my throat, irritated to find myself so tender out of nowhere. "It's not what you imagined for me."

Her embrace tightens again, the ratchet straps of her arms cinching me down, closer, tucking me into her motherly affection and attempting to shelter me from the reality neither of us can ignore. Despite my being a man of forty years, I think there's still a part of her that wants to tuck me back inside, to swaddle me up and hold all the bad, hard things at bay.

I'm tired enough that the ridiculous notion almost sounds nice.

Except no, it does not. I'm a grown man, and it's time my beloved mother respects it.

However, this is a reality I'm forced to confront more and more often lately. In a room full of ten similarly ranked officers, I'll be the only one who hasn't at least been married once. Poor old JJ hasn't even made the attempt.

And the one time I thought I knew what I wanted? Well. Everyone got their hopes up, only to find out how naïve they were. She refused my proposal because I was already married to my job, according to her, and she wasn't going to be the other woman in my life.

I turned forty last year. I'm maneuvering up the ladder, doing my time and gaining rank in the Army, and I'll be able to retire with full benefits after twenty years in, which is coming right up. Until recently, I hadn't thought about what else I might do, because why would I leave when I'm thriving? If I did, I'd still practice law, just not for the military.

I've always assumed I'd stay in longer than twenty, though. Moving around can be exciting, and I don't mind someone else calling the shots on where I land, because I know the system. I like succeeding, like seeing my success measured by years, by job title, by rank. I'm the straight A student who enjoys studying and taking tests.

And I haven't minded the nose-to-the-grindstone life. What else would I be doing? What would I even do if I did retire soon? If I don't have a chance to keep going in the Army, to progress and promote, then what?

That's where the dangling carrot of retirement turns into a very large stick.

Because the truth is, the thing that stings? I always imagined retiring with a partner. I assumed I'd be factoring in how my kids were doing and what my wife thought. I'm not sure when I shifted from someone who held out hope to someone who accepted there is none and decided the job mattered more—that being "married" to work was enough. Maybe before I ever realized the change had taken place.

And looking at my mom's shining eyes and shaking head, I know she and Dad had thought I'd be someone else, too. They'd dreamed of being grandparents, and here I stand, childless, single, with no prospects. It'd be one thing if I didn't want all of it, even if I could fully admit it to myself, but...

"It's not that I thought she could help you. I thought you, my gallant, handsome, incredible son, might be able to help her. Provide her a roof and a safe place to land. I mean, if she'd ended up here, she would've been in your room. It's just a case of *a* room in your fancy apartment, for a little while, until she gets back on her feet."

She cups my cheeks, shakes her head again like she can't quite handle how much she loves me, how maybe that love breaks her heart a little right now, but she wouldn't trade it.

An alien grunt-sigh combo trips out of me, and I pat her hand before she releases me. "Good recovery, Mom. But marriage? Why wouldn't we just date? And what do you mean about her living situation? Can't she just find a place to rent?"

She heaves a giant sigh. "I suppose. But there are other things to factor in. She is struggling a bit after her time away. And you—" She dips her chin. "It's not that you need saving, but you do need someone. Not to fix *you*, son, but if nothing else, to help with all these social engagements and obligations you have. To get your boss and whoever else is to blame for overworking you to see that you, too, deserve space and time and rest. And mark my words, you should have those things whether single or married or whatever else, but I wonder if maybe being a newlywed might... give you some breathing room."

I nod, trying to sift through the mêlée of reactions running wild in me.

"I know you meant well. I'm just—I don't think it's right." Or legal. Or ethical. Or beneficial. Or possible, frankly. Because after this morning, I doubt Grace wants anything to do with me.

Not that I want her to want this. It's a fanciful idea straight from Marcy Justice's mind and absolutely taken from a Hallmark movie she likely started binging after Halloween, and it's not something that can actually happen in reality. Nor should it.

People don't get married to solve a problem unless they're in a book or movie. This thought repeatedly plays through my mind as I reassure my mom everything is fine, I'll be talking to Grace, then I make my exit.

In the silence of my car, I send the woman in question a text. *"Clearly I need to apologize. Please let me know if you're free tonight."*

A few minutes later, she responds indicating she is. I hope she'll be able to figure something else out about her living situation, as this can't happen. I owe it to her to tell her so in person, and even if there's an uncomfortable strain of thought whispering that maybe this *would* be the solution to both of our problems, I ignore it.

I know what's right and I'm going to do it. Like I always do. Tonight.

CHAPTER THREE

Grace

I am *not* arriving early for dinner.

Honestly, I was sorely tempted to ignore Justin's text or to simply say I'm unavailable. But instead of listening to the devil on my shoulder, I agreed to meet him and hear his apology. I can tell by the fact he's asked to meet in person that this will be an apology and a letdown. And my pride won't allow me to no-show and let him think I'm sad about it.

Sure, I'm scrambling to find a housing option with even more urgency, and I really shouldn't have been banking on this wackadoo idea, though I'm getting used to living dangerously. I've never been less organized or prepared than when I returned from my years in England without recommitting to a third year like I'd planned. Why? Because I'd also told the hospital where I'd worked for eight years and had taken a three-year leave from for this specific tour with the NHS in England that no, I would not be returning.

Even though I had a free year because I'd bailed on applying for the third and final year in the UK. And even though they needed help and could've used me.

The administration was *not* amused. Neither was my old boss, or the chief of the ED, or any number of my friends still in what can often feel like actual trenches.

It's about as close to danger as I get... and right now, *right* now, it feels wildly dangerous. I have no plans, and the only decent prospect I'd lined up has fallen so far through it's likely about to penetrate the earth's core.

How did I think all this not-re-upping for a third year would work? I thought I'd have my parents backing me up. Though I have to point out, it's not their fault I'm in this ditch. They believed I was happy being a nurse, being in those trenches—and I was. Emphasis on *was*, because at first, the change of scene worked to distract me from the burnout I can now see had already started. It only worsened as time went on. Meanwhile, my parents imagined I'd double-down for a third year in England, possibly not even wanting to come back stateside again. To be honest, I'd thought so myself at some point, so I can't fault them.

Cue, then, the whole burning pile of ashes. Justin's offer had sounded like a temporary urn for that little lot, a break until I could figure out if we could revive a phoenix from all this raw material. Like I said, the only decent prospect out there—

Oh, wait, there he is, sitting with such rigid posture and a ridiculously cut jaw, he's casting his own shadows. This man would look like a movie star if his general aura wasn't so entirely void of charisma.

"You came." Justin says this as he stands a few seconds

before I reach the table, a hint of relief or surprise in the words.

Interesting. The show of human emotion hits me and makes me just a touch less annoyed with him. After all, that's been the worst part of this—feeling like I'm the only person in the room. Chatting with a handsome robot is the pits, especially when he's making you feel like you're the odd one for mentioning something he should've known about.

But that's not the point anymore, and here he is with a very human flicker of feeling on his face. Maybe he's a cyborg? Those are the ones that look like humans yet... you know what? Not important.

Instead of all that noise, I respond with what feels like the truth. "I had to."

His usual frown deepens. "Of course you didn't. You're always free to say no."

I let those words sink in and wish they were true. I'm not sure I've felt free to do anything in years, but at least I did say no to picking up right where I left off at the hospital. I did do that for myself, and it's a nice thought I could've done so tonight, even if it doesn't seem like this person is used to having anyone tell him anything other than yes. *Curious*.

"Right. I just mean I needed to know how you'd handle this. Based on this morning, I'm just along for the ride at this point."

And he can't know how true it all is—that I have so little gusto for fighting any battles right now, I'm still going to agree to this even if he's made two bad impressions in a row.

His irritation is palpable, and though I can't say whether it's with me and my honesty or the entire situation he undoubtedly doesn't want to be mixed up in, he has made no efforts to mask it.

Good to see we're both being honest, then.

"Have you had a moment to review the drink menu, or shall I give you another few minutes?" the waiter asks, hands clasped behind his back.

My dinner bud snaps out of his frowny face and raises those mercurial brows as though to ask me. Never one to turn down a cocktail when I'm having a deeply awkward dinner non-date with a man I almost fake married, I say, "An Old Fashioned, please."

The waiter nods an approving smile at me and turns to Justin.

"I'll have a Strawberry Crush, please. Thank you."

The waiter nods again and turns, disappearing in that magical fine dining way that tells me he's been trained to be neither seen nor heard until he materializes to either take or deliver an order. I let my eyes trail him so Justin doesn't see the way his drink order charms me—the way my lips curve into an unbidden smile and I feel such a lightness in my chest at this discovery. Not that I had any expectations of what he'd order, but if I had, it'd be something like Scotch neat or maybe bourbon and Coke. Something manly and traditional and obvious.

Strawberry Crush? Never saw it coming.

Justin shifts and draws my attention.

"I apologize for this morning. My mother told me you were looking for a connection at the State Department, where I happen to know someone. I thought our meeting was set so I could tell my contact about you after lightly vetting you. I had no idea about the"—his voice drops low—"marriage idea."

As the hours passed, I assumed it had to be something

in this vein. While I didn't love the interaction, in retrospect, I can't blame him for being both completely confused and shocked when I dropped the bomb on him. He was blindsided, poor handsome cyborg.

"I guess that accounts for the confusion." It's not a complete cop-out of a response.

He nods. "Certainly. And I hope I didn't offend you. I didn't mean to seem so incredulous. You are a—" He clears his throat, and his eyes flick over me like he can't stop them. "You're an objectively beautiful woman. And I'd be lucky to, well, to enter into a legally binding situation with you."

Disregarding his stumbling over admitting I'm *objectively beautiful* and absolutely ignoring the way my stomach flips without my permission at the same, I prepare to nudge this whole thing forward. I'd planned on dinner here, but maybe we could just call it at drinks.

"Here we go, folks. Are you ready to order?"

Our waiter sets my Old Fashioned down, the squatty tumbler full of amber liquid and a giant circular cube of ice. The orange garnish is twisted and almost looks like a double helix, with a cranberry held by the curl at the end in a festive little nod to the season and bringing color to what can otherwise be a fairly drab drink. Super cool.

Justin's drink is gorgeous, too, if not at all seasonal. It's a tall, skinny vessel flaring out at the top and filled with what looks like crushed ice, sliced strawberries, and crystal-clear liquid with carbonation bubbles creating little jewels of air dotting the sides of the glass. A strawberry perches on the edge and has been carved into an ornate flower with a lime peel as leaves.

Honestly, this drink feels extravagant and fancy and entirely *not* what a man whose personality seems best described as "gray" would order.

When I register the waiter is still awaiting our orders, I speak, since Justin appears to be disinclined. "Wow. These look amazing. But no, we're not quite ready."

Sorry, guy. We may not ever be.

The waiter disappears again, and Justin and I both take sips of our cocktails. I knew this was a fancy place, though I've never been since I only make it into DC every now and then. Or, I used to. Today is the first time I've been in the city since my flight landed at Dulles International last week.

I may or may not have had a mild frustration-fueled tantrum and booked it into the city to see apartments I could never afford after the madness of the morning. Then of course, Justin texted to ask about dinner, and though the petty, silly part of me wanted to force him to drive back to our small town, I was here. And once I said I was here, he suggested this place, which I'd read about, so I showed.

I've never chosen to indulge in the finer things, though that doesn't stop me from appreciating them. Including this earth-shatteringly good drink and a moment to enjoy it without rearranging every line item in my budget to compensate for it.

"Good?"

Justin's rough voice interrupts the internal rhapsodies about the oaky, perfectly balanced drink.

"It is excellent. Do you want to try?"

The brows again. They arch high like I've asked him to strip me naked, not sample a beverage.

"I don't actually drink bourbon."

"Oh, okay. Well, how's yours?"

His eyes narrow with a little tug at his mouth that makes me think he wants to smile. No dice, but he does say, "Excellent. Uh, would you like to try it?"

It's the tone, that little stumble, and the way I can tell

he's got a slight blush starting, even in the dim light. I would've said no, but those things compel me to accept. The force of this short moment is an unexpected jolt to the foggy, sludgy feeling I've been carrying around. It's something light and sweet and bubbly like the carbonation in his drink. "Sure. Thanks."

I take a small sip from the edge of the glass, the wildly surreal moment shooting heat to my own cheeks.

I'm sharing a drink with Justin Justice. I am sharing a drink with hottie nerd Justin JUSTICE!

The drink is light and refreshing, a cold zap to my senses that stops me from flaming red as the bizzarro return of my teenage inner monologue takes over.

"It's not as sweet as I expected," I say, because I need to say something.

His chin dips in confirmation, though his eyes snag on my mouth right as I lick my lips. It's the weirdest sensation because until just now, this exact second when his eyes narrow as my tongue flicks out, I'm not sure he has any idea I'm a grown woman. And no, the *objectively beautiful* comment doesn't count because it's still squarely situated in cyborg territory. It's the equivalent of saying "I'll look at you and confirm you're kind of pretty—for science!"

But now, the way his eyes jerk away and cast to the table in front of him only confirms what I caught.

He may not like or even be attracted to me, but he's *aware* of me. *Oh, hello.* And suddenly, the tween who always had a crush on her nerdy-hot neighbor is dancing a jig.

The grown woman in a very awkward situation? She just wants to drink her Old Fashioned in peace before skulking home to browse rental listings on Zillow and console herself with something happy on Netflix or settle into the new Josie Wade novel on her e-reader.

The waiter returns and instead of evading placing an order, Justin dives in, selecting an appetizer and suggesting I do the same or get dinner if I want. I'm tempted to order one of everything but promise myself when I get the finances and living situation under control, I'll be back.

I opt for an app, too, fully aware he might be about to escalate the discomfort by telling me I'm silly for ever expecting him to agree to this scheme and how unethical it is, or whatever other objection he has. Never mind that he's noticed me—it's not going to lead us anywhere. But I've also decided I'll take that in stride because he'd be right to say so, and I'm still going to enjoy my appetizer.

With our waiter gone, quiet descends between us again. I can feel the need to fill the silence coming, bubbling up uncontrollably. I will it away, knowing anything I say will likely make me look more immature and foolish.

Because here's another reality—I feel like a child. I may only be six years younger than him, solidly in my midthirties, yet I feel like a complete fool for having placed so much on my plan to live with my parents, for their decision to put themselves first for once throwing me for such a loop. Somehow, I've ignored this ugly reality—that *he'd* know about all of it, too—until right now.

Justin has likely never had to worry about money or a place to live. I cannot imagine a world in which this stalwart fellow has anything but clarity and confidence and *certainty*. Basically, everything I lack and have been sorely lacking in the recent past. Who abandons a life in the UK, then refuses to resume the one she'd left here at home even though that'd always been the plan? Not a man like Justin Justice, for sure.

"So, uh, drink still good?" I ask, because of course I stick him with something thoughtful and mysterious as my brain train runs off the tracks internally.

One side of that stern mouth might lift. Probably did—it's just indetectable to the human eye. Yes, fine, I'm reading into it all.

All of it.

Sue me.

"Yes. Yours?"

This man. He's not giving me a thing. And when someone gives you nothing, it's hard to volley back with much. So I let a meager "Well, good" slip out.

His face remains unchanged, and yet there's a sense of humor there. The knowledge it's in there somewhere sends fizz into my veins and an odd buzzing sensation up my arms, raising the small hairs a touch. I can swear it's hiding underneath the sharp cut of his jaw and the fine style of his hair. He really does have a beautiful face—it'd be too pretty if he were any less angular. This way, he's just kind of... strikingly handsome.

So. You know. Totally not distracting.

Totally not making me twitchy with nerves on top of everything.

Cause folks? Nerdy-hot Justin John Justice—let's pretend it *is* a J middle name—is just plain ol' hot now. The gangly teen, the wiry college grad... it all led to filling out his suit in a way I have to work not to appreciate too much.

But chatty the man is not, and if I don't keep us going, who will? We'll likely slip into the oblivion of a silent whirlpool and get sucked down the drain of indifference in a cool ten minutes. So, I keep this baby cranking.

"Really good."

And again with the conversational artistry because it's

normal to agree with oneself minutes after speaking in the worst, most boring form of small talk. Maybe something about how unseasonably warm it is for November? That'll slay him.

And he's still giving me an engaged presence yet nary a word unless I lasso them and haul them out against his will, apparently.

This guy must wow 'em in the courtroom.

I can't tell whether I want to huff in frustration or grin because something about this quiet between us makes me want to laugh. I've only had a sip of my drink, so it's not the alcohol. I'm not in as much of a rush to bolt out of here now that we've ordered dinner, but I want to get the ball dropping over with. I don't like the feeling that this strained conversation is ultimately leading to one place and one place only—him letting me down easy. And I don't want him to think it's a topic to be avoided. We can just cut to the chase and get it over with.

Our waiter delivers our food in the fastest turn around in the history of all restaurants, and I'm relieved to have something to do with my hands and mouth other than fidget and toss more verbal spaghetti at the wall of our conversation.

I slip a bite of the roasted root vegetable and goat cheese tart into my mouth and suppress a groan of ecstasy at the flavor, momentarily forgetting the pure work of this meal in favor of focusing on the light pastry, the perfectly balanced earthiness of the vegetables, and the buttery crust and creamy tang of the cheese. *Glorious*.

I don't realize my eyes have fallen closed until I open them and find him watching me. Heat floods in, embarrassment blooming in my chest and cheeks faster than I can swallow. I dab my napkin at my mouth, hoping I don't have a big smear of goat cheese across my face and mentally scrambling to make an excuse for myself. Something about how I love cheese and can't deny it, even in the presence of someone who gives me nothing but a blank stare.

Before I can decide how to excuse myself, Justin speaks.

"I think we should do it."

That effectively shocks the wind out of me and I cough, choking on air. *So elegant.* "It?"

He nods.

Then he says the words I never really could imagine coming from his serious, handsome face.

"I think we should get married."

CHAPTER FOUR

Justin

Grace might look a bit like I did earlier when she dropped the fake marriage bomb on me.

Her dark hair is pulled back from her face this evening, though one strand has escaped and frames it on one side. Her blue eyes are wide, and even in the low light, I can tell they'd have the power to mesmerize me if I looked closely enough. Right now, lips that are plush and far too appealing hang open, and her formerly slightly pink cheeks have drained of color. The only question is, why?

Never one to be anything less than direct, I ask. "Why do you look like that?"

She rears back a bit, another wave of surprise layering over the shock already there.

"Um."

Her lips press together and disappear, and I do not pay close attention to this. I am already too interested in those lips, and therefore I wrestle the desire, the near need to keep watch for them, into submission.

"Be honest," I prompt, wanting nothing more than to understand her.

So far, I don't. While I do spend a great deal of time observing people professionally, I haven't spent time with someone romantically in years. It's an entirely new muscle I need to develop, even if this isn't actually romantic. It's business.

Perhaps I hadn't entirely planned on this eventuality either. No small part of me had planned on telling her that while she's a lovely woman, I can't engage in this Marcy-Justice-style nonsense. Then she sat down and... something shifted. A voice in the back of my mind asked me to engage with her, to see who this woman actually is, and after a few short minutes and a shared sip of my drink, I took the bait.

She squints a little, taking my measure for the umpteenth time since we sat down. The longing to understand her hits me again, but I force myself to wait and give her time to share what she wants.

"I've been expecting you to tell me this isn't happening. Then you just said you think it should. And I'm having an—an out-of-body experience, or something."

Like so much about her, this turn of phrase catches me by surprise, and a laugh trips out. I clear my throat in a belated attempt to cover it. "That bad?"

A shaking hand rises to smooth along the vibrant arc of her right eyebrow. It must be a nervous motion, because now that she's done it again, I realize I've seen her do it at least three other times. I've also never particularly felt the need to trace someone's eyebrow, and yet here I am noticing the pads of my fingers and how stupid they feel resting on this white tablecloth when they could be put to good use.

Perhaps the Strawberry Crush is stronger than I realized, though this thought is nonsensical since I've only taken a few sips.

"Not bad. I just really didn't think you were going to go for it after this morning and everything." A furrow notches deeper between her eyes. "So in the spirit of transparency, since I think that's important if we're even talking about this, can you tell me what changed between ten this morning and now?"

Fair.

"This morning, I was blindsided, as I mentioned. Admittedly, I wouldn't have agreed to it even after I'd discussed with my mother and learned of her plan. I'd prepared to tell you it wouldn't be wise right up until..." I can't tell her all the reasons everything changed the instant I saw her walking toward the table tonight. But at least one, I can. "Until I got another gentle reminder from my boss about how statistically, my probability of advancing past a certain rank without a significant other is lower."

This being but one of the motivating factors in deciding to pursue something as ill-advised as a fake marriage would not be up for discussion.

The main reason is exactly what I've said—my promotion chances will be augmented. Fair? No. Legal? No. Reality as I know it? Based on what my borderline despicable boss has said, yes. He's a remarkably successful officer who has repeatedly promoted early and made clear he has connections on the board who will review my file. The pool is growing smaller at this point in my career, and any little thing can give them a reason to deny promotion, including something as maddening as my marital status.

Had my boss meant to suggest I find someone to marry for the sake of the job?

I highly doubt it. I can almost guarantee it isn't what he had in mind. I don't like it, but I don't like the thought of seeing an avenue that may increase my odds of early promotion and choosing not to take it even more.

So here I am.

"Your mom did mention you were getting pressured."

She says this like she's frustrated by it, and her expression makes something in me wind tight.

I ignore whatever this is because it doesn't matter. Nothing does but the ultimate goal and the reason I'm here.

"It's an odd situation. But military life does conflate the workplace with homelife. At times, this means a superior or mentor might speak to that side of your life in a way they might not if you worked in another industry."

She's still disgruntled. "It's messed up."

I clear my throat to avoid outright chuckling. "A little, yes."

"How is it only a little? That seems like crossing a line."

At this, a quiet laugh does slip out. "It's hard to explain to someone who hasn't lived this life for nearly two decades. Let's just say that being in the Army feels like a whole-life commitment, not just a job. And that's without having hauled along a wife and kids. Many of my peers move their spouse and families all over the world, sometimes with very short notice. Their spouses can't find work and are often, at best, underemployed. At least for me, it's just me."

She's looking at me with earnest blue eyes, and I can't help but feel the pathetic reality of my own words. *It's just me.*

I'm not a needy man. I'm introverted and appreciate experiences I have with myself as company. I'm not someone who has been wandering around feeling incomplete because more often than not, I'm requesting a table for one. I like working hard and focusing on advancement. I like being able to measure my efforts and see what lies ahead without messy variables like partners and children gumming things up.

And yet...

In the last few years, some of my hold-out friends, those who've been single right along with me, heads down and grinding in our jobs without establishing families, have dropped away into the partnered category. Nate Reynolds, formerly a perpetual charmer who'd seemed fairly comfortable with the title of bachelor, is now married to the love of his life and they've already started having kids. A few of the men I knew at EMU have partnered off. Wilder Saint, of all people, a man who epitomized brooding soldier and rarely bothered with complete sentences, has a wife and at least one kid now.

These thoughts might seem uncharitable, yet the truth of it sits buried underneath all these observations. Though I haven't felt incomplete, I do want more. I always have.

But I've accepted it's not more in terms of family and what we've traditionally identified as happiness. I've embraced that my *more* will be based on what I and I alone control.

"Sounds challenging. But... interesting. You must like it to have stayed in for so long." Grace spears a piece of her goat cheese tart.

I avert my eyes so I don't watch her take the bite or enjoy the way her eyes flutter shut. That's... not my business. "I do. It's been meaningful for me. And though my mother's meddling is nothing short of humiliating on one hand, I have to appreciate her problem-solving."

When I look up, she's gazing at me with an expression I can't read. "Did I say something wrong?"

She blinks and shakes her head. "No. You're good. It's good. You're a little different than my first impression and memories made you out to be so I'm just... readjusting."

There's a tinge of red in her cheeks, and I find myself leaning forward without checking the impulse. "I can imagine your first impression, but memories? What about me in your memories is so different now?"

She chokes on her drink and pats her napkin to her lips as she coughs out her recovery. "Um, well... you're chattier than I remember. You were always so quiet."

"I am still, most of the time."

I leave the rest unsaid because what good would it do to tell her I feel instantly comfortable with her in a way I don't with other people? No good. *Chatty* has never once been used to describe me, and I'm sure she knows it.

Quiet settles between us again and forks clink. I can't figure out why I'm this at ease with her other than the fact that she's familiar. Even though Grace has grown into a beautiful woman, and we haven't had a conversation in years, I've known her pretty much all my life. *Has to be it.*

"You were always kind, too. You stood up for me with those mean Nelson kids more than once. I had a little hero worship going on, honestly."

These gently spoken words reveal a lot. They acknowledge some of the history we haven't spoken of yet. They remind me of how awful I felt every time Corbin and Dayton Nelson showed off by bullying little Gracie. And then, that last part. I can't let it lie, even if it is past tense.

She doesn't know everything about me, of course. She has no idea how those words burn through me—she can't. I hope she'll hear me now.

"Not much of a hero. Don't get that confused, Grace."

CHAPTER FIVE

Grace

There's more than meets the eye to Justin Jeremiah Justice, and it's the adamance in his voice as he speaks that reels me in. I mean what I said—I worshipped him a little, thinking of him as my periodic savior. The Nelson kids had been... rough. And once they were significantly bigger than me, they got mean.

However, the tone in his voice is saying something more. He's not refuting that he saved me as a child. It's something else and it's gripping me, making me lean closer, sending my eyes over the planes of his face in an attempt to read between the lines and finding words to deny his matter-of-fact statement.

"I know you're a good man, Justin."

His gaze shutters somehow. "If we're serious about doing this, we need to hash out a few details. I can write up a contract with confidentiality clauses and parameters. Tell me what you want included."

Hello, topic change. Apparently, any more discussion of what kind of man he is has been outlawed. Fine for now, though if we're really doing this thing, we'll need to circle back to it. But I can get on board with the brass tacks since, in the end, I do need this situation nailed down so I can move out of my parents' house on time. "Okay. I—I just need my own room. I think that's all."

He blinks. It's clear from how long it takes before words emerge from him in the deep tenor I instantly like whenever I hear it that he hasn't ever even considered living arrangements or bedrooms.

"Of course."

I nod because *thank goodness* and scramble through the other questions I planned to ask this morning when I thought we were both coming into this on the same page. "I'll need your schedule."

He waits for more, so I continue, my heart beating wildly in my chest for some reason. "Your mom mentioned you had a lot of events over the holidays. That if we were doing this, we'd want to be seen together at as many of those this season as possible. How it would lend credibility before they get to the job decisions in the new year."

His jaw flexes, but he doesn't clam up. "Right. Yes. I can get the main dates to you. There will be a few that pop up, and unfortunately, several center around the holidays. Are you planning to—" He cuts himself off, and I can practically see the gears in his internal GPS shifting. *Recalculating...* "Will you travel to see your parents?"

Ah. Ten bucks says he was about to ask if I was going to go home for Christmas. But when my parents dropped the bomb that they were moving in a matter of weeks, they also revealed their plan to launch on an around-the-world cruise for the next year. How they hadn't mentioned selling the house *or* going on the cruise in the times I'd checked in from England, I have no idea. In any case, they won't be anywhere near home or what home used to be for me, so no. I'm very free to assist.

"I—probably not. I'm not going to have the—uh, the time to fly to them. And I want to be there for you."

And away from them. He can read this with no help.

He studies me for a moment. "Okay then."

He asks a few more questions, though his voice has shifted to something businessy and he's got this still energy that tells me he wants to leave. I don't know how I know, but maybe it's because I feel it, too. Talking about the past and my parents has done nothing to make me clearheaded, nor did the drink and the whole situation. He needs space, as do I.

A few minutes pass and we've paid—and by that, I mean Justin paid and I don't object since he invited me and this place isn't in my budget—and we're walking out. We're agreeing to meet next week at his place at eight. He's telling me I don't need to hire a moving company. He's telling me he'll send me the contract within forty-eight hours. Then I'm waving in an awkward gesture I regret and parting ways and I feel confused, just messed up in a way I didn't expect going into this.

I get into my car and begin the drive back to my parents' house, where I've crashed for a matter of days and the same home where I grew up. The same place that created some of the impetus for this situation I've just agreed to be in before the professional cleaners come to scour it top to bottom and my drop-dead move-out date is nigh.

I'm not sure how to feel as I wander inside and try to

savor the last vestiges of the homey scent I associate with this house where my whole childhood happened. This has me wildly emotional, and I don't want my parents to know how sad I am—about their moving, and about hating a job I thought I'd always love, and about Justin. So I let myself ignore the feelings and settle into some sweatpants, turn on an audiobook, and start packing.

Justin sends me the contract a few days later with a severe warning not to sign until I have a lawyer review it. When I reply that he is the only lawyer I know, he responds with a clipped text that reads *"That's a conflict of interest. We'll discuss this Saturday."* And that's that.

Except it's not really that because I've done nothing except mildly obsess over the details and what I may or may not be understanding. I don't believe the Justin I used to know would do anything to harm me, though I'm starting to wonder if maybe this new person is someone who would. Why else did he insist I get my own lawyer? But then... maybe that's just how cyborg Army lawyers are?

So now I'm pulling into the space he said is *mine* at his apartment building in the city. My hands are a little sweaty, and I double up on deodorant because I can tell I'm just an actual hot mess despite the chilly November air. I've bundled up too much and am likely shiny from overheating, but when I see Justin approaching the car before I can even exit, I snap out of my daze and throw open the door. *Let's do this.*

Only problem is, I push it open right as he walks up and

nearly kneecap him. Or maybe worse, based on the sound he emits. It's a kind of *oof*, and he steps back while placing a hand on the door to stop it slamming into him any more than it already has.

"Oh my gosh, I'm so sorry. I didn't realize you were so close. I didn't mean to hit you, I promise. Are you okay?"

I fly out of the vehicle and drop to my knees to get a closer look. The dirt from my door is smeared across the thigh of his jeans, and it's only when he says, "Grace, it's fine. I'm fine," that I realize I've probably overreacted.

Humiliation is my new accessory, lighting me up like I'm wreathed in multicolored twinkle lights and making me sizzle with embarrassed heat as I push off the ground before it gets any worse.

"I'm so sorry," I mumble again.

"Not a problem. Is this all of it?" He nods to the trunk where I've stuffed everything I own.

"Yes. That's it."

His eyes flick to me, but I don't catch them. I'm grateful to avoid seeing the pity I know is there. Two suitcases and some plastic totes. A few pillows and a quilt. I sold all my furniture before my time in the UK, and other than one more small load of clothes and knickknacks, this *is* it. I thought I'd move back to the US and want to revamp, so I sold or gave away every bit of furniture I had before I went overseas. I thought I'd feel something other than total inertia. *Silly girl.*

Instead, I crawled back home, tail between my legs in submission to the brutal reality that I am not tough. I'm not the put together career nurse I thought I was. I'm not coming home having had a broadening experience that augments my practice—no. I'm coming back feeling small and sad and just... beaten. I'm an egg who should've stayed in the carton but instead got cracked open and swirled around, thoroughly scrambled.

Without another word, he hauls the suitcases out, which both easily weigh over seventy pounds based on the struggle I had shoving them in there. They must not actually be that heavy, because he lifts them, one bag per arm, like they're full of stuffed animals and cotton balls.

It shouldn't be appealing, but there's something undeniably sexy about seeing this buttoned-up man have stealth muscles. I mean, he's clearly fit, but lifting my gargantuan suitcase one-handed? *Weirdly* hot. Like, I have to look away so he doesn't catch me admiring the way his biceps strain his shirt.

After realizing I'm just watching him unload and not doing a thing for myself, I jolt into action and grab as much as I can carry from the back seat. In minutes, we're stepping into a clean, well-lit elevator, and it's only now that I fully register what I'm doing.

I am ascending toward the apartment I'll share with Justin Justice. At some point very soon, I'll marry this man.

What am I doing?

"It's to the left," he says, the door sliding open at the same time. He wraps a hand around one of the panels so it won't start to close, and I scurry out, my body mercifully clear on what's supposed to happen even if my mind is moving slow and wrapped in too many Christmas sweaters.

He catches up to me and paces right behind, then at the door, I pause. Eight fifty-two. He gave me his address, and I know this is the door and recognizing *this* will be my door, our door, has my breath getting stuck in my throat.

What is my life that I'm about to do this? Moving in with a man I only barely know? How did everything I imagined for myself fall to pieces?

I startle from the spiraling thoughts when Justin's arm brushes against mine as he reaches to tap a key fob against the lock.

"Sorry," he says, quiet and almost gentle, like maybe he can sense I'm internally panicking a bit.

"No worries." My voice is froggish. Maybe the sound of the door opening might've disguised it.

Okay, no. There's no way, especially because I can feel his eyes on me, checking for external damages most likely.

And then, he steps over the threshold and holds the door open, swinging it wide as his gaze catches mine.

He's always had amazing eyes. I haven't let myself think this, but his somber stare feels heavy in a way I can't define and yet settles me. I do know him. I mean, I don't *know* him, but I know he's not about to murder or hurt me. I know that here, even though I haven't been inside, I will be safe.

And that is not something I've been guaranteed on a fundamental level in a while, so I waddle in with my things and start taking in the details while he slips out behind me to drag in my suitcases. Before I can take in the space, he zips back by me, out the door.

No words. No "I'll be right back." No "Make yourself at home." No "Your room is down the hall." No "Your butt looks cute in those jeans."

Fine. That's unlikely to emerge from his stern lips at any point in the future, though I did wear my best pair. I'm sporting sneakers I haven't scuffed up yet, and I have on a stainless bright red T-shirt. Even thinking through those choices makes me feel like a dirty little female Pig Pen standing in what is an absolutely pristine apartment.

Steel gray appliances. Gray cabinets and a cooktop I wonder whether he knows how to use. And so much more... gray. It's a sterile landscape of bland, and if I hadn't seen flickers of his sense of humor, I'd be feeling a much larger sense of doom about this setup.

As someone who loves color and vibrant palettes, this drab gray has a bunch of things flitting through my mind. He's too busy to decorate? He has no sense of style? He isn't home long enough to bother?

I've been mentally maligning the early Christmas décor popping up in more and more places as Thanksgiving approaches, and suddenly, I find myself missing it. A little garland, maybe a bright bow. Some lights on and a tree would look great in the corner. A soft throw blanket and some *Ho! Ho! Ho!* pillows would make the gray couch a little less... well. Gray.

I'm staring at what will be—*is?*—my new living room, when Justin pushes through the door loaded down with the rest of my worldly goods. He's got my two reusable grocery bags crammed with stuff looped over one wrist, two large plastic totes that weigh a ton stacked and held in front of him, and the handful of random bags I stuffed the straggler items into hanging off the other arm.

"I'll take these to your room." He moves past, barely looking at me.

Right. My room. Where I'll be living for the foreseeable future. I follow, nervous energy twisting through me so aggressively I feel dizzy. His posture is somehow impeccable despite being covered in bag straps and holding what has to be a hundred pounds of my junk. Must be that miraculous military bearing.

He comes to the end of a small hallway and enters the last door. I'm not sure what I expected, but this is both more and less than I imagined for this arrangement. Justin moves to the far corner and leans down to stack the totes against a wall while I take in the space.

A double bed is shoved up against the wall on one end. In the space opposite, there's a tiny corner desk. Good spot for journaling, so I'll take it. There's a decently sized window on one wall, a closet on the other, and then... well, that's it.

"It's not much, but I haven't had time to make improvements. If you'll bear with me for a week or so, I have a day off coming up and I can—"

"It's fine. Really. Bed and a closet are all I need. The desk is a bonus."

That's true. In England, I had little more space than a single bed, a small side table, and a very dingy old bathroom. The luxury of a slightly larger bed and a desk? And after a few days, I'll make it my own. I have to. It's the only option.

Justin is quiet for a moment, and when I finally glance up at him, he's watching me. When our eyes meet, he nods quickly.

"Good. And of course, you can use whatever else you need. Your bathroom is on the left, and you can help yourself to anything else, but we'll discuss all that in a few minutes. Let me get your bags, and you can have some time to settle in before we nail down the... details."

For some reason, his cheeks look a little hot and maybe even flustered.

I take mercy on him, or me, or both of us, and smile brightly. It's my "everything's fine and I'm not at all melting down internally" smile. The one I use when I'm triaging and the news is real bad but I'm not the one who's going to tell the patient.

It's the same smile I pasted on for years, even sometimes in the mirror, to convince myself I was fine—that I was handling myself and the work and the imminent danger of a meltdown and not... *not* handling it. My smile is a lie I've been telling myself since I left Virginia in the first place, searching for some relief from the pressure and exhaustion and promising myself a change of scene would do the trick.

But in England, after the shine wore off and the grind set in—far faster than I'd imagined it would, foolishly—the same smile became harder to summon. The physical and emotional exhaustion paired with distance from family and isolation, and in retrospect, some real depression, stripped me of even that.

The fact I can conjure it now means maybe there's hope. Not that I want to lie to Justin or start lying to myself again—I'm never going back to such nonsense. But maybe regeneration is possible... eventually.

In this situation, obviously Justin's completely convinced. He slips out, and the smile fades from my lips as I take in the room and the reality I've just willingly signed up for and very foolishly jumped into.

CHAPTER SIX

Justin

A V notches between Grace's perfect brows. I'm doing my best not to push her through this. It's going against every instinct in my being, ignoring this need to explain. Doing what I do, it fuels me, the way people say if you make your passion your work, you'll never work a day in your life.

Normally, I love reviewing the details of a contract. The satisfaction of sewing up every angle of an agreement, of making sure no one is taking advantage of anyone else—it carries a sense of purpose, of things done efficiently. I do a variety of things for the Army, and reviewing the legality of a given thing—an action a unit plans to take on a mission in another country or the contract for materials, and a whole host of other things—brings me a fair amount of joy.

But right now? I just want all of this over with. I wish she'd found a lawyer and had them review it. I wish I wasn't sitting here itching with the reality that if I wanted to, I could be taking advantage of her. She's been a nurse for over a decade and is clearly highly intelligent, yet legal jargon is its own language and she isn't trained.

"This all sounds reasonable to me," she says, eyes sifting over each line in the document.

"Are you sure? Read closely." I can't say it any other way, especially not when her gaze flicks up to mine and sends me a look I'm smart enough to read as a warning.

"If you're worried I'm misunderstanding, let's talk it through." She straightens, folds her hands on the table in front of her, and waits.

She's almost royal with this look—a little aloof. She's looking down on me, the peon, the one who's indebted to her. For someone who's desperate enough to marry a person she hardly knows in order to find a decent place to live, it's perhaps a bit misplaced.

Still, it intrigues me. At the same time, I want to knock some sense into her. Maybe into me, too. She should be far more wary than she is, and I should be less... whatever it is I am by her posturing.

"This contract states we will remain married for no less than three months. Any extension of the contract will be mutually agreed upon at least fifteen days prior to the end of the initial term," I summarize.

She nods.

"There are basic prenuptial agreement elements here—you will be entitled to a portion of my income accrued while we are married, but nothing I have saved or invested prior to our marriage. I will not be entitled to anything you accrue during, or have accrued at any point prior to, our agreement."

"And why shouldn't you be getting anything from me?"

The defensiveness isn't hidden from her tone in the slightest, and the way she pulls back her shoulders makes me want to... I don't know.

It just sort of makes me *want*.

Ignoring this, I address her question. "While I appreciate that you will bring many things to this agreement, I don't believe it's fair to expect you to financially contribute considering the demands on your time that fulfilling the obligations outlined will require."

While I don't make anywhere near what I would in private practice, I live frugally aside from the rent thanks to the location of my apartment, and I have few expenses. Perhaps it can all be considered a bonus to my lack of dependents, as the military would call them.

But this doesn't seem to settle well with Grace.

"Let's talk about the obligations I'm going to need to fulfill."

Wariness has entered her tone, and I wonder why. The concept of the agreement is clear, black and white on the paper right in front of us. "You'll be my date, behave as my wife in public settings, and for all intents and purposes, *be* my wife when we're in a situation where any coworkers would witness us together."

She swallows. "*Be* your wife."

I nod. Is this not obvious? It's the purpose of this fake marriage, isn't it?

She squints a little. "Can you clarify what that entails? I think this is where we might have different definitions, and I'd like to confirm what exactly our arrangement is."

Logical, even if it feels as though we've already been through this.

"We live together, so that's step one. We'll have a quick courthouse ceremony, and we'll have some professional photos taken so we have evidence. Afterward, I have a series of events ranging from casual to black tie, during which I hope you'll be amenable to pretending like our marriage is not one of necessity but one borne of"—my voice is rough, so I clear my throat—"love."

Her gaze is steady on mine, and I can practically hear the wheels turning. She has a question or a concern, though something is keeping her from asking. I have work to do, and I need to move on from this. I need to step away and take a breath without the peppermint-sweet scent of her assaulting me.

"Please say or ask whatever it is you're not saying." The words slip out almost against my will.

Her gaze doesn't waver, though one of her brows lifts a touch, like maybe my tone sounds more pushy and less direct. Wouldn't be the first time I came off as brusque, though I've worked on that. I've been doing... better with it.

"Fine. I guess we should just... address it head-on."

She shifts in her seat in a way that speaks of physical discomfort. I'm not the kind of lawyer who spends hours interviewing people, though as a natural introvert and a person who tends to listen before speaking, I am adept at reading body language. Hers is screaming something, but for all my experience, I'm just not sure what.

"We have different bedrooms. But you keep saying I'll *be* your wife." She swallows again, then reaches for the glass of water she must only now be remembering.

"Yes. Correct. And?"

She stares at me with those bright eyes over the rim of the glass as she gulps down half, no, three-quarters of the water. Is she that parched? Is it too warm in here?

"And I want to make sure you plan on respecting the fact that I have one room and you have yours."

I wait for more, but when nothing comes, I nod. "Of course."

Her lips flatten and she sighs silently, her shoulders dropping a half inch. "And I have a bed in my room and you... have a bed in *your* room."

As her cheeks bloom poinsettia red, finally, *finally,* it clicks. I rush to reassure her.

"Yes, of course. We will not—" I clear my throat because apparently I'm the kind of man who can't say regular words out loud without prefacing them with throat clearing. "We won't consummate the marriage physically."

A relieved breath escapes her. "Thank you. I assumed as much, but then with all the *being my wife* business, I realized we should be very clear on that."

I didn't expect to sleep with her, and clearly, she doesn't want that. Neither do I—I mean, I don't know her. Call me old-fashioned, but I can't even think of that when we've barely gotten reacquainted.

Grace and I, we've hardly touched, save our accidental run-ins that have been more painful than anything else. And yet, opening the door to this topic makes me realize we will need to discuss this aspect of the relationship. To be any amount of convincing for possible promotion board member interactions and to truly alleviate the constant refrain as to how I might as well be the one to work late, to come in on the weekend, to take the TDY trip even though I just got back... to make it clear I have a life outside of the Army and my office, we'll need to *act* married.

With all that entails.

"Fair enough. On that note, I didn't delineate any physical boundaries, but I imagine it would behoove us to discuss this now rather than wait until our first official outing."

I have remained completely still to this point, but right now, I feel like pushing to my feet and pacing the floor. Not the discussion I was expecting to have today, now, here.

Grace's lips twitch just a touch, and I see her bite the inside of her cheek like she's trying not to smile, or maybe attempting to hide a grimace.

"Sounds wise. What do you have in mind?"

I reach for my water and guzzle down the full drink because suddenly, I've gone from having absolutely nothing in mind to imagining my finger tracing her brow, then sliding back into her hair and tilting her face up to mine. She's medium height, but I'm tall and I'd need the angle just right. Where before, I hardly thought of her, hadn't even considered anything more than passing appreciation of her beauty, in this inconvenient instant, I am struck by just how much I could very easily have *in mind.*

The glass in my hand makes a loud *crack* as I set it onto the table with too much gusto. It does the trick of shaking me from my shockingly vivid daydreams and gives me a beat before I say, "Holding hands, I imagine. Maybe a kiss on the cheek. Depending on the dress code, that may change since there are rules about public displays while in uniform. We can plan to discuss before any given event—perhaps choreograph some moments that feel okay."

She doesn't hide her smile now, and it's doing nothing to ease my jangled nerves. It's a truly lovely smile—the kind that is all warmth and delight. It's snow outside the window while you're snuggled on the couch with a good book. It's dessert for dinner.

"Choreograph, you think?" She tilts her head to one side like this shift in perspective will help her make sense of me.

That's when the last few seconds hit me. I've been an

idiot. She's sitting there, gorgeous and confident and somehow relatively unaffected by the previous minutes of conversation, save a pretty blush, and I've been daydreaming of things, babbling on about how we'll plan out our touches. She's not worried about it because she's not a work-obsessed freak like me. She's... natural.

"Well, only so you're comfortable. So we both are. But we don't have to. I only mean we'll be clear. Communicate everything—ideas, concerns, boundaries. I don't want you to feel uncomfortable with anything. Ever."

Her piercing gaze is back as her smile fades bit by bit into the serious expression that must match my own. She has placed me on a slide and shoved me under a microscope, and she's looking for something and I don't know what.

After a second and before I can ask her, she's decided something. She flips to the last page of the contract and uncaps a pen, scribbles her signature by the flagged *X*, and stands.

"It's a little late for that, JJ."

Her blue eyes flick to me, and the expression there sends my stomach tumbling. I don't know what to say to her, but it doesn't matter. I'm not fast enough, and she's already walking down the hallway to her room, sending me a "See you in the morning" before I can figure it out.

CHAPTER SEVEN

Grace

After a fitful sleep, I wake tangled in a sheet and absolutely starving. By the time we finished discussing the contract, my brain had shut down. I'd sat down at the table expecting a simple read-through and review of the plan, but somehow, we started talking about boundaries and plans and it all took it out of me.

First, there was the part where Justin couldn't say *consummate* without clearing his throat and getting a little blush on his cheeks. I wouldn't have been surprised to see smoke coming out his ears, all those gears grinding away to figure out how to make the moment less awkward, though there was no help for it. And *that* was incredibly endearing —especially after I clarified I wasn't signing a contract with a... benefits plan.

Okay, I guess technically I do get benefits like health insurance, which is great. But no other *physical* benefits.

And then there was this moment where—I shake my head, clearing it of the asinine thought. Just because I'd felt a weird swoop of attraction toward him doesn't mean a thing, and it certainly doesn't indicate he has interest in me. The man was no less robotic than he had been during our first few interactions, with the possible exception of the night we went to dinner.

I need to keep my wits about me and remember that underneath his stunning gray suits, he's likely a motherboard and his native tongue is ones and zeroes. One of these days when I notice the angle of his jaw or how weirdly pleasing his nose is, I need to focus on this.

Thinking of that first dinner and my need for food, I shuffle into the kitchen to find it gray, sterile, and void of anything other than a red light blazing on the coffee maker. I'd switched to tea with gusto during my second year in London, but that had been the result of too many disappointing attempts at getting something other than instant coffee. Even the coffee pods there weren't right. My parents had a serviceable drip machine that would've worked just fine except they only brewed seasonal blend flavored coffee from a local store. The flavor names were all cutesy like "Thanksgiving Spice and Everything Nice" and "Oh my Gourd, it's Pumpkin Spice," though they mostly just ended up tasting like someone tried to brew burned potpourri.

Justin's coffee machine and the scent of what I detect is pure, dark blend coffee stands as a beacon of hope and sanity in the dull slate kitchen. I find a mug (black) in the cupboard and fill it to just shy of the brim before I notice a small note with clean, handwritten words in neat rows. Not a cursive loop to be found, to no one's surprise.

Grace,

I'm working a long day but have us scheduled at the

courthouse tomorrow at one p.m. I'll only have an hour. I've hired a photographer and my mother is insisting on being there. If you'd like to invite anyone, please do. I'll wear my green service uniform unless you have objections. Please feel free to wear whatever is comfortable.

I'll be working late, but please make yourself at home. It is, in fact, your home now. See you at one tomorrow.

—J

I read through the note a few more times. Can't decide if I love or hate it, so I land on a neutral feeling. The emotional overload of last night and accepting that my first marriage will be a total sham has calmed. I spent a few hours falling down a search engine rabbit hole that revealed all kinds of motivations pushing people to get married for reasons other than love. One recurring theme I decided to cling to around two a.m. is the idea this is like any other contract. When I think of this, it makes me feel mostly better, because I wouldn't feel like my life is ending because a contract came to an end. Been there, done that, still here to tell the tale.

But the other part of me that has just refused to resume my employment contract with the hospital is feeling distinctly like a failure, and like maybe this is all a very, *very* bad idea. As I find a seat on Justin's very gray, though very cushy, couch and take in the charming little fireplace and envision what it might look like with some garland hanging on the mantle and logs lit inside, I relax.

Justin has made all of the plans. He even found a photographer. All I have to do is find a dress. And now that I'm not facing paying rent, I'm not quite so stressed about finding something appropriate I can afford.

I think about calling any of my friends—Alaine is in the UK and in the thick of a shift right now, plus we were really only friends of convenience. And Angela and Cammy... they're so angry with me for not coming back to the hospital. They haven't said as much, but when I admitted I didn't plan to come back to the hospital, they'd ghosted me completely.

I wasn't shocked since our communication had been sparse at best. They'd planned to come visit while I was there, then didn't make it—though they did manage a Caribbean cruise and another trip out West just the two of them. We kept an active group text for the first few months but it dwindled, then practically died, until I told them I was coming home. It reignited, energy injected into our chats, until I admitted I wasn't sure whether I'd return to work at the hospital.

I've grieved so many things these last few months, and my old friends have been part of it. But in truth, it makes sense. Maybe we'll reconnect when I start back at the hospital eventually.

If admitting something is half the battle, then I've done it—I have no friends. Not really. And I'm not an introvert or a loner like Justin, who seems perfectly happy to live a solitary life.

So. Part of this new life will be finding new friends, then. And though he's far too serious for his own good, I wonder if maybe Justin and I can be friends again. Or, in truth, friends for the first time, since I was too young and he was too shy all those years ago to offer each other anything other than familiarity.

After finishing the coffee and dressing, I'm determined not to sit and wallow in the weirdness that is today, so I bundle up and venture out. I haven't explored Old Towne Alexandria much, and there's no time like the present. I need a boutique for the dress, but first, breakfast, and I recall some kind of coffee shop or diner on the first floor of the building.

Sure enough, Alex Brews is a quaint little shop nestled in the corner of the apartment building. My heart flips at the cuteness, and even the cutesy name—Alex being the local nickname for the city of Alexandria. Maybe it's silly, but this feels like I'm actually here, living in the city. I'm not even in DC proper, though I can't deny the bustling feeling, even in this historic downtown that feels more like an idyllic small town main street than most small towns themselves do.

The windows are decorated with hand-drawn pictures of steaming mugs of coffee and pastries with faces, all saying adorable things like, "Come grabba cuppa" and "Don't be shy, get some joe!" and my favorite, a cheery croissant saying, "Friends don't let friends skip coffee." Inside, there are about fifteen tables. A third of them are occupied, mostly with people chatting, and one or two with singles and their laptops.

"Welcome in! What can I get you?"

The chipper greeting draws my eyes, and I see a girl with blond braided pigtails and a giant smile. As I approach, I see she's not a teen, as the hairdo might've suggested—more like midtwenties, maybe—and she is stunningly beautiful.

"Oh, hi. Um, just a flat white?" I'm not sure why I sound like I'm asking a question, but lately, everything in life I thought I knew has become a little tenuous, so that has to be it.

"Excellent choice. Dairy milk? Whole? Skim? Something in between? Oat? We do have soy but..." She makes a face.

I chuckle because her energy would be overwhelming if

she weren't just so darn charming. I instantly like her, which is so very not like me lately. "How about middle of the road two percent?"

She nods, winks, and taps at the screen in front of her. "Perfect."

I pick something from the food menu and she grins, apparently completely pleased with my selection, though I suspect this would've been her response no matter what I chose. She gives me the total and I pay, enjoying the calm of the shop and the way they haven't transitioned into Christmas just yet. There are still a few gourds and a large cornucopia drawing on the chalkboard where the menu is etched. The flavors are all still in the Thanksgiving zone—more pumpkin than peppermint. And don't get me wrong, I do love those things, especially since there was nary a mention of Thanksgiving in London this time last year, but for some reason, thinking about the holidays makes me melancholy.

Yes, melancholy, like I'm some nineteenth century old maid nursing her wounds after a bout of nerves rather than a modern woman about to marry a man to help his career and solve her housing crisis.

"Here we go. One flat white with two percent and one breakfast burrito with eggs, bacon, and cheese. Anything else I can get you?"

The spritely woman is blinking back at me like getting me something else would absolutely make her day, having brought my food to my table rather than calling out the order, and therefore catching me totally off guard.

"Uh, no, thanks." Then I remember the one thing I have to do today and say, "Wait, this might be odd, but do you know anywhere around here where they sell wedding dresses?"

Her reaction is instant, and like the flashbulb of a camera snapping, though the brightness comes from the utter delight shooting across her face like a star. She slips into the seat across from me and beams. "Oh my gosh, are you looking for a wedding dress? Are you getting married?"

I laugh, warmed by her enthusiasm even though I'm not sure I've ever felt as much excitement over anything in my life, let alone the idea of someone else shopping for a dress. "Yes, actually. I'm getting married tomorrow and I—"

Her gasp stops me. "I'm sorry, you're *getting married tomorrow?!*"

It's a borderline shriek, except she seems to be aware of the setting enough to drop into a whisper before she says the last bit.

Still, I glance around to see if anyone has heard her. It's not like anyone here cares or shouldn't know this, or that my getting married tomorrow somehow means it's a legal agreement and not a love-fueled elopement, but it still sends my pulse climbing.

"Yes. Bit of a story there. Basically, I need a dress for a courthouse wedding tomorrow. I'm new to the area, and I don't want anything super fancy, obviously, though I'd love to..." I trail off, realizing for the first time I mean what I'm about to say. "I'd love to feel nice. Love my dress, at least."

Her energy shifts and her eyes soften. I didn't say it, but we both heard the unspoken reality that I don't love much else about the wedding. She might not realize I don't love the groom, even, but something in the way she tilts her head, then nods, tells me she gets that this isn't a great love story.

"I actually know the perfect place. They're pretty fancy, but the owner is a regular and she loves me. Give me a minute and I'll call and see if they can squeeze you in."

She pats the table twice, and the clink of several silver rings draws my attention to her hands. She's got bright orange and yellow fingernails alternating across one hand, and I'd bet the pattern continues on the other one. She wears a little glove that leaves her fingers and thumb free, and I think I see another layer or something underneath—a brace, maybe?

"That's so kind. I can't ask you to do that, though," I say.

She shrugs one shoulder. "You didn't."

And that's how, five hours later, after a quick stop in a nearby salon to refresh my hair and get rid of those dead ends dragging my locks down, I'm standing with barista Andy and the owner of En Mode Blanc, admiring the fourth dress I've tried on in the mirror. Somehow, it's the perfect dress—one that makes me feel oddly choked up, and I can't tell whether it's because I love it so much, or I hate that I'm wearing it to marry a man I hardly know.

CHAPTER EIGHT

Justin

I have jumped out of innumerable airplanes.

Well. Not *innumerable.* I can, in fact, count them quite precisely as it's listed in my service record under my Airborne Qualifying Jumps. I may be a lawyer, but I've served in several elite units, more than one of which require even someone like me to jump out of a perfectly good airplane and stick the landing.

And that expression is also not at all accurate since, if one did try to stick a landing, one would likely break one's legs. There's a very specific way to land after jumping out of an airplane at twelve hundred fifty feet in the air—the aptly named parachute landing fall.

Entirely off topic, though, because the point is that I have done things I hate doing for this job, things that send my stomach into my throat and make me feel like another second of stress will end up with the contents of said stomach all over whatever is near me or simply with me passed out from anxiety.

Jumping out of an airplane has nothing on marrying Grace Murphy.

I wouldn't have thought it. In fact, I have explicitly *not* thought of it for the last twenty-four hours. I've been working on a contract review for a proposed plan of action that needs to be implemented as soon as possible, and this provided me blessed refuge from the rampaging thoughts that have plagued me after Grace's first night in my house. I stayed away by design—I wanted to let her settle into the house, and frankly, I wanted to remind myself what my real life is like. Grace might be signing up to be my wife, but I'm doing this for my career.

I'll no longer be the single guy, the one who has never even tried to marry, the one who has no dependents or life outside of work and therefore should always take the TDY, always take the more demanding schedule. And though it's less an issue and more of an annoyance, I won't mind not being accused of being married to the military. *No, fellas. I don't see the Army as my wife.* I'm doing this to make the next promotion board early and then lock in retirement at a higher rank.

I'm doing all of this, and Grace living in my apartment and being my date to a handful of events over the next few months won't change a thing, except ideally those delineated as the reasons for all of this nonsense. It's business. An agreement. A contract with clauses and an end date.

Then I walk into the courthouse and I see her.

I didn't realize how much I've been worried she might not show—or in truth, how much I hoped she would. It doesn't make sense because I can move on with my life just fine. This fanciful idea brought to me by one Marcy Justice is just that—a bizarre fantasy belonging in a book. And yet, in my subconscious, I've gotten myself wrapped around the idea of this—what it might do for me, where it might lead me. In my career, that is.

There's relief and a crush of other instantaneous reactions when I see the woman has followed through, and she hasn't done it by halves.

She is—

I am—

I exhale, summoning the calm I can reach for whenever I need to. It's right there, a little well I can dip into.

But just as the little bucket rises up, full of all the cool calm I'm desperate for, a large hand slaps me on the back.

"This her? She sure came out of nowhere now, didn't she?"

At this voice, the bucket plummets back to the depths of the well, back into darkness and far from my reach, back to a metaphorical Timmy who'd fallen down it and whom Lassie will never, ever find because he's been brained by a bucket falling from above. *Might be a little dramatic...*

"Sir. What are you doing here?" It emerges as a croak as I turn to find my boss, Colonel Gruff, standing at my side looking as austere and borderline angry as ever. His dark hair and severe widow's peak give him the air of a villain, and his demeanor doesn't help. He's got sparkling blue eyes that would be mesmerizing if they weren't always narrowed in suspicion.

He embodies the adage mothers used to tell us—*If you keep making that face, it'll get stuck like that.* Here he is, his face having gotten stuck in a perma-scowl with six-foot-four stature to match.

"Couldn't miss my JAG's wedding, could I?"

His brows lift, and I can't tell if it's an actual question or more of a challenge. Between his height and the Imperial Death March playing to accompany him wherever he goes, it's formidable.

And no, he doesn't have a soundtrack, but if he did, that'd be it.

"I—how did you, uh, hear about it?" I sound like such an idiot, it's painful. I'd cringe, but I'm too busy scrambling with the implications of his being here.

"Your mother, of course. She came by the office to see if you wanted a ride and when I noticed how lovely she looked in her wedding attire, I inquired. She seemed shocked I hadn't been invited in the first place." He lifts one thick brow. "I was, too, as you can imagine. This all seems rather sudden, especially in light of recent conversations we've had."

His words come at me like a hailstorm, and I'm left gaping at him, my mouth slightly open and my eyes no doubt bugging out to complete the picture. He took me aside a few months ago and not so gently suggested my chances for an early promotion from lieutenant colonel to colonel are more likely if I'm married. "*It never hurts to show you can be faithful and committed to something*," he said, as though my nearly twenty-year career in the Army didn't demonstrate that already.

As a colonel himself, he knows the process, and he's even stated he can put in a good word, maybe introduce me to a few generals who are likely to sit on the promotion board in January.

Now, he's directly pointing at the weakness in my plan —the reality that no one has seen or heard about Grace and how, months before the board, I'm getting married. And yes, it's a silly thought that marriage would help it, but he made it sound like talking to the general *would* make a difference.

A lot of times, these small, personal connections are how things happen. It's how it might happen for me.

"Sorry, sir. I just assumed you'd be too busy. Didn't want to trouble you." It sounded... legit.

Not like I purposefully avoided all mention of my marriage to the Sith Lord who is my boss.

His brows dip into a perturbed vee. "Not a trouble."

The moment stands there, awkward and more personal than anything I've experienced before with this man. He's not a warm boss, but he's an excellent soldier, what I imagine the Army really wants—someone who has given his entire life to the military. Like me, he's single, and so like me, he's happy to work and travel and pour himself into the job. Unlike me, he has at least one marriage that has suffered for it.

But his being here changes all of this. My mother bearing witness to this sham of a wedding is one thing, especially since she knows Grace and everything going on with us. Having my commander here puts this whole situation at risk. It ratchets up the need to perform, to be a man in love with his fiancée, and it has only just now occurred to me I have no idea how to do that.

I have never once felt romantic love for a person—even the failed proposal. She refused, yes, but also, I didn't love her, exactly. Not like she wanted to be loved. That was a factor in her rejection as much as my devotion to work, I suppose.

So love? No. Attraction, yes. Affection, yes. I already feel those things for Grace purely by the fact she is a beautiful woman and I have known her all my life. But love?

"JJ, are you coming? Grace and her friend are waiting."

My mother bustles up to me and inspects my uniform. It's squared away and she wouldn't know if I have a ribbon in the wrong place or whether things are at the right angle, but she will never not make sure I'm presentable, no matter how old I get.

"Yes. I was just greeting Colonel Gruff." I don't need inflection to hint at the surprise his being here is, or how much I wish she hadn't invited him.

She grins like she's done me a favor. "Oh, I was delighted to run into him. So glad you could come, Colonel. Tell your mother hello for me when you talk to her."

The colonel just nods like this is a normal request. I know he went to the military academy, just like I did, and I know the mothers of soldiers who go through there have a tightly knit network, but it hadn't occurred to me that my sweet, small-town mom would know Gruff's rather high-brow mother.

"Hi, I'm so sorry to interrupt. I'm Andy, Grace's friend. She's getting a little nervous since we're being waved in and you all are just standing here. Any chance we can get this party started?"

A petite blonde grins at us, then knocks her head toward Grace.

And just like that, the nerves have shifted to a messy tangle of dread, anticipation, and awe. How did this woman end up agreeing to marry me?

She's standing fifty feet away in a white dress grazing her calves. It's fitted up top with sleeves to just below her elbow, the material hugging her torso and then tucking in at the waist before it spreads out into an elegant skirt. I don't know the language for all of it, but it's stunning. It's demure and lovely and sexy and chaste, and I have to clear my throat.

In the back of my mind, I think I hear the same chipper voice say, "You should try smiling. It'll make your day even better," and Gruff's irritated grumble snaps back with the audible version of an eye roll.

Grace must hear all that, somehow, and her gaze swings over and collides with mine. I attempt to swallow, but my throat has forgotten how.

"Oh, JJ, she's so beautiful."

My mother's voice has a softness, a dreaminess I'd like to correct. I'd like to remind her this isn't real and getting her heart wrapped around this moment will only lead to disappointment. But I still can't figure out how to swallow.

"Doesn't she look gorgeous?" Andy says, her tone just as full of fantasy as my mom's.

"Congratulations, Justice. You have a beautiful bride." Gruff says this with sincerity, and even though it feels lightly out of character for him, of course he does, because Grace is an utter vision.

And through the clamor of the room, I manage to hear her say, "Shall we?"

I nod, because yes, we should.

Even if walking toward her, I feel raw and exposed in a way I'm not sure I ever have.

Even if I can see the tightness around her perfect mouth and the way her shoulders are tense, and I know with a gut-level certainty she's as nervous as I am.

Even if I sense that what we're about to do is going to change my life, and it won't be simply by having a roommate and a plus-one for a while.

Despite the warning flares shooting off in my head and the butterflies in my chest and the stress wrapping around my heart and squeezing, some wild and primal instinct in me says she's mine. And yes—yes, we should.

CHAPTER NINE

Grace

We walked in ten minutes ago. Ten minutes and the officiant, someone who Justin's friend of a friend knows and agreed to squeeze us in at this time thanks to the short notice, has introduced himself, reviewed the requirements, and presented a marriage license we will sign. I fleetingly see Justin's middle name does in fact start with a *J*, as I have always fantasized it does, but I won't ruin the surprise and look too closely, nor can I even manage to focus long enough to read it. I have hardly heard a word, though I'm trying to focus and take this in—to absorb the moment even though I'm strangely pained by it.

Actually, I've been focusing on the way this kind man's bushy eyebrows and mustache are months past needing a trim. They've got bright white and orange hairs intertwining in a way that reminds me of a tabby cat, and I have to tuck my lips between my teeth to keep from stress-induced giggling at the image of this man's eyebrows and 'stache masquerading as a tabby cat's tail.

Cruelly, my brain reminds me of Garfield, and now I'm fighting an awkward smile and lightly hungry for lasagna, yet also mildly nauseated by the thought of the dish.

So clearly, I'm doing just fine and this is fine and I am completely fine and not at all freaking out.

A simple band is slipped onto my finger, and somehow, my brain engages in the moment long enough to slide one onto Justin's. He must've bought these, because I hadn't even thought of it. Probably odd I wasn't wearing an engagement ring to start with, but I can't even worry about that.

It's intimate. Unnerving. Then again, I've already frazzled every nerve ending I have, so what's a bit more?

And now the man is speaking again.

"All I need to hear is that you both wish to enter into this legal marriage." He raises his brows and waits, eyes swiveling back and forth between us.

I'm on the verge of tears and have been since seeing Justin in his uniform, looking tall and handsome and completely unfamiliar to me. This person is a grown man, not the teen who kept the mean kids in the neighborhood from ragging on me endlessly. He's such a grown-up, and despite being thirty-four, I feel like a child. I feel like my head is a balloon on a string and I'm going to float away only to pop when a strong gust of wind hits me at the wrong angle.

"I do," Justin says, and my eyes snap up to his.

He's waiting, those hazel eyes patient and full of things I can't hope to decipher. Because again, this man is a stranger to me, and I've been a fool to think of this as no big deal. I didn't walk down an aisle. There's been no pomp and circumstance, no party to plan, no bridesmaids, and yet the formality of the courtroom and this man reminding us this is a *legal marriage* feels like a concrete necklace.

I open my mouth, and I know the words to say. *I do.* I do. *Just say it!*

But I can't. I can't hear anything over the pulsing beat of my heart in my ears, and my tongue is thick in my mouth. I can feel the eyes of everyone—his mother, his boss whom I've just met, this nice man with his bushy brows waiting for me to respond.

Garfield help me, I can't do it. I don't remember how to form the words, and if I did, I'm not sure I could vocalize them anyway.

I have lost every single marble I've ever had—must be how I got here. I've been dropping them one by one, scattering them from the UK to here and everywhere in between, and now here I am, entirely marble-less and about to marry a man whose apartment is gray. *Gray.* With black accents.

I'm marrying a hot gray-and-black robot lawyer I weirdly have a crush on, and I don't think I can stop this because I walked in here of my own free will.

My heart jumps into my throat and starts tap dancing or doing something that makes it feel like it's actually bouncing around and clogging up my airway. I've only had one panic attack in my life, and it started a bit like this, though my hands aren't going numb yet, so there's hope I can reverse course.

Problem is, how does one not panic when one is doing a thing that is very much panic-worthy?

I want to scream at someone, but I'm the only person to blame here. I stepped right into this, dazed and beaten down by the last few years and gutted by the change in my life's plans. I stumbled forward and let this plan catch me and give me shape, ignoring the warning voices in my head telling me this isn't just an agreement, and I don't want this to be my story.

I'm Weird Barbie, about to get her hair chopped short, but I'm also the weird little girl holding the scissors because this is my fault. This wedding is the last stop before I'm left in perma-splits and wearing clown makeup until the end of time.

A warm hand cups my elbow, and Justin ducks his head to speak low in my ear.

"Whatever you want here, Grace. You don't have to do this. Please know that."

When he pulls back, our gazes lock and I see he means it. With every bit of him, even those parts I can't read, he means those words. He might be uptight and robotic in many senses, but there is a heart there somewhere. I could walk out of here right now and he'd likely let me keep living at his place. Or, if I didn't want to, he'd probably help me pack my stuff back into my car. He'd probably help me find a new apartment.

Well, maybe not quite, but he won't be horrible to me, at least. He'd probably *Bleep Bloop* some consolations and help me with the logistics.

It's this that reminds me I *do* know him. Despite his protests the other night that he's no hero, he's proving himself wrong right now. We might be marrying for the optics for his job, to make sure he gets that promotion, but I am in no way coerced.

Honestly, he's not a robot, and I can't keep pretending he is, especially now that he's made clear I can still say no. This, more than anything to this point, proves it. He's not forging ahead with no concern for anything but the end goal.

And it's this thought that gives me strength and sends my fancy little tap-dancing heart back into my chest. It's doing more of a clog now, pattering away on some cut-rate piece of plywood behind my ribs, but I can breathe. With a bolstering inhale, I straighten my spine and press forward as I've planned to do.

I nod, hoping he understands how much his words freed me, and turn to the officiant. "I do."

The man smiles, seeming genuinely pleased. "Very good. Then by the legal authority granted to me by the state of Virginia, I now pronounce you husband and wife."

I'm relieved to hear this, relieved it's done, when applause from just behind us has me turning, and then Mrs. Justice says, "Kiss the bride! Kiss the bride!"

That's when I register the officiant didn't say it. It's not a legal requirement, which I am fully aware of thanks to the aforementioned late-night internet scrolling, but it's tradition and I suppose we've shirked any sense of tradition so far. We could avoid this, especially since Marcy knows very well what's happening here is not a love match, though Justin's boss is standing there like a tall, judgy winter storm cloud, and I realize there's no choice in it. This moment is the beginning of the ruse, and if we don't start now, we aren't going to succeed.

Justin must feel the same way, because I register his hand back on my elbow, then the other sliding up to cup my cheek as he rotates us thirty degrees. Our eyes lock and I duck my chin a touch so he can see. We haven't talked about this—fools—but it's okay. It'll be fine.

He holds my gaze another moment before dipping to press a kiss to the corner of my mouth. With my back to them, they won't know the difference.

His lips don't linger. There's no heat or passion in the touch—and that's all it is. Just a touch, and the kiss is done, the marriage sealed, and we are husband and wife. My husband just kissed me, and I can hardly feel my face let alone anything having to do with his proximity other than a fair amount of shock.

Not medical shock, thankfully, even if I do have a handy basketful of symptoms that could combine to fool any nurse—clammy skin, rapid heart rate, rapid breathing, though I've calmed a bit. It's just that this moment, the impact of his lips on mine, feels like it's happening to someone else's body—some other girl I'm watching who looks a lot like me.

Justin pulls back with this severe, intense expression so far from what a man who just kissed his new wife would be wearing. It sends a wild hair through me and makes me want to tickle him or jolt him in some way, but I'm rattled enough that I simply take the arm he has held out and let him turn me to face our witnesses.

"If you folks will head out, we've got another group ready to go."

I take one last look at the nice officiant who just married me to a man I used to describe as my hot, shy neighbor, and then we're moving.

"Well, simple, but now the fun starts. Marriage is a wonderful journey. Don't you agree, Colonel Gruff?" Marcy says, eyes a sparkle as we process through the lobby area. Justin hands me my coat as Marcy tilts her face up to welcome the colonel's agreement.

"I have found marriage to be a journey with only one kind of end."

Andy scoffs outright. "My, you are just absolute sunshine, aren't you?"

Gruff blinks once as if in slow motion, then simply continues without acknowledging Andy in any way. "Justice, I assume I'll see you at the briefing at four?"

His stern expression leaves no room for adjustments, though I know Justin is planning to be there.

"Of course, sir," Justin agrees, even as his mother barely hides her scowl.

"It was great," Andy chirps, a little smile on her face that, even after knowing her for just over a day, I can tell means we'll have things to discuss later. "I'm going to head out, but thank you for having me! I'll see you soon?"

We exchange a quick hug, and I marvel at how natural it feels, maybe the only thing that has felt natural lately, and then she trots off and it's just me, Marcy, and Justin.

As soon as the colonel and Andy are well away from us, Justin turns to his mother and says, "I suppose it was wise to have him here."

She sniffs. "Of course it was. And now you have a full two hours before you need to be back at work. Take your wife to a celebratory lunch." She mumbles something along the lines of *or back to your apartment to have your way with her*, but then she brightens up and waves from just three feet away. "Goodbye, you two! See you in a few weeks!"

And that's it. She's practically jogging to the parking lot down the street, and it's just me and Justin. Or, me and him and however many hundred people are milling around the courthouse and this city block.

I don't know what we do now—it's not like we're actually friends, and now we're married, and I almost lost my crap back there. I'll need to address it. But I haven't been able to eat all day thanks to the glut of nerves that hit the second I woke up this morning, so I'm relieved when Justin squeezes my arm lightly and asks, "Have time for lunch?"

M.O.M NETWORK

M.O.M. Network Message board:

JusticeLVR: It's done! They're married! I'm messaging from the car and they're going to a post-nuptial lunch date.

SCLDG: Here's hoping this works.

Vic: Seems rather unlikely.

CoolyKay: I hope they're happy together!

JusticeLVR: Let's not get ahead of ourselves. This was step one. Or, really step ten, but that's ten of twenty at least.

Vic: Well at least she's realistic...

CoolyKay: I'm so hopeful for you and them!

SCLDG: Keep us posted. I want to know if it gets good, and I won't hear a word from my own son about it.

JusticeLVR: More to come soon, ladies. More to come.

CHAPTER TEN

Justin

The polite clinking of utensils against plates and the low hum of conversation surrounds us even this late in the day. I love and hate this about DC—how there's no stopping. It's not the city that doesn't sleep, but there's a hustle here that borders on desperation at times.

Right now, the only desperation I feel is for Grace's thoughts. I've never been someone who dreads silence—I enjoy it. Yet the quiet from her is unnerving, especially after the little pause before she said, "I do." Compared to her fairly constant stream of talking at our other interactions, save the possible exception of the day she moved in, I know all is not well.

I've picked at my salad and watched her pick at hers. Neither of us is being dainty—in fact, we're both having salads and main dishes. Oddly, I'm second-guessing even this.

"Are you okay?" I finally ask because I can't take it anymore.

Why is this bothering me so much? It's not that I need her to be happy, but the idea she's... I don't know. I honestly don't know what this is except I can't stand it.

She gives me those stunning eyes and nods slightly as she finishes chewing a bite. "I am. Are you? This is a lot of change."

"For both of us."

A smile pulls at one corner of her mouth. "True. Though it feels like I should be used to it by now."

"Why?" I wonder aloud.

Her brows drop, and I forbid myself from looking at her and instead focus on my salad. It must be the heightened sensations from the events of the day, but I'm feeling oddly drawn to her, like my hands are tied to little strings trying to attach themselves to her, and I keep having to remind myself she's not really my wife. She's not mine.

This all has a purpose—a means to an end. It's an end I've worked for and wanted, and so we checked the box this afternoon, did a passable job in front of Gruff, and that's all. Simple.

Hands to yourself, Justice!

"I guess it's a silly thought, but it feels like everything about my life has been centered on change—moving, ending my contract with the hospital, my parents selling their home, and now this. At some point, I should probably stop being surprised by it and accept this is my new state." She tips her head up and opens her arms in an odd yet charming show of acceptance.

I don't laugh, exactly, but make a sound *like* a laugh. "I disagree. You should now begin to accept you are through the change and can settle in to find a new sense of normalcy. It'll be smooth sailing from here."

Amusement flickers across her face. "Yes. I absolutely know what I'm doing as a newly minted Mrs. Grace Justice, and the total collapse of my career, support system, ambition, and overall life are totally normal."

My mouth drops open, then I pull it shut and scramble for purchase here. "I didn't realize it was... so much going on."

I also didn't realize just how much hearing her refer to herself as *Grace Justice* would tilt my axis. I'm a little teapot, and I just got turned over. It's stupid how much I like the sound of her name with mine, how lovely the combination folds together.

It's also utter nonsense I even for one second think she'll change her name. I know she won't. What a legal hassle for a short-term agreement.

Still. Grace Justice is just so... pretty.

She snickers and it's tinged with equal parts disbelief and frustration, and I'm brought back to reality.

"No? You thought anything shy of borderline desperation would have me entering into this agreement?"

That lands, though based on our interactions thus far, I don't think she means it to be an insult. Still, it drives home all of the reasons our connection here is purely based on the agreement. "I'm sorry. Of course."

She heaves a big sigh. "No, I'm sorry. Because as much as that is all true and I'm at a point of major transition, I'm also glad to be here. I know you're doing a lot for me, but I'm glad I can help you, too. And I hope—" She swallows thickly. "I hope my hesitation didn't cause any trouble with your boss."

"I'm not worried."

In truth, I think if anything seemed unusual, it would be our lack of affection and excitement. The couple who married right before us was practically weeping with happiness. Another pair came out, and everyone in their wedding party *was* actually crying happy tears, with smiles stretched wide.

The contrast was stark. I can't be certain, but I don't think the colonel noticed any of the other people. I'm not sure if he'll say anything since he is neither talkative nor prone to share his feelings. The fact that he showed tells me something is off, but maybe it's simply that I hadn't told him and he wanted to make a point.

Or maybe he just felt like he wanted to be our good luck rain cloud on an otherwise lovely November day. *Who needs a wedding march when they can have the Imperial Death March instead?* It would be par for the course, and now that I've had the thought, I'm certain that's the gift he was giving me today.

"I hope not. I didn't realize he'd be there. I wasn't... prepared."

She seems genuinely concerned, which is unnecessary, so I do what I can to reassure her.

"I wasn't either. He wasn't supposed to be there." I briefly explain my loving mother's invitation to him, and then add, "I'm sorry about the kiss, too. She was clearly too pleased with herself."

She grins. "She was, wasn't she? She knew she had us."

I'm relieved to see her good humor on the subject. "She absolutely did."

We chuckle together at her, though there's a niggling concern my mom is hoping all of this is more than just an agreement. She's enough of a matchmaker to think she's done the job and this will end up with all her dreams for me coming true. While a lovely sentiment, it's a misplaced thought to be sure.

We move on to talk about her new friend, and I tell her a bit more about the colonel. By the end of our meal, I've nearly forgotten what we've done. That is, until Grace stands up and I see her in the dress again.

It's not particularly formal, though it does look like a bridal dress—or it does to me. I hadn't noticed the narrow, plunging vee at the neckline until we sat down for this meal earlier, and it's one more thing making it hard to swallow. The beautiful line of her neck and the dip at her collarbones. The expanse of skin at her sternum stopping just before it'd be something more than alluring.

"Do we have plans this weekend?" Grace asks, slipping her arms into her coat as I hold it for her.

"Didn't I mention? I've got a trip coming up. I'll be out of town through December second." I shrug into my own jacket and gesture for her to move ahead toward the elevator bank.

"Oh. I apologize. I assumed you'd need me for Thanksgiving."

And oddly enough, she sounds disappointed. That can't actually be the case, but nevertheless, it's what I detect.

"No, it's my fault. I thought I'd made a note of it on the schedule. But you're off the hook for the next twelve days. I'll have the first work obligation I need you for that Thursday."

She nods and we step inside the elevator. With this talk, work begins to edge its way into my mind, and I'm restless with it. I've just gotten married, and yet my default setting is returning before I've even said goodbye to my new wife.

This is solid proof that a fake marriage is the only kind for me, to be sure.

"You know, I think if we're going to be successful, we may need to use the time you're traveling to get to know each other. If it's possible." Her gaze rises to meet mine, then drops away.

"How do you mean?"

"Just basic get-to-know-you things. What you like and don't. Allergies, hobbies—all the things we'd learn over the course of a dating relationship and well before marrying."

"Right. Makes sense. I meant, how do you envision doing this? By what medium?"

She blinks at me like she's sifting through my words, then says, "By text? Or, I suppose if e-mail is the only option, we could do that, though it seems simpler to text."

"Yes. Should be fine. There will be times I won't have access to my phone, but we can agree that instantaneous responses are not a given and see how it goes." I sound downright breezy, which is not a word anyone would use to describe me.

The smile on her face tells me I've done something right, and though I'm not sure exactly why, I'm glad for it.

"Perfect."

The elevator car springs open, and I gesture for her to go ahead. The bottom of her dress swirls around her legs as she walks in her heels, and I have to bat away an image of me slipping off her shoes and running a hand over the curve of her calf.

"Thank you for lunch, Justin Jacob Justice."

Even with the little tease about my—wrong, I must point out—middle name, why does she seem so earnest? Or pretty? Or... I can't pin it down, yet everything she's doing right now feels a little like she's casting a spell.

"Not my middle name."

Her lips quirk, though she doesn't say anything.

"Thank you for joining me," I add. And interestingly, it speaks to something true. I *am* glad to have had this time with her, even when it has taken me away from work a bit longer than I'd planned.

Her rideshare car pulls up—I hadn't realized she'd even gotten one, and suddenly, I have this frantic feeling inside me like I can't let her go without—without something. She's walking toward the car, and I fumble and reach for her hand.

"Grace, I—" Her gaze snaps to mine, and I suck in a breath because she is so insanely gorgeous and I've known it, but I cannot unsee it now. It's like those two words, "I do," have suddenly made the scales fall from my eyes. "I just wanted to say, you look incredibly beautiful today. Thank you for being there."

She bites her lip like my words genuinely please her, and then she paces toward me, leans up onto her toes, and presses a kiss to my cheek. With another pretty smile, she winks and says, "See you at home, husband."

CHAPTER ELEVEN

Grace

I planned to stay up and greet Justin when he got home.

Though we're married in name only, our lunch was great, and there's something in me telling me to just go for it and at least try to be friends with the man. We have enough history that it makes sense, plus, on the very most basic level, it'll make my life easier to be friends with my roommate if any issues come up.

Instead, I fall asleep on the couch watching a movie, wishing I had something to do with my hands, and wake up when the front door shuts this morning.

He's come and gone in the time I've been asleep, and though it makes no sense, I am immeasurably disappointed by this. And a little embarrassed because I often sleep with my mouth wide open and there's every possibility I snore.

Honestly, it's exactly how I dreamed of this man seeing me for the first time after our wedding—mouth agape and nasal cavities whistling with the sweet, sweet evidence of my lungs working perfectly in repose.

Ideal, really.

Not that I care.

Because why would I care what he thinks of me?

I don't.

Obviously.

Anyway...

It's not a surprise Justin didn't wake me up. He's tiptoeing, not unlike I am, and we had this huge thing happen yesterday. Or, rather, we *did* this huge thing. But it's also, if we take it for what it is—simply an agreement—*not* a huge thing. It's just a thing.

He's probably not as jumbled up about it as I am, but it's still not nothing. The exhaustion from not sleeping the night before and the up and down and up again emotions of the day absolutely hammered me, and I passed out cold enough I didn't hear him come in, leave, or even brew coffee, which I see evidence of.

I fumble around and move to get dressed, then pour myself a giant black mug of coffee before noticing he's left me another note.

Grace,

Didn't want to disturb you as it was an exhausting day. Feel free to text at will.

Best, J

I can't help but smile at him. Who signs "Best" in a handwritten note to his wife slash roommate? Justin Jared Justice sure does. Nerd.

And also... seeing his handwriting and hearing his voice in my head as I read the note reminds me of that last moment. When his hand snagged mine and he said I was beautiful in the tone of his that felt so... real. I couldn't resist pressing a kiss to his clean-shaven face. It almost felt like I couldn't resist *him.* I'd wanted to lean into the moment, and it was so weirdly comfortable and exciting compared to the rest of the day.

I'd been an anxious, second-guessing mess all day. Andy did her best to reassure me, telling me I'd made the choice to go ahead with this for a reason and I should trust myself, unless I wanted her to whisk me away, which she'd happily do. After yesterday, we are better friends than most people I've known for years.

But it was the moment when he'd said I could choose. Even then and there, even with his mother and especially his boss witnessing. He didn't try to tell me to buck up and do the thing or cajole me into remembering our agreement. He'd just been that kind, calming presence I associated with the person he used to be. That man is still Justin, and it flipped something in me. It made me want to find him again.

Underneath the workaholic soldier and beyond this gray existence where he's working more than he's doing anything else combined, that sweet, kind man is in there. And no, he hasn't been unkind, but he's... something. He's dulled, maybe, or just so used to being on his own that he's walled himself off. And I'm realizing I have this chance to dig under those walls and open him up.

Maybe I can find his electrical panel and recircuit his settings so he lets his feelings show.

I don't want to be too eager or overwhelm him, so I opt to pop downstairs and see if Andy is working and grab an application for a job opening there. I've decided to apply for menial, no-stress jobs and see if it will help me regain some sense of what I *do* want to do since I've already identified one very clear thing I *don't* want to, at least until I can stomach it again.

I hate how nursing, even the thought of it, fills me with a bone-deep exhaustion, like the total burnout seeped into the marrow and leached out any regenerative properties that once existed. I am professionally spent, and I hate myself for it, though I'm working on accepting this and trying to look forward.

Not to be dramatic, but it was a thousand tiny cuts until I was bleeding out. It was no one thing that pushed me to my breaking point.

And yeah, it sure is dramatic. I've embraced that much, at least. Now, a break is what I've promised myself and it will help... it has to.

I'm going to channel the Instagram influencers and self-care the crap out of this situation so I can, eventually, look myself in the eye and not feel quite so much like something the proverbial cat dragged in.

Then there's also the issue of needing a new roof over my head come February, when my agreement with Justin will be over. I don't see us doubling down on it—he'll already have made it past the promotion board earlier in the new year—so I'll be moving out. Which means rent, aka money, therefore I need a job to bring some income in.

I spend the afternoon submitting applications for jobs along the street where I now live—Alex Brews, the wedding dress shop, an adorable paperie and bookstore, and a few restaurants. I'm not particularly excited about any of them, yet I feel excited about all of them. This is all a clanging cymbal in my head alerting me to the reality that I shouldn't feel so happy and accomplished for applying to jobs far beneath my education and experience, and yet, who's to say?

Going back to the hospital or taking a third year in the UK system would've been a fatal move, even though it was the original plan. But staying here and never having gone abroad would've garnered the same result—I'd needed a change, though simply transplanting to the UK wasn't it. There's no other way to say it. And so, I'm taking the break, making a change, and hoping somehow I find a way back. The only way out is forward.

While Andy wasn't able to chat when I stopped by earlier, she asked if I could meet her down the street at Tacos y Tacos, and of course I said yes since I have absolutely no schedule to speak of.

I've been snacking on deliciously crispy tortilla chips from a basket and tangy-hot salsa, patiently waiting on Andy. I've been sitting here for about eight minutes, and I haven't heard "Feliz Navidad" once, so I take this as a good sign. Anywhere that dares to play something other than Christmas music this close to Thanksgiving and the holiday itself is alright by me.

Also, any number of wrongs can be righted by chips and salsa. I only needed guac and, truly, all would be well.

Career burned to a crisp?

Have some chips.

Basically homeless?

Grab ya some salsa.

Married a man you used to know for mutually advantageous but non-romantic reasons?

Grab. That. Guac.

Andy barrels in the door, waving to the guys and woman up front and finding me instantly. I'm facing the window, and she saw me when she walked by and no lie, did a cartwheel on the sidewalk.

This woman is something else.

"Oh my gosh, aren't the chips amazing?" She slips off the gloves she was wearing, then dives into the basket and shoves a chip into her mouth like it's oxygen and she's been under water for two full minutes.

I already like her, but I appreciate her obvious adoration of chips. Clearly, she's good people.

"I ordered guacamole and I got myself a margarita. I wasn't sure whether you drink, so I just said a water for now."

She smiles sweetly. "That's so nice. And yes, a margarita for me, too, but they know. I'm here at least once a week, and always for Friday happy hour."

I register this—oh, yeah, it *is* happy hour, though we're early. It's not quite five, but the tables are slowly starting to fill. In seconds, they bring a yellow-green drink the size of my head to me and something that looks like its base liquor is a deeply green substance and definitely not of this world.

Andy holds it up proudly with a giant smile. "The Grinch Margarita."

"Yikes," I say, because I'm nothing if not honest in my curiosity and dismay, though I'm definitely chuckling.

She laughs, too, full and bold and with so much abandon, I'm kind of jealous of her. I don't know her all that well, but she has this way about her that feels like she's just wringing every bit of goodness out of every single moment she lives.

"It's actually amazing, but fine. Have your very normal margarita and tell me all about your hot new husband." She waggles her brows.

My cheeks heat. Because yeah. In the midst of all of the *stuff* of the last few days, I have fully ascertained that Justin is incredibly and deeply hot. And in his uniform yesterday? *Whew.* I mean, I've seen his formal photos, but there's no comparing to the man in person. Maybe especially when said man is becoming my husband. Hard to say what leaves a bigger impression, though I dare say it's because I now realize I really like a man in uniform.

See? I've already learned and grown. What good that realization does me, I can't say, but there's one point for this little catastrophe paying off with housing and a refreshed me.

"Oh, I see the blush. Is he a good kisser? Did you, uh, ya know..." She winks one eye three times like this finishes her sentence.

I cover my cheeks, which are now blazing, laughing and feeling embarrassed and a little foolish, too. After a long sip of margarita, I admit, "He kissed me right here." I point to the spot.

She's waiting for more, rapt for details as she slurps Kelly green Ninja Turtle juice through her straw. "And? Then? What?"

I get it. There should be more. Alarmingly, some part of me wishes there was, but I'm also not too deep into my marg to know that'd be too much.

"Nothing. We went to lunch and talked. He told me I looked beautiful, and I kissed his cheek and went home. He went back to work. And then I had planned to stay up and try to talk with him, but I passed out on the couch and woke up when he left this morning."

Her mouth drops open, then closes, then opens again. I already know she isn't often speechless, and embarrassment fills me up until I'm brimming with it. She must see this and realize I'm... whatever it is I am, because she reaches out and grabs my hand.

"I know you said it was an *agreement*." She drops her

voice on the last word. "But I don't think I realized it was... that much of one."

I release a pent-up breath. "Yeah. And you may have caught how I nearly didn't go through with it yesterday." We share a look because *yeah, she caught* that. "But something clicked for me overnight. It's not like this is normal, but I just feel... safe, I guess. Like it's maybe an odd choice, but not a wrong one. So now, I keep waffling back and forth between feeling kind of excited about it, weirdly, and then just the occasional wave of *what the heck did I do!?*"

She's already shaking her head. "No. No second-guessing, because it's already happened. Plus, it's... not a long-term obligation, right?"

"Three-month initial agreement." It sounds insane when I say it aloud but it's helpful to remember right now.

Andy nods once as though this settles it. "Perfect. That's all you need. Three months with this man and you'll know if you want to keep him."

I barely manage to swallow my drink before I burst out laughing.

"I don't think there's any chance I'll get to keep him," I say, ignoring the odd little pang the admission gives me.

But Andy isn't going to let that lie. "We'll see, my new little newlywed friend. We shall see."

CHAPTER TWELVE

Grace

It's after seven when I get back to the apartment, and I have been overserved—that second margarita was probably not my best move. Not so I'll be sick in the morning, but enough so I laid out aaalllll of my business for Andy, and so she did the same. And as we were leaving the restaurant, she also made me promise to text my "hot soldier" and start getting to know him.

She's not wrong about the hot soldier part—I have eyes, don't I? So does she. She saw the man in his uniform and he is truly, madly, deeply good-looking. It's actually quite inconvenient. Why couldn't he look like a troll or something? Not a cute troll voiced by Justin Timberlake, obviously.

The old freaky kind that lived under bridges.

I flop down on the couch a little harder than I normally would and eye my phone.

"This is silly," I say to the empty room. Didn't expect it to reply, though. I'm not that far gone. Now if I'd had a talking cat like Sabrina the Teenage Witch, we might be in a different situation. Note to self: get a cat when I settle into a new place. Which isn't for the here and now. At the moment, the focus is Justin. My hot husband.

Why am I nervous? Why do I feel little drunken butterflies careening around in my rib cage, ramming into my chest wall? Or maybe it's my heart pounding like I'm about to do something important and not send a text message to a guy.

It doesn't matter that it's Justin. That should make all of this easier at this point and should certainly *not* make it so I feel like I have carbonation fizzing through my veins. Good thing I don't because that's basically me dead on the floor in a heartbeat, stroke material instead of romantic, silly notions of champagne veins.

Maybe I would've been able to stick with it if medical ailments had catchier names like champagne veins or sparkle face or... yeah. No. Wouldn't have made a difference and probably would've slowed the whole process down.

I heave a huge exhale and settle my wild train of thought, tucking my hair behind my ears and glaring at my phone, then promptly grabbing it and tapping out a message.

"Did you make it to your destination?"

Totally normal and not weird or tipsy sounding, so I internally high-five myself.

It's a few minutes before I see his response because I've gotten changed into sweatpants, popped some popcorn, and poured myself a tall glass of water. I've also cued up one of my favorite Christmas movies, and I've ignored the thought that I wish he were here so we could watch it together, because that doesn't make any sense.

We aren't friends yet, not quite. And he's so... stern. Quiet. Workaholicky.

Still, my heart flips when I see he's responded.

"Yes, all settled in. How was your day?"

Look at that! He's learned from our first exchange when he thought I was trying to use him for a job connection. Granted, I'm using him for a house, but he's using me right back. And arguably, he'll get more use out of me than I will him because—you know what? This is a creepy way to think of it so I'll just focus on him.

"Really good! Sorry I missed you this morning. Hope I wasn't snoring when you left."

And by *hope* I actually mean *I will be horrified if it turns out you heard me snoring on your couch.* I have resisted the mental image of me slack-jawed and sawing logs while he exits the house in a crisp uniform after one last look at a disheveled me that strikes him with a searing pang of regret.

Mostly, I have succeeded in not imagining the scenario... until now.

It takes longer than I'd like for him to respond, but when he does, it's not the worst news.

"You looked very peaceful. I was hoping I wouldn't wake you."

Okay, well, maybe not the worst? Or maybe he's just being polite. I have suspected that what can seem robotic is more his less than gregarious personality paired with persistent formality rather than an actual circuit board under his crisp shirts. *"I'm not sure if you're being honest or being vague, but I'll take it. Are you allowed to say where you are?"*

"London."

My mouth drops open because, what? *"Seriously? Did we just switch places somehow?"*

Another minute of me shoveling popcorn and drumming my fingers impatiently, and his response pops up. He explains he's only there for about forty-eight hours to see a friend who's stationed there on the way to his actual destination, which is Germany.

It's only after an hour of chatting about my day collecting job applications and a bit about the pub he visited with his friend that I realize it's the middle of the night where he is.

"Wait, shouldn't you be sleeping?"

"Can't."

How atypically eloquent of him. *"Are you working?"*

The response bubble pops up, then disappears a number of times before it solidifies.

"Yes."

I sigh. "This man just won't stop," I say to the empty room yet again. Then I tap out, *"You should get some rest. Send me a picture of something you enjoy tomorrow."*

"Why?"

I roll my eyes because really? *"It'll help me get to know you."*

He doesn't respond, and I decide to try a more direct approach. *"It will help us be comfortable with each other and be more convincing. That's the goal, right?"*

"You do the same."

That's all I get back, and I assume it means send him a photo. Better than outright refusing, I suppose.

For the next few days, it's like that. Quick little snatches of conversation peppered here and there throughout my exploration of his neighborhood, searches for jobs online, and existential dread over how I'll ever feel ready to return to the hospital in a matter of months. It's actually seven months until my official three-year leave of absence is up thanks to the logistical time suck of moving home, but that feels like a gut-wrenchingly tight timeline. Even if Justin and I extend our agreement to six or nine months, right now, it all feels too soon.

And that's what it feels like—like while I'm with him, I can have this time. No rent, no real obligations, save a basic job that *isn't* nursing. Until we're done, and then it's time to face reality. Racing heart when I step inside the hospital, and the scent of the place, familiar and foreboding, fills my nose. Strung-out appearance when I forget to take care of myself. The empty, hollow feeling that gnaws at my gut and has turned something I know I loved once into something like a waking nightmare.

But for now, I'll live in this dream world where I'm not such a mess.

Honestly, it's a lovely vacation from the self-recrimination and burnout.

Even surrounded by Justin's gray universe, it's pretty freaking great.

He's sent me a few photos—a classic Big Ben shot but from a distance, which tells me he didn't wander by Parliament. A gigantic fluffy white dog sitting on a bench next to his owner in Hyde Park, which has me wondering if he likes dogs or just liked the moment.

If Justin is an animal lover, I'm going to be doomed. Seeing him pet a dog, let alone get mushy for one, would probably cause instant expiration.

That said, if he did like dogs, wouldn't he have gotten one if he wanted? Although no, he wouldn't—he didn't even let himself have a nice throw or comfortable pillow on his couch, much less a dog.

Eventually, he sends a shot of the *Look Right* painted at the crosswalks. To this, he asks, *"Does this make you homesick for your time in London?"*

I snort when I see it. *"No. I loved London, but it wasn't home."*

It's hours later before he responds, right before I go to bed, when he must be waking up inordinately early.

"Where do you feel at home, then?"

I look around and know I shouldn't feel the odd sense that this place feels more like home than any I've had in a while, but it's true. I've added a soft red throw blanket to the couch and a cute Christmassy pillow that says "ho ho ho" in red against a cream background. I've arranged the fresh pine garland I envisioned so it's hanging cheerily off the mantle, and even though I'm sure I'll have to replace it before Christmas, it smells amazing.

I've started a bit of Christmas crafting, too. I never have been much into such things, but I'm realizing it's only because I was working so much, and when I was home, I was too tired. Now that I'm not generally spent the moment I walk through the door, I'm cutting paper snowflakes to hang from the kitchen ceiling, and soon enough, I'll start making popcorn and cranberry garlands for the tree.

It's too soon for a tree, of course, so I haven't set one up, though there's a nice open space behind a small sitting chair that would work perfectly. I even bought wood, then realized I should probably find out whether this is a working fireplace before I get too eager and end up burning down the building. Maybe Justin knows, and if not, I'll ask the building's super.

These small changes, along with settling into my room

and adding more food to the pantry and fridge, have quickly resulted in me feeling quite at home here. No, it's not perfect, but it somehow feels a lot more like home than anywhere else has in years.

The apartment I'd rented in my twenties, then the house I'd rented up until I left for the UK, and then my tiny flat in London... none of those were ever homey. They weren't right. My childhood home no longer belongs to my family. There's a small piece of me that feels raw at the reality that the place I thought I'd come home to and find to be a soft landing is gone. That said, I should be past needing a safety net, shouldn't I? At this age?

Answer? Yes. Yes, I should.

I should not be floundering like a fish on dry land in my early thirties with advanced degrees and years of experience under my belt. Alas.

Alas!

Real life isn't always pretty, and it doesn't always go the way we plan. Maybe this is the lesson I'm learning more than any other.

I won't tell Justin I feel more at home here than I have in a long time, or how my heart is a little broken that my parents have sold my childhood home. I don't mention how this formerly gray place starting to liven up thanks to my presence is something I hope he'll appreciate. If not, I certainly do.

I'm waking up the longer I settle in here, and in some odd way, the more I let myself embrace the season. I've missed reveling in the holiday cheer and indulging in some of the things I've always wanted to do but never had time for.

I don't need pity from Justin about any of this, and I

don't want him to feel weird, so I tap out something a little less personal.

"TBD I guess."

I send it off, yet the ache is there. It's carving into a soft spot in my chest, hollowing me out a little as I try not to sink into the gaping unknown that is my future or the bizarre reality of my present.

For now, I'll embrace the past—good memories, old habits, and a bit of romance—and let a Christmas movie and my snowflakes keep me company tonight.

When Andy asks what my Thanksgiving plans are, I tell her honestly—I'm going to eat my body weight in Thanksgiving side dishes, choke down a few bites of protein, and then wait a half hour before having dessert. After that, I'll do it again a few hours later.

I know myself, and I'm determined to make sure she knows me and not some idea of me. Plus, she seems to get a kick out of me and how much I missed the holiday last year.

She already knows Justin isn't coming back until next week, and I've managed to make my excuses with his family. Marcy invited me to join her and Mr. Justice, but when I told her I was having a Friendsgiving dinner, she seemed pleased enough.

What surprises me is that Andy is free, and because of this discovery, we have a Friendsgiving feast. Instead of ordering an entire Thanksgiving meal for a family of four at the fancy grocery store down the street and having every intention of eating the entire thing by myself over the next few days, I happily end up sharing it with my new friend.

While part of me considered getting fancied up and setting the table with Justin's nice stoneware dishes and shining cutlery, Andy is all for a casual meal from the couch with a movie going. We decide on *Love Actually* because at the stroke of midnight last night, it officially became legal to watch Christmas movies according to her—I don't mention I've been consuming any available Christmas content since the day after my wedding.

We're surrounded by food—half-eaten servings of dressing, corn pudding, sweet potato casserole, some kind of green bean thing that's a grave disappointment and far too healthy, and decent enough turkey, but I mean, it's still turkey, so what can one expect?

There will be glorious leftovers, even though we'll keep pecking at these delights for a while until we shift to pie mode.

"You know, it kills me so much that these two don't get together. It literally makes my heart ache for them," Andy says as she gazes at the screen where Laura Linney and Rodrigo Santoro play a couple who both deeply like each other but ultimately don't get together thanks to her family obligations and his unwillingness to burden her.

"It is painful. They're so close to having something. She's so close to—" My voice catches and I shake my head as my stupid eyes fill with tears.

Andy looks over at me and presses her hand against my knee. "She's so close to doing it with this gorgeous man—I know. It makes me want to cry, too."

I burst out laughing at this ridiculous statement, but relief rolls through me. "Well, definitely that. It's so brutal because she's all alone with her brother, and it's such a challenging situation. If she just let Karl in a little, she wouldn't be so alone."

Andy gives me another minute to collect myself because my voice has broken again and I'm a little watering pot out the eyes for nonsense reasons.

"Right. And she'd have a gorgeous Brazilian man ready to make all the bad things disappear. I mean *come on* with the bronze skin and dark eyes and those thick-rimmed glasses and the pining." She mimes stabbing herself in the heart and falls back against the couch.

This is enough to give me a break from my sudden rise in real feelings and focus on her movie-generated angst.

Once I finally look back at her, she raises a brow. "So what you're really saying is, you need to let your sexy soldier in so you're not all alone?"

A breathy laugh escapes. "Yes. My ridiculously handsome husband slash roommate slash the stranger I married is the answer to all my problems."

When she doesn't say anything, I look up to find her inspecting me.

"Does he really feel like a stranger?"

This woman isn't giving me an inch, is she? She couldn't possibly know about the flash of discomfort that shot through me when I said it. But what's the point in denying it? It has felt good to be honest with someone.

Yes, I'm still getting to know Andy, but she's been lovely, so far. And even though I've only seen the blazing sunshine parts of her, the fact she's here right now, with a friend she's known for less than two weeks, and not with family or a boyfriend or friends, tells me maybe she knows something about the need to let someone in, too.

"No. He hasn't for at least a solid week," I say, flashing her a smile.

She chuckles. "All that texting is helping, so it must mean he's actually telling you about himself."

I smile, and the photos he's sent each day flash through my mind. Each one has had some kind of thoughtful question to go along with it, like the *Look Right* one. As resistant as he was to the idea, he understood the assignment. I am certain this has nothing to do with a desire to know me more intimately and everything to do with our primary objective, but still. I'll take it. It's both entertaining and making it easier to embrace the situation.

Then there's the discovery that a lot of what I remember about him is still true. Yes, he's changed and grown, yet there's enough that's familiar about him, I know this feeling of closeness is partly due to our shared history, even as distant as it sometimes seems.

Earlier, when I asked what he was doing today since I know he's at a US Army base in Germany and figured most people would be off the clock, he sent me the most unexpected photo I've ever seen.

It was him with his arm around a stunningly beautiful blond woman on one side and a wildly good-looking Latino man on the other. There were three little kids, two standing and one being held by the man at Justin's side, all grinning with gap teeth or gums. And Justin was smiling in a way that made me kind of achy.

This was the accompanying message.

"I'm sorry I'm not there with you because I know there's been a lot of change for you lately. This is Rae Jackson, her husband Gabriel, and their three kids. I've known Rae for years, all the way back to when we were both stationed at Fort Campbell. For some reason, she and G have kept up with me and I end up visiting them and a few other friends about once a year."

He seems like such a loner at first glance, and yet here he is with friendships he's maintained for years. It's almost mind-blowing, except he sent me a selfie of him with a man he also called a dear friend before he left England.

What I assumed was a solitary, work-driven life is one that is surprisingly deep, just like the man himself. And the more I uncover about him, the more I'm baffled by the fact that he was available for me to marry at all, much less amenable to that being the solution to his predicament.

And yet, there's the stern, work-focused part of him that clearly drives the train. I suspect getting these real insights into him is painful for him to share based on the amount of prying it has taken to get to where he's giving me full sentences in exchange with my texts.

He's a mystery, yet also one I'm feeling more and more compelled to solve. So far, he's been willing to answer my questions and has been a rather engaging texting buddy. And all of it has added up to Justin Jerry Justice feeling not at all like a stranger and more, each day, like a friend.

"For someone who seems very private, he's doing a very good job letting me in," I finally say.

Andy wears a soft smile when she says, "I love that. Now don't be like Sarah and keep him out when he's trying to get in. Just let him in." Her gaze narrows on me. "Just let the gorgeous man into your bed, and don't answer the phone if it rings, no matter what!"

My cheeks flush instantly, but I laugh. "Yeah, not about to happen."

Because it's not. We're getting to know each other, but we are so far from anything more than just that. Plus, he'd need to be in the same city, at least.

"Well. Tuck the advice away for when the day comes. And trust me, it's coming."

We turn our attention back to the TV, but my mind is circling her words and the photo of Justin from earlier. Even a week ago, I would've said she was crazy, but something about seeing him with his friends, about learning even just a little bit more about him, has me thinking all kinds of things might be coming soon.

CHAPTER THIRTEEN

Justin

I've been looking forward to this TDY trip since it popped up on the schedule earlier this year. No one else wanted to be gone for Thanksgiving, and for once, being the single guy with no family worked out well.

In the absolute pandemonium that is the Marquez-Jackson household, the depth of my lack plunges in like a dagger in my side. It's an odd thing to see these old friends with what feels like exponential children. I haven't gotten to visit them in two years. They only had Tori then. Now they have Matthew and Michael, one by adoption, one by what sounds like a grueling birth. And here they are, Rae flourishing in her career, Gabriel her unwavering champion and the part-time nurse, full-time dad his family clearly loves beyond measure.

I watch the baby in his arms gazing up at him as he pinches Gabe's chin in his little fist.

"He's a daddy's boy," I say, though it's one of those weird things I can't imagine saying out loud until it's out. Is that a thing people say, even? I've been in the cave back in Virginia for too long, and I've forgotten how to function.

Rae wanders in and hands me a high ball with vodka and cranberry. In her own glass, she's got something golden with a slice of lime—probably tequila. I'm impressed she remembers I don't really like hard liquor if I can taste it, but then that's her way. She's a person who excels at anything she does, whether it's carving her way through the ranks, mothering her children, or hosting a friend for dinner.

"Thank you," I say, still enjoying the sight of this baby so enraptured with his dad. The other two are already tucked in for the night.

"He's absolutely a daddy's boy. Though the other two are obsessed with him, too." She sips her drink, then grins. "Can't say I blame them."

Gabriel grins even as he winks at her. Ever since the first time I saw them together, they've been like this, and apparently, growing their family has done nothing to stifle their connection.

"Ah, you two," I say, taking a long slug of my drink.

"It hasn't always been easy, but I wouldn't change a thing. You?" Rae asks her husband.

He's shaking his head one way even as he's started rocking their youngest, who is almost passed out in his arms. "Nada. I love our story."

He glances up to send Rae a fiery look that makes me aware of how late it is and that their kids are almost all asleep. They could use this time for other things.

"I see you getting shifty in your seat, Justice, but you're not going anywhere."

Rae's voice brooks no argument, and I feel pity for

anyone who tries to cross her. It's almost incomprehensible how we met years back when someone was harassing her at work, but we've both come a long way, and I couldn't be happier to see it.

"Yes, ma'am," I say, even though I do technically still outrank her.

She shakes her head at me. "You're not getting out of here until you give us the update. You can redirect our questions all night, but you need to know I'm not letting you leave without an explanation."

She nods toward my left hand. The very place I'm now wearing a tungsten black wedding band on my ring finger.

Fair enough. Plus, I want to talk about it, surprisingly.

I started the trip grateful to escape Grace and the myriad thoughts crowding me at home and work in the wake of our nuptials. Her texts have pushed her to the forefront of my days even at this distance, though, and as the days have passed, I've found myself looking forward to those moments of connection.

It has to come down to the fact that our doing this, our talking, is helping to position us for success. What's the point of any of it if we aren't convincing when the time comes for Gruff to talk to the general who's on the board? I don't intend to do it in half measures, and even though I initially balked and saw no purpose to investing any more time than necessary, I now see this *is* a necessity.

That I also, more and more, *feel* it is a necessity to communicate with her is something I have chosen not to examine further.

"I got married."

Gabriel and Rae stare at me for a beat, then his shoulders start shaking and Rae slaps a hand over her mouth to muffle the sound of her own laughter. I give them a minute, bracing for the inevitable barrage of questions.

Gabriel sobers first. "Don't sound so happy about it, man."

Rae's smile drops off, though the humor lingers in her eyes. "Seriously, Justin, what happened? Don't act like this isn't a surprise."

I'm not sure whether it's the way they shoot each other another loving, amused glance, or the way being with them makes me feel better and worse at the same time, but my chest pulls tight when I see it. I consider spinning it to make it sound better, but ultimately, I trust these two. And after the last week of texting Grace and feeling more and more attached to her, I need to talk this through.

Apparently, I'm fairly vague, because after I explain, Rae is still baffled.

"So this woman, who you sort of grew up with but also hadn't seen in over a decade, is now living in your apartment and is your wife?"

I nod. "Pretty much, yes."

She gives me a stern look I know must make subordinate soldiers shake in their boots if they've crossed her.

"I know you're working a lot, but I didn't realize you were so..."

Embarrassment colors my cheeks, and I fill in what she must be thinking. "Desperate?"

She huffs and I can see Gabriel shaking his head.

"No. I don't believe for one minute you're desperate in the true sense. I guess I just didn't believe you'd given up on finding something real. And I don't mean that to sound like it's something weak or a failing to have stopped looking, I just..." Her brow furrows, and she glances at Gabriel before continuing. “I want you to find someone who can really love you.”

Throat tight, I nod. “Not everyone can have what you two have. You must know how rare it is.”

They both agree, and Gabriel continues. “It is rare, but it’s not impossible to find. And make no mistake, we fight. We work at this.”

Rae leans forward, her glass of tequila hanging between two fingers. “I don’t know what you’re not telling us, but it feels like something. Probably plenty of somethings. The only thing I want to know is whether this is really just a three-month thing or if it could be more.”

Her blue gaze doesn’t waver, and I scramble at her direct question even though it’s exactly the one I wanted her to ask. “We have a clause that allows for three-month extensions as long as both of us wants to proceed. So I—”

“Justice. Man up.”

Gabriel’s softly spoken words hit hard enough. If he weren’t holding a snoozing baby, I imagine they would’ve come out a bit more gruffly. However, the thing I know about Gabriel is this—when he says “Man up,” he means be honest about how I feel. He means own the situation and my part in it, and don’t be so darn scared to get a little vulnerable.

And maybe it’s the vodka cranberry or the fact that I know these two want to support me, I do.

“I don’t know what’s going to happen. If you’d asked me this ten days ago, I probably would’ve laughed in your face,” I admit.

Rae eyes me. “And?”

I say what I have been unwilling to admit fully to myself. “And now… it feels like maybe, *maybe*, if we weren’t in this weird situation, there could be something between us."

Gabriel beams and Rae makes a gesture like, *there you go*. But then she keeps prodding. "And why does the current situation, which is clearly the reason you're interacting at all, preclude you from having something between you? Why wouldn't it just... solidify your interest?"

I'm shaking my head like that's impossible before I find words to explain. "It's like coercion or expecting someone to fall in love with you under duress. It'd be like Stockholm syndrome, and it's ultimately beside the point. It's business, in the end."

Rae bursts out laughing, and the bundle in Gabriel's arms shifts. We all freeze, waiting for him to settle, and when he does, Gabriel gives his wife a look and stands, presumably to settle the baby into his crib down the hallway.

"I don't mean to sound like I'm laughing at you, my friend, but that's nonsense. This woman sounds like someone who is doing this because she's getting something from the arrangement, yes, but also like she's a very kind person."

"She is." I recognize it more every day. Not only is she a nurse who genuinely wants to help people professionally, but it's clear to me one reason she ever even considered a situation like we're in is thanks to her desire to help, even if it's someone like me whom she doesn't really know. Even if it's for my career, which she has zero investment in.

"So why not use this time when you're going to be together so much and just... try?"

I swallow down the instant protest and take a measured breath. "It seems a little outlandish, doesn't it? Starting a relationship like this? Or if not that, then kind of sneaky or something?"

She grins and Gabriel sits back down, his hands free now. He reaches for her, and they twine their fingers together.

"Life is always happening. You know better than most we can work ourselves into a situation where we're missing everything but the j-o-b. Unless you're going to start on dating apps, there's little chance in your current version of life to meet someone." She raises one brow in a pointed expression. "Except for the beautiful, available, kind woman you've known for decades who is now living in your apartment."

I make a sound that's just shy of an actual grumble, and it rings alarmingly like something Gruff would do.

They laugh lightly, but when Gabriel raises Rae's hand to his mouth and kisses the back of it, I know he's about to lay it on me. When his dark brown eyes pin me, I brace.

"It's always a risk, JJ. I don't know this woman, but I know you well enough to know if you see something in her, she's probably a great human. And in that case... I'm on team take your shot."

We move on, mercifully, and start discussing Gruff, since they've heard about him a bit already and he's a not-small part of the impetus for this mess anyway. But my mind is still stuck on their suggestion—on how ridiculous it is, and how hard I'm working to ignore how much I can feel myself wanting to take it.

But I can't. Or won't. Either way, it doesn't matter. This whole thing has a purpose, and it has nothing to do with anything except the agreement we made in the beginning.

CHAPTER FOURTEEN

Grace

It has been ten days since I last saw Justin in the flesh. So much has happened.

Our communication has become increasingly frequent. Despite the time change, he's managed to continue our conversations far more capably than I ever would've imagined a few weeks ago when I first contacted him.

What I thought would make me feel more comfortable living here and smooth the way for roommate-style interactions has turned into something much… more.

I can't explain it, but I am both more and less comfortable here on his couch as the clock ticks down to his arrival. He said he'd be in by nine tonight. I am determined to stay awake and not end up a snoring, gaping-mouthed rock in his living room.

And as significant as our texting has felt, I've also made progress here in terms of what life looks like. I got hired on at Alex Brews fairly quickly and ended up going in on the Friday after Thanksgiving because they were short-staffed. Not having been a barista since college, I did menial things until Andy could train me.

I come home smelling like finely ground espresso—and I don't come home feeling frustrated, worn thin from angry patients or irritable doctors or the ridiculous hurdles of the health care system. I don't carry the weight of those we helped or those we didn't, and more especially, the drudgery and infuriating realities of the American health system or the breakneck pressures of the NHS coupled with a suffocating feeling like I can't escape. Instead, I come home feeling like I've worked a satisfying shift… and that I have a lot more to learn.

I feel grateful for the time I've had here alone. Though there have been moments when I've wished I had company —maybe Justin, or maybe my future faithful little cat to weigh down the sofa next to me—I'm ultimately glad I had this time.

I was never alone in London and yet always felt lonely. The feeling intensified when I returned and met with my old friends from work, and they essentially bid me farewell since I wasn't ready to come back to the hospital. That, and soon after finding out my parents had sold their house where I'd hoped to crash and collect myself for a minute, were truly the loneliest moments I've felt.

So these days in this clean, less-gray-than-before apartment have been a gift. They've given me time to myself in a safe place with no pressure. No one watching me and waiting for me to realize what a mistake I'm making in walking away from nursing.

Because I'm not, I don't think. I'm taking a breath.

I'm not ready to go back, but what won't help is more

judgment on my friends' and colleagues' ends and more inability to relate to their lack of burnout and desire to stay. I certainly don't want them leaving their professions. Maybe it makes me weak for needing this break—I've never pretended to be particularly strong.

But this time without Justin, without my parents, even, and with a new friend who's seeing me as I am and not as she thinks I should be... it has given me room for my lungs to expand fully, for my sleep to deepen and heal me in the darkness, and to wake up ready for the day.

And then there's my Christmas spirit that has shown up in full force. I am maybe a *touch* nervous about how he'll respond to the decorations I've set up, because the apartment is now vastly more Christmas cheery than it was before he left and, if I had to guess, than it ever has been before. It might be a lot, but I hope it'll feel cozy and Christmassy and lovely like it does for me.

When I hear the sound of the door opening, I bolt up from my spot on the couch and fumble for the remote to stop the movie I'd been watching. Anticipation lights me up, and my mind jumps back into the litany of ideas of how this time will go. Maybe he'll join me on the couch for cookies and hot chocolate, and we'll chat about his trip. Maybe he'll ask about my job. Maybe we'll just sit here and watch the movie a while longer, or maybe he'll be exhausted and need to go to bed.

I am a golden retriever whose owner has arrived home from a trip to the grocery store. I have to mentally glue my feet in place so I don't start jumping around and pawing at him, begging him to tell me how he is.

Okay, maybe that's a bit much, but still.

Should I hug him? Is that weird? Probably too soon. We've gotten to know each other, but we've only touched a small handful of times, and all of it happened before. For someone who has been relatively isolated, I'm actually a pretty tactile person. I like hugs and holding hands and snuggling. I just... well, I haven't had that in so, so long. And I don't really have it now. I need to keep that in mind.

Justin slips in and shuts the door gently, my excitement cresting at the sight of him in a suit, because of course this man travels internationally in a suit.

"Hey—"

My words cut off because he's startled so intensely, he drops his phone and stumbles back against the door. With a hand over his heart and his chest heaving, his eyes meet mine. "Hello."

The word is breathy and thin, and I'm on the verge of laughter. "Oh... dear. Did you forget I'd be here? I'm so sorry I scared you."

He huffs. "I didn't forget. No. I just thought you'd be asleep, so I was trying to be quiet."

Adorable. Honestly, he's just freaking adorable there with his breathing still a little erratic and his cheeks pinked. Having him here has sent my pulse racing, and I'm trying to stifle my laugh but it's coming anyway, despite my trying to press my lips together and banish it.

"I'm so sorry," I say, chuckling through the words.

I see the moment he shifts from the terror of his lizard brain screaming *invaders!* to when he fully relaxes and embraces that it's me... just me. And then his eyes do this thing where they drop to my fuzzy sock-covered feet and slide up my red leggings, over my baggy green sweatshirt, and take in my hair in a ponytail and my makeup-free face.

I specifically chose not to remain dressed from the day and instead changed into comfy clothes. This was cause for much internal debate because after the last week-plus of chatting, I can admit I want him to like me. As a friend, as a person, and as a woman. Maybe it's the last vestiges of the crush I had growing up, but I want him to *see* me, to have the same look in his eyes he had when he first saw me in the courthouse, or when he held my arm and told me how beautiful I looked.

Not that I've had those thoughts running on a loop lately or anything.

Strangely enough, I could swear it's this same expression, like he's a little hungry and a little lost, reflecting on his face now.

"No need to apologize. Now that my fight or flight has decided you're not trying to murder me, I can appreciate that it's nice to come home to someone." His eyes skip away, and he sets his keys, wallet, and a few other small things from his pockets onto the little landing zone he has set up just inside the door.

This is one thing I really like about the way Justin lives. After being in his space and seeing past all the monochrome, I've realized how many smart, small details he's included. One of them is the tray and hooks he has set up to hold things by the door. Another is a well-programmed remote that controls his very fancy surround sound speakers, giant TV, and the various systems connected to it.

There are small details like how the cabinets in the bathroom I'm using are stocked with spare items like toothbrushes and fancy bars of soap and basic over-the-counter medications. I'd think he entertained frequently except I can't believe he actually does. He's simply that thorough, that determined to get things just right in order to be comfortable.

"Have you eaten? Are you hungry?" I ask, moving into

the kitchen. I'm not much of a cook, but I'll find something for him.

"No, I'm fine. I've got some work to wrap up before I turn in," he says, hesitating where he stands, then his eyes catch the snowflakes. His brows jump slightly, and he follows the trail of them through the winter wonderland of the kitchen and into the red-and-green-decked living room.

"I did some decorating. I haven't had time to do that in a few years, and I thought it'd be fun. I hope you don't mind," I rush to say, supremely nervous he's silently cursing himself for ever letting me move in.

He finishes inspecting the space, and if I'm not mistaken, his jaw flexes. *Oh.* Not happy, then. Shoot. I can ease off some of the garlands and maybe tuck a little snowman or two currently sitting on the mantle amidst the greenery back into my room.

"No problem."

That's it. That's all I get. The man version of him is lost over the Atlantic, and in his place is my friendly neighbor-hood robot again.

Whomp whomp.

And though I wasn't decorating for him, per se, I had hoped he'd at least enjoy it. But he's stiff, completely still as he sometimes is, and he appears downright irritable. He's making no move to appreciate the details and clearly just wants to get out of here.

This shouldn't bother me, but it does, and I deflate a little. "Oh, okay. Sure. Well, then I'll see you in the morning."

I grab my glass of water sitting right next to the one I poured for him. I'm halfway across the apartment because I'm not going to hang around on the couch if he's not either before I hear him say, "Grace."

Hiding my jumbled feelings, I turn back to him. Our eyes meet and my stomach flips.

"It's good to see you."

Warmth is a slow drip into me, but I feel it, and my smile is small yet very real. Decorations, shmecorations. *This* is what I'd hoped for.

"Likewise, Justice."

CHAPTER FIFTEEN

Justin

It's seven the next morning, and I'm shocked to find Grace's door open, until I remember she's got a job at the coffee shop downstairs now. The woman is certainly not going to laze about in the apartment and fritter her days away. Not that I expected that, but she certainly didn't need to take the first job she found.

I know she said she wanted to work, and of course she needs to since this is all temporary, but there's a part of me that feels twitchy and irritable that she won't just... rest. She needs it. I may not understand everything about what she's leaving behind, but I know she needs time off. Something inside me wants to take care of her...

I bypass the pot of brewed coffee for reasons I don't examine too closely and carry my empty insulated mug along with my briefcase, keys, and phone down the stairs. Along the way, I choose not to inspect the utter glut of

Christmas that has thrown up all over the living room. It's an anxiety-inducing conglomeration of things I can tell Grace enjoys, and I'm not going to let myself drown in how to handle it for the next month.

It's not the colors so much as the... stuff. There's just stuff everywhere—on the mantle, on the couch, hanging from the ceiling. I know it makes me stodgy and boring, but it's different. I know there's something festive there, but I haven't had time to really *look* at them, and I don't want to.

It feels homey and familial in a way I worry things between us shouldn't be. It's not that I'm a Grinch who hates Christmas. It's more I go *to* Christmas—to my parents' house or I see friends for the holiday or I take a ski trip. I don't try to make my own version of it in the apartment by myself.

And maybe there's the rub—I'm not by myself. I'm with someone, and that person is slipping into every nook and cranny of my space. Soon enough, she'll fill it up and there'll be no room to retreat—nowhere to hide.

I've bundled up because the December chill is starting to slip in, and though it's nothing compared to Germany's weather right now, I won't be back until late tonight, and I'll be glad for the layer.

Before I can think twice about it, I enter Alex Brews for the first time since moving into the building close to two years ago.

The place is bustling, and to my dismay, there's a line four people deep. How do people build enough time into their schedule to account for this variable? What a waste.

Then I spot Grace, and she grins at me even as she's tapping away at the screen before her, presumably assisting the person at the front of the line, and something seismic shifts in me.

"Justin! What's your order?"

All of my plans to swing by and simply wish her a good day, to congratulate her on her job in person since I'd failed to do so last night, and to then head to work and go about my day as usual, drain from me. I sputter, awkwardly saying, "Uh, um, a large black coffee."

Grace shoots me a smile that is practically a weapon, it's so potent, and I shuffle forward a few feet on autopilot. So I don't just stare at her, I take in the tinsel lining the bar and framing the large chalkboard menu. There are paper snowflakes hanging from the ceiling at intervals and a tree in the corner.

After my trip to Germany and seeing old friends, I feel surprisingly ready for the activity that comes with the holiday season. Just not the décor carried over at home, possibly. And though I'm nervous, there's a decent part of me looking forward to taking Grace to the first social event of the season.

Not because I'll have *her* there as much as the payoff of her being there, of course. The whole having a wife thing Gruff has more than insinuated will gratify the top brass on the board is the point. Not the woman. Not being with the woman, obviously.

Two minutes later, while the bustle of the two baristas and various chatting patrons fill my oddly empty brain, Grace catches my eye and tilts her head to the right. I'm sure I'm frowning like she's speaking a newly discovered language, and eventually, I gather she wants me to go that direction. Someone jumps to the register to take her place, and Grace slides down to the very end of the counter near the takeaway lids and stir sticks, a large cup in her hand.

"Large coffee to go, though of course you can stay if you

want. I just figured you'd need to get into work sooner rather than later after being gone."

She crosses her arms and leans a hip against the counter, and I find myself stepping as close as I can, wishing there weren't three feet of gray-black counter space between us.

"Thank you. I could've waited."

She gives me a sly smile. "I guess you could've, but you've got an in now." She winks.

That's when it hits me—Grace's energy is different. Last night, I was worn out from the travel and the trip overall, so I failed to notice any evidence of it then. But here? Now? She's got an ease to her, a joy. She seems… happy.

"Guess I do. I'm a lucky man."

Her smile flashes wide and full, and I'm having another revelation. It's one that keeps dawning on me at inconvenient moments but in new ways—when I see Grace for the first time in ten years in the coffee shop. When I see her walking around my apartment. When I see her in her wedding dress. When she's standing in my living room in sweats and slippers. And now.

To be fair, it sounds like I have this realization whenever I see her, and I'm not sure that's wrong.

It's this—Grace is utterly and completely gorgeous. Even if I didn't know anything about her, she'd turn my head, but the way she's smiling at me, the few things I know she's dealing with behind those lovely eyes and the way she's just dived in here with an abandon I've literally never had… it is captivating.

Logic aside, she's glorious.

"Guess so. Is black coffee your usual order here?"

She's got that tilt to her head, and I'm still marveling at

how happy she seems to be just standing here talking with me.

It's probably the reason I'm distracted and admit, "I've actually never been in."

Her confusion hits her face in the furrow of her brows. "Wait, how is that possible?"

The familiar embarrassment of the choices I've made over the last few years hits, but I tell her anyway. "Never had the time."

It's mostly true.

It's also a lie.

Because the more I settle into this fake marriage, the more I'm admitting to myself I've actively chosen not to have a life outside of my career. I've allowed my coworkers, Gruff, and even my previous commander to pile on the work, and I've refused to create boundaries.

It's sickening and weak and also a product of my selfishness. It's also a cultural value that's part of the doublethink in the military, and I've fallen for it.

Grace isn't going to berate me or even make fun of me for it, though. Either she knows there's no point, or she senses my discomfort with the truth, so she shifts things back to coffee.

"Well, do you ever order anything besides black coffee? What would it be?"

I honestly don't know why, but I ask, "What do you think I'd order?"

She laughs softly, then taps her cheek as though deep in thought. "Hmm. If I didn't know you at all, I'd probably guess black coffee or maybe even a doppio would work just fine. From the little I do know..."

For some reason, I'm breathless, waiting on tenterhooks to learn what she'll say. It feels like she's admitting something with this, like she's not only taking a guess but acknowledging she does know me, at least a little.

Why this gives me so much hope, such a burst of adrenaline, I couldn't say, and I have to look away from her and press a lid to my coffee cup to keep from staring at her.

"The evidence suggests you'd like something sweeter, and by *evidence* I mean the sweetened creamers in your fridge. Probably the last thing someone would guess for you, like a peppermint hot chocolate with extra whipped cream, although I know you do need caffeine, so probably some kind of mocha, extra whip."

The way she's looking at me, waiting to see if she's right, spears right through me. Did I not sleep last night? Is there a glitch in the matrix to explain why I can't seem to think straight or do anything but admire how beautiful she is and hang on to her every word this morning? What happened to me while I was away?

Curse you, Rae Jackson!

"Actually, yes. Yeah. Love a mocha."

She brightens. "A few weeks ago, I don't think I could've fathomed you saying the words, 'love a mocha.'"

She's so joyful here, so warm and lovely, I can't help but smile, too, even if she is teasing me. "The wonders never cease. Marriage must suit me."

Her lashes flutter and it's like a wall comes down, then the closed expression disappears just as quickly, though her smile isn't as sweet.

"Must be the case." She glances toward the door, where another patron has just entered and the line is now six-people deep. "I better go. Have a great day."

She's gone before I can say, "You, too, Grace."

I worry the whole drive to work—practically obsess over the way she shut down, then rebooted in a slightly different version of herself a millisecond later. I wouldn't have caught it if I hadn't been looking right at her, but I had.

By the time I show my ID at the gate and find my parking spot, I've worked myself up into something of a tizzy, as my grandmother would've said. I exhale and tap out a message.

"Thanks for the coffee. You seem to enjoy the job."

I cross my fingers and pray the morning rush is in a lull. Mercifully, as I pour the coffee into my mug—which I would've done before putting a lid on it or even leaving the shop if I hadn't been distracted—my phone buzzes with a response.

"Great to see you. Hope you have a good day."

Generic and kind of maddening, yet what do I expect? Why am I acting so oddly? Still, I send one more message.

"I don't think I've mentioned that I don't have cell phone access during the workday unless I'm off-site, so if you text and don't hear back, don't worry. I'll be home late tonight, and we've got the ball tomorrow as long as you're still free."

The thought of her *not* being free is loathsome, but it's possible her plans have changed. I don't recall the hours of the coffee place, and around here, you never know. Yes, our agreement laid out my needs and does technically stipulate her presence at this event in particular, but I will never force her and she seems to know it.

Before I exit the car, she responds again.

"I'll see you tomorrow night, if not before. Already got my dress."

And it's this thought that keeps me going long into the night and all the next day, until I'm straightening the bow tie of my dress blues and taking one last breath before I go out to see my date—my wife.

CHAPTER SIXTEEN

Grace

I thought I was nervous for the marriage ceremony, but I might be even more nervous for this military ball.

The day we got married, I was numb. Dazed. In a place that doesn't quite seem like a distant memory—wouldn't that be nice—yet does feel very much like a hole I've started climbing out of. But right now, I have champagne veins again plus tachycardia and a mean case of dry mouth I keep trying to swallow hard against to fix.

Tonight, we'll have an audience. I missed Justin last night—I passed out in my bed instead of on the couch, thank you very much. I thought I was used to early mornings since I've had plenty of schedules in my previous job that required early rising and long days, yet something about the blissful exhaustion of physically being tired but not mentally worn down has me slipping off to sleep before I even realize it lately.

Because of this and Justin's insane work schedule, I didn't see him last night. He didn't stop into the shop this morning, and I'm not sure if this is good or bad. Obviously, it's not his usual habit, so I shouldn't be disappointed.

I mean, I wasn't.

I'm not.

I totally haven't been thinking about him and this night and all of the traditions wrapped up in military balls and the fact I'm pretty sure I haven't worn a formal gown since my senior prom incessantly for the last thirty-six hours at all.

Which means I'm preoccupied as I pace his living room in this red dress that cuts just above my collarbones in the front and then dips into a dramatic vee ending at my lower back. I slide my hands along the material fitting close to my ribs and waist and over the curves of my hips down to a mermaid skirt that swirls and is miraculously the perfect length for my heels.

It is utterly gorgeous and the red is deep and vibrant and feels like the formal manifestation of a black-tie Christmas. I rented the gown from the same boutique where I bought my wedding dress—the fact that Andy has an in with them has turned out to be a miracle. But even getting fancied up hasn't distracted me because it's all leading toward the thing, or person, I'm anxious to see.

And there's the small potential issue the dress is so conspicuous, it might be embarrassing, and I am terrified I've done everything wrong. It's a floor-length dress, after all, and it's about as formal as formal gets. I love that about it, but I can't pretend I'm not paranoid I've gone *way* overboard.

My hair is curled, and I've pinned it up in a stylish chignon after watching a few online tutorials. I'm wearing dramatic eye makeup and red lipstick, and I cannot stop thinking he's going to walk out in his camouflage or whatever you call it and I'm going to have to run and change.

I know he won't be because I asked about what to wear last week in the flurry of our texts. On the schedule, he'd noted attire was formal, and I had to make sure I wasn't misunderstanding.

I've searched the internet until I'm blue in the face and have learned what I can about a military ball, including all kinds of things one should *not* wear. Shockingly, dresses short enough to show your underwear? Not a great idea. So much cleavage you could take an eye out? Also, seemingly frowned upon. Beyond that, it's all a choose-your-own-adventure and, again, my pulse knocks up and I am praying I'm somewhere in the zone of appropriate.

A sound pulls my attention, and I whip around to see Justin standing in the room with his hand braced on the kitchen counter. And he's not wearing his camouflage. He's got a black tux jacket with deep navy on the lapels and gold buttons down the front, a chain attaching each side of the jacket in the middle, and golden cords whirling around the sleeves. Under it, he wears a black bow tie atop a crisp white tuxedo shirt. There are small colorful ribbons with circular medals attached in neat rows on his left side hanging above his heart, and I hope I'll learn what each one means. The slacks are close to a royal blue hue, with a gold stripe on the outside of each leg that matches the cording on the jacket. His shiny dress shoes reflect the light from the kitchen.

It is by far the fanciest uniform I've ever seen. This means little since my exposure to military finery is minimal, and yet it packs a punch.

And none of it is his face, which is so gravely handsome,

it makes my nerves quadruple even as I feel a little melty and soft looking at him. It's both the hazel eyes that seem darker against the black and deep blue of his jacket, and his lips that are generous and firm at once. It's the way his cheeks hollow a bit in that manly way, and the close shave he must've given himself very recently that makes his jaw look like it could cut glass.

Okay, getting a little fanciful there, aren't we? A jaw? Cutting glass? What kind of anatomy is that?

Not the textbook kind, for sure, but nothing about my life is textbook anyway.

"Grace, you're stunning." His voice is quiet yet firm.

My cheeks burn. "You are, too."

He only nods in acknowledgment, like he knows what he looks like and it's good, and yet this man isn't that kind of confident. He's the forty-year-old male equivalent of the One Direction song "What Makes You Beautiful." His obliviousness to exactly how handsome he really is just piles on more allure.

He's still standing there, his eyes taking in every inch of my face like it's that and not this fabulous dress making the moment balloon between us, taking up all the air and shifting the beat of my heart into my ears.

"Should we go?" I ask, because I cannot reliably stand here any longer. My knees are absolutely going to give out under his intensity.

He blinks, coming back to himself. "Of course, yes. Do you have a coat?"

The sharp, close shave of his jaw is giving me an arrhythmia, and my palms are in danger of sweating, so I welcome the excuse to pace away from him and retrieve the black thigh-length wool jacket where it hangs in a hallway closet. It's not as fancy as the faux-fur stole Andy wanted me to get, but that just isn't me. I'm not this glamorous person who wears gowns and has ridiculously good-looking dates. I don't know how to do this.

In a matter of minutes, we're in the car he called and moving swiftly along the winter evening road. We've made small talk that is less painful than it was before we knew each other, yet more uncomfortable in that I'm starting to worry I may not be able to shake these nerves. I look at my hands and enjoy seeing my French-manicured nails. I got them done for this occasion and it made me realize how long it's been since I last painted my nails. Years ago, I used to celebrate my days off by painting a new color every week, but it's been so long. It's one more thing I let drop during the last few years of shrinking and shriveling up.

"Are you alright?" Justin asks, that same quiet, steady quality to his voice.

I don't look up, keeping my focus on my hands. "Just a little nervous."

When he doesn't respond for a full minute, I look up. Maybe admitting I'm nervous made him nervous, too? "Are you?"

His gaze is on me when my eyes meet his, and he nods slightly. "Yes. But it's going to be fine."

A laugh slips out. "Well, then. If it's going to be fine, I guess I'll just shut off the nerves altogether, right?"

One side of his mouth slides up like he's genuinely pleased. "There you go. Well done."

I would chuckle, except he seems like he might actually think I've banished my nerves. "I wish it were that easy."

And then his large hand reaches over and covers mine for a moment. He squeezes gently, and it's a little odd, but his palm covering the back of my hand is warm and comforting, too. He retreats before I can flip my hand and accept the gesture.

It's so... sweet. So genuine. I can't tell if it's the nerves or something else, but a little ice-skater in my belly does a double axel.

"Nerves are your body's way of preparing you. You already know the hardest case in there, and Gruff will likely be so irritable at having to dress up in his mess dress that he won't be watching us all that closely."

"Mess dress?"

A hint of a smile again, then his eyes slide over my face before shifting to watch out the front windshield. "It's from the British uniform. They wore something vaguely similar back in the mid-eighteen hundreds, and typically, military formal events were held in mess halls. So... mess dress." His eyes come back to meet mine again. "It is far less comfortable than any other uniform."

I press my lips together because the boyish look on his face is killing me. It makes me want to cup his cheeks or kiss his forehead and give him a cookie. I can't hold it in—especially when his brow furrows—and a snicker escapes.

"Laughing at my discomfort?" There's another small curve to his lips.

"Oh, never. I can imagine it's horrible to wear pants, a shirt, and a jacket with shiny shoes. I bet you have something awful on under there, like underwear and an undershirt, too." I blink my lashes at him, waiting for it. He's a very smart man. Surely, he can make the connection.

His eyes narrow. "Are you suggesting you are also uncomfortable in this very fancy dress?"

I grin. "Now you're getting it."

"I feel silly, but I've honestly never thought about it. Women never seem to be uncomfortable. You don't seem ill at ease, beyond your nerves, I suppose. But is that due to the dress?"

His eyes are running over me, not in a lascivious way, as though he's looking for the particular areas of discomfort.

"It's adorable that you both haven't thought about it or noticed. But it's also thanks to the fact that women are often in situations where they are uncomfortable and have to manage the feeling, whether it's circumstantial or due to the various circus tricks we do to be comfortable in an outfit like this."

Clearly intrigued now, one of his brows lifts. "Circus tricks? Can you elaborate?"

I consider being coy and elusive, but I don't have much of that in me, and with the nerves and the ever-approaching destination nearly in our sights, I decide honesty is best.

"Any dress like this requires excellent posture, for onc, though I am sure a fancy mess dress uniform or anything else looks best when you're standing straight as well. Then there's the dress itself—this one's lovely, though the material is actually fairly heavy. By the end of the night, I'll be exhausted from holding it and myself up, and doing it in three-inch heels." I tug the dress up a few inches to reveal the gorgeous and not-yet-but-definitely-eventually painful shoes.

His gaze tracks the movement and he swallows.

"And that's not including the time it takes to do hair, makeup, and find the right underthings to accommodate whatever style of dress you wear."

"Underthings?" he asks, and I see the moment he realizes it isn't particularly appropriate.

I don't mind, though. Because it's part of this, and I know he's not saying it in a creepy way. Plus *maybe* I want to push him a little... see what he does.

"Yes. There're all kinds of shapewear that use spandex and Velcro and hooks and eyes to strap in or tie down a woman's curves, to *shape* them into submission so we satisfy a contemporary beauty standard that has nothing to do with a real woman's body. They're usually hot and make using the bathroom a process."

He looks genuinely troubled by this, and I see his eyes dip to my waist, then jerk back up. "And you're wearing one of these contraptions?"

I chuckle at his word choice. "No. I can't stand them, even if they do smooth things out. I just hate the whole concept. Instead, I wear as little as possible and hope the dress does me favors."

He swallows again and this time, his voice is low, low, low. "As little as possible?"

I flush, suddenly realizing just how TMI this whole situation is. But we're this far in, so I finish the thought. "Uh, yeah. Just underwear that doesn't leave lines, and since this dress is basically backless, that's it."

And yep. Yes. I did just tell my husband slash a man I think I may have a crush on slash the man who is kind of my landlord that I'm not wearing a bra. He might even realize I insinuated I'm wearing *barely there* underwear since this dress is rather fitted and very few things allow for no panty lines.

Really, the question is, why on earth am I talking about panty lines with him?!

I wouldn't be entirely shocked if smoke started coming out of his ears, though it's just as likely he's completely unfazed by the discussion of underwear. He's an attractive man, but there seems to be no history of broken hearts following him. I don't really want this information anyway, but it occurs to me he may not be moved in the least by the discussion of undies and the like.

He clears his throat. "Ah, well. That does sound unpleasant. I'm sorry you had to go to so much trouble."

He won't look at me now, and I sit back and sigh as silently as I can. *Mmkay* so, maybe not entirely unfazed.

This is perfect, though. I mean really, what better way to kick off a fancy evening of pretending I'm in love with my new husband than to talk about my underthings in borderline graphic detail and make things even more awkward between us?

If there is one, I sure can't think of any.

CHAPTER SEVENTEEN

Justin

I thought Grace was a kindhearted woman. I know she is, at least on some level.

But after the drive here and that last bit of conversation, I am now reexamining all my previous notions.

I'm not a man easily flustered. Though I can be anxious, I have worked long and hard to keep the manifestation of that anxiety inside and not let it seep out onto my face or into my body language. It's why I tend to stay very still rather than allowing my knee to bounce or my eyes to shift around a room like they're sometimes tempted to do.

It took every ounce of self-control I had not to react any more than I did to Grace's statements about her stunning red dress. And most especially, what she is—or is not—wearing underneath it.

I am making a truly valiant effort not to picture in detail what may or may not be under the dress and then mentally slapping myself for thinking about what's under it at all. She's not my real wife. She's not someone whose underthings I get to consider at all, in any way, ever.

And even though the more I'm around her, the more I *want* to be able to, it is not appropriate to be feeling such things for my wife.

Do not think about your wife like that!

It's not the first or last time I've thought it.

We've made it through the formal receiving line, a custom I find tedious but am happy not to have to stand in myself. We've found our table, and Colonel Gruff has just shaken Grace's hand and greeted her rather cordially, so someone must've slipped him his nice-boy pills. He has a pretty woman with him whom he introduces as Janie and gives no explanation of who she is to him, so a mystery to be solved another day.

We've mingled and each had a drink. I have forbidden myself from setting a hand on Grace's back, though I'm finding *not* doing so may appear abnormal, particularly as I watch colleagues and friends escort their dates around in just such a way.

The more I think about it, the more I find I'm lightly obsessed with the desire to slide my hand against the bare skin there, the dip of her dress a tantalizing glimpse of skin and fabric.

Along with Gruff and Janie, we are also, mercifully, seated with the person I like best in the unit. James Ashley and his wife, Megan, are both delightful. I know James from his time in Rambler Battalion back at Fort Campbell years ago. It's good to see he and Megan have survived these long years. Rumor has it he'll take command of the Old Guard here in DC soon—an illustrious position and certainly one of honor. These are the soldiers who guard the Tomb of the

Unknown Soldier and many other important duties. James stands and shakes my hand.

"Good to see you, old friend," he says, his smile bright against his dark skin, and he leans in to give me a pat on the back.

"Oh, JJ, I'm so glad to see you!" His wife reaches for a hug and kisses my cheek. "And who's this stunning flower of a woman?"

I grin, because Megan Ashley is over the top in exact proportion to the way her husband is steady and understated. I reach for Grace, who steps close and extends a hand to Megan as I say, "This is my wife, Grace."

Megan's eyes grow wide, and then she screeches loudly enough several tables swing their attention to us. Then she knocks Grace's hand away and launches at her for a hug.

"I am so freaking happy to meet you!" She pulls back, holding a dazed Grace by the shoulders. "Yes, you are stunning. No surprise since our JJ here is a handsome devil. Aww—"

She glances at me with a look far too sentimental for someone I haven't seen in years, then pulls Grace back in. I could swear she whispers something to her, and when they separate, Grace is smiling and clearly a bit dazzled. Megan's beauty queen energy has that effect on people.

"You're out of your league with this woman, JJ," Megan says to me with a big grin and wink.

"I can't argue with that."

I pull out Grace's chair and she sits down. I do my best not to let my eyes linger on the long sweep of her spine down her bare back or the jut of her shoulder blades. I've never thought of these parts of a body as something intimate, but suddenly, I'd like to clear the room and make sure no one else gets to see.

"You call him JJ?"

Grace's voice snaps me back into the moment, and I sit next to her as Megan answers.

"I think we met his momma one time when she came to visit, and I just loved how she called him JJ. I've taken to using it, too, though James still calls him Justin."

James casts me a look of apology, though he needn't. "I'm always sensitive to using the name someone uses to introduce themselves. I've had people call me Jim after I've introduced myself as James—it's an entirely different name. Strikes me as very odd. So until Justin tells me to, I won't be calling him JJ."

Gruff must catch this leg of conversation. "His mom called him JJ in front of me, too. Maybe I should start up."

There's no humor behind it, but I scrape from the bottom of myself and try. "As you wish, sir."

Everyone chuckles and Grace gives me a quiet little grin. I haven't stopped thinking about how *she* called me JJ. She's slipped once, and it gave me an odd pang. I haven't known whether it was nostalgia or longing, and I'm still not sure. I don't really care what people call me, but I like the idea of hearing Grace use JJ like she did when we were kids.

"So do you call him JJ or Justin? That'll be the tell-all for name preference."

Megan's question is perfectly on topic, yet dread kicks at me. This is the first question that feels like a real test.

Grace's blue eyes flick to mine. I can't read her expression.

"Usually, I call him Justin."

I'm not sure if I'm seeing it right or not, but if I am, there's something like a shade of regret there.

Megan smiles broadly, though I know any answer would've garnered this response.

"Can you tell us how you met? And about the wedding?"

She's a good woman, but I wish she'd stop asking. She has a romantic heart and she and everyone else at the table seem genuinely interested in the answer. Gruff's gaze sharpens and he narrows all his attention on Grace.

"Yes, do tell," he urges.

"Oh, uh, we've known each other for years. He was my neighbor growing up."

I can read her now, and she's practically mentally screaming at me that we didn't go over this—any of our answers.

Right about now, a Jedi mind trick would be handy. *You already know our story and it's great. Move on.*

How did I fail to address this? After Gruff showing up at the wedding, I guess I grew complacent in thinking he'd witnessed the act itself and therefore wouldn't have questions. I should've known he'd be reluctant to take anything at face value, even if he witnessed it.

Megan says something about a sexy neighbors-become-lovers situation, Grace's cheeks heat, and Gruff cuts through all of it to begin the real inquisition.

"I thought Justin's mother told me you'd only just reconnected? I wonder why he hasn't said anything to anyone at work if he's been so smitten."

The accusation rings loud and clear, and I respond with a smile. "It surprised us both, I think."

I reach for Grace's hand and link our fingers. Normally, any amount of contact with her would send my heart sprinting, but it's already at a jog from this line of questioning, and I'm fairly certain my limbs are feeling a little numb.

There is no motive to defraud the government here. I have no insidious plan other than to help Grace with a place to live and help myself get a life. Yes, I've played into the odd pressure to be married in order to appeal to certain board members for early promotion, yet it's not fraud. It's actually simple prejudice and shouldn't enter into the equation at all, but at this level, the games are rampant, and with this move, I've decided to play.

I always knew there would be this moment when Gruff pushes back and tries to make it feel like I've done something wrong, though he can't prove it based on anything we've said or done, and I'm not about to let this go on a second longer.

Before I can say anything, Grace is leaning close, sliding her hand up my arm, slipping it into the short hair at the back of my neck and pressing a kiss to my cheek.

I suck in a breath because, whatever the circumstances, this touch has my attention. It feels... decadent. Almost indecent in the way it's happening here, in front of all these people, when it should be happening in private so I can respond how I'd like.

But that's not what I should be thinking about. And I'm not. Definitely not thinking about getting her alone and what it would be like if maybe this closeness were real.

No.

Instead, I watch her at close range as she pulls back and turns to speak directly to Gruff.

"I always had a little crush on him, but between the age difference when we were young and life happening, nothing came of it until recently."

She shoots me a smile, and the pretty blush on her cheeks sends a thrill through me.

Did she really always have a crush on me? The six years between us meant I'd never thought of her that way, not until my last visit to her family home before I deployed the first time.

It shouldn't matter if the Grace of more than a decade ago had liked me. This is a grown woman with life behind her. It is her opinion now that should really matter. But my idiot brain just has to get hopeful about the now because of this tiny mention of then.

"I love it," Megan sighs, and Janie says something along those lines, too.

Still, Gruff isn't having it. "Sounds nice. But how did you go from ancient history to marriage when we haven't heard a single word about you?"

CHAPTER EIGHTEEN

Grace

Colonel Gruff is a terrifying human being. He was none too friendly at the wedding, but I hadn't gotten this vibe from him. I've been working hard to understand what would be asked of me tonight, and silly me, I've focused on knowing the military protocols and what *not* to do so I don't embarrass Justin.

Insanely, we haven't talked about this—the backstory!

How have we not talked about this?!!

I haven't been all that worried about people not believing us as an *us*, maybe because I was more preoccupied with being around Justin in this intense, unique atmosphere.

Justin slides his arm along the back of my chair. "You know I'm a private person, sir, and we don't exactly gab about our dating lives."

I've learned Colonel Gruff is one of few officers who

aren't married in this unit—thus part of the issue with Justin taking so much of the workload on himself. Gruff apparently liked long hours as much as Justin did, but he's already climbed up the next rung *and* his previous marriage doesn't seem to have held up to the pressure... or his attitude problem.

"It doesn't appear your colleagues know anything either," Gruff points out.

Justin doesn't falter, though. "Again, I'm a private person. Grace has been overseas, so much of our relationship has been virtual." He glances at me, and the steady look in his eye gives me faith we can make it through this. "We've known when she was getting back, and we wanted to be together. There was no reason to wait."

"I didn't realize you were so decisive, but I'll offer my congratulations again nonetheless." Gruff says this like he's bestowed a gift on Justin, and my hackles rise even higher.

That is just about the rudest thing a boss could say, and why on earth would he say it here, now, and in response to this?

Megan exclaims loudly when a server comes to bring salad plates to everyone, effectively cutting off conversation about us. She then launches into a loud recounting of her kids' Christmas letters to Santa, which is both hilarious and so well timed, I could kiss her.

Throughout the dinner, defensiveness on Justin's behalf lingers close to the edges, on the tip of my tongue. For some reason, I feel like crying, and it's the weirdest response. Yes, he's my husband in name, but not... emotionally. We aren't married because I fell for him and know what a wonderful man he is and couldn't live without him.

Though you could because he is and... we'll see about that last one.

I shake off the thought and focus on the guest speaker who is now talking about the valuable contributions the military personnel in the room have made in the National Capital Region. Instead of just saying NoVa like a Virginian, or DC like someone who's moved into town would, all the people here refer to the *region*. Maybe it's because this is a conglomeration of units and organizations around DC and not specifically a single-unit event, as Justin explained to me earlier.

Justin's hand is on the back of my chair again, and I feel the brush of his fingers against my neck. That little contact makes me gasp, and my gaze snaps to him, but his eyes are firmly on the speaker as though he has no idea he's touching me.

Is it possible he doesn't feel the same sizzling intensity whenever we touch? Does he not have an inner voice sounding like a greedy little thing begging for more, more, more, and then a rude, intrusive conscience saying "This ain't even real"?

Apparently not, because the pads of his fingers tickle up and down my neck, then lower. I'm tempted to sit forward and offer my whole back to him—*here, have at it, baby. I very much do accept your physical touch whenever you want to give it to me.*

Before I embarrass myself by leaning back into his contact even more and audibly moaning, the crowd begins to applaud, and the emcee announces it's time to dance. I'm relieved to have a reason to stand, and I do, offering a hand to Justin. Sure, I should've been calm and cool and not asked *him* to dance, but it was that or beg him to keep tickling my back, and I feel like this is the less odd thing.

"Dance with me, husband?" I say, hooked into those hazel eyes of his.

"My pleasure."

I'm simultaneously hungry for waffle fries and his nearness. Since I'm actually quite full of dinner and dessert, I ignore the Pavlovian response to the phrase used by my favorite fast-food chain I missed while overseas and enjoy the sight of him rising from his chair without breaking eye contact.

He guides us to the dance floor as several others, including James and Megan, find their way as the band begins to play Nat King Cole, and I realize I'm not sure I've ever danced with someone to Christmas music.

Justin takes my other hand and cuts off my momentary panic at not remembering what to do or how to position my arms by sliding one hand to my left shoulder blade and holding the other out to the side. Muscle memory from some long-forgotten high school dance reminds me to place my other hand on his shoulder. And just when I think, "This feels a little formal," he takes a large step closer so only inches separate us and begins to move.

After a moment of swirling around the floor, it all feels so much like a fairy tale I might've dreamed up as a girl, I can't hold in a joyful laugh.

"Are my dancing skills so bad?" Justin asks, his eyes on mine before they return to the space where he'll lead us next on the floor.

"Not at all. You're wonderful." And if that isn't the whole truth, I don't know what is.

He rewards me with a small smile I absolutely love. In this amazing, light moment of swirling around a dance floor full of couples dressed to the nines with the band playing Christmas classics and Justin easing up on the controls he has himself under, I forget.

For a few minutes out there, I forget this isn't real. I'm

not sure how, since Justin and I are only starting to know each other and we clearly have a ton to discuss. That doesn't seem to matter to my fluttering heart and gleeful little brain. Maybe it's the champagne I had in cocktail hour or the half glass of wine at dinner, but I don't think so.

I think it's Justin—JJ. The man I always liked, always *saw*, and here he is with me, years and years later. His hand is gentle yet firm on the skin of my back, the contact there a delectable bonus to this gorgeous dress.

"You're handling all this very well," he says, slowing us down in time with the music, which is now beginning "I'll be Home for Christmas."

"I'm not so sure about that, but I hope we convinced everyone," I say as quietly as I can so no one hears.

Two things happen next. First, the hand steadfastly pressed against my shoulder blade makes a sensual, purposeful slide down my spine and rests against my lower back. Second, he brings our clasped hands much closer to our bodies. I readjust so the hand on his shoulder slides up to the back of his neck.

We are now in a dancing form far more intimate than before, and it feels perfect. He hasn't stopped moving, swaying us around in tiny pivots as the singer begins the verses. This has always been a favorite song, but in a room full of soldiers who've likely missed many Christmases with their loved ones, it hits me with a melancholy sideswipe.

"You handled everything well, Grace. Thank you. I'm sorry for the resident rain cloud."

Our faces are close, so he's looking into my eyes. I haven't been this close to him since he kissed the corner of my mouth at the courthouse, save the quick peck on his cheek earlier, which hardly counted.

We are in each other's space, legs brushing as we dance,

hands linked, and faces so close, we could kiss without breaking stride. My heart is fluttering because JJ's touch and surprisingly good dance skills and gorgeous face *right here* are overwhelming me.

"He is a delight."

JJ chuckles low and the sound does something to my insides, and then he pulls me even closer, sliding his other hand around me so our bodies are a fraction of an inch apart, and he responds at just above a whisper.

"I don't fully understand his issue, but I've never been more thankful for Megan."

We laugh together now, though his breath warm and soft against my ear is no laughing matter. The singer reaches the bridge of the song, singing her heart out, and I find myself wondering aloud, "Have you missed many Christmases?"

"A handful."

That twists through me like a thorny branch, yet he says it so casually.

"Is it hard? You and your mom seem close."

He huffs a small embarrassed laugh. "Do we? What gave you that impression?"

I pull back enough to see his eyes glittering with good humor, and I am struck anew by exactly how handsome he is. I'm a broken mental record, and yet, *where's the lie?*

He continues. "I don't like being away. But I have been able to step in for people who would miss time with their families, and so I try to keep that in perspective. I try to imagine that if I was in their shoes, it'd make a difference to me."

"In their shoes how? You're missing time with your family, just like they are."

When I search his face, I find a key to a little lock I

hadn't expected to stumble on in the expression on his features, and he clinches it when he says, "Their spouses and young children. That's different."

His jaw flexes, and I don't bother to check the reaction in me or the impulse to press onto my toes and kiss the smooth edge of that very jaw. My heart feels achy and too big for my chest, this man stealing any bit of me that might be Grinchy and turning it into empathetic mush.

"It's a lovely thought."

It's not enough or even the right sentiment, but I want to acknowledge what I know has been a sacrifice at times. I can't figure out how to tell him he deserves it, too—the time with family, or maybe even just the feeling he can rest and be at home with his people, whether they are his parents or his future wife and kids. It feels like something I'm too close to now, so instead, I ask, "Are you looking forward to Christmas with your family?"

Megan and James twirl up next to us, and Megan flashes her brows before she juts her chin up. "You know, it's time you make use of that mistletoe."

James winks at me and guides her away with another turn.

And that's when JJ and I look up to see a sprig of mistletoe hanging from golden ribbon. There are little clusters of it strung up at intervals all around the dance floor.

And it'd be adorable if it didn't mean I now needed to kiss him in front of a crowded dance floor.

CHAPTER NINETEEN

Justin

I see Grace's throat move as she swallows. My stomach clenches and I catch her eye.

"We don't have to—"

"Just do it. Quick."

Her eyes flare and I take the warning, not because I'm particularly attuned to what she's warning me about, but because I can tell she *is*. She's not simply trying to get it over with, which means someone must be watching.

So I slide one hand to her neck and stop short of the ornate updo so I don't ruin it, though the desire to slip my fingers into her hair is absolutely there. I meet her eyes for a second before they close, and I lean in.

The instant our lips meet, I regret it. Not the meeting, but the context, the setting, the moment we've given ourselves to experience this first. Because more and more,

I'm convinced I want many things, many firsts, with Grace, and this first kiss, this first true contact between our lips, feels too close to something real.

It's with this in mind—the thought that maybe we could have this again, for ourselves and not for show, that leads me to press my lips to hers in an insistent yet soft moment of contact, then pull away.

An exhale gusts out between her plush lips, and I mentally arm wrestle the need to devour her right here, right now. It might seem like a newlywed thing to do. Really, what would be *more* convincing than a man fully captivated by his wife? If the goal is making this appear to be a love match, there must be a magnetic pull between the parties, right?

But we haven't prepared for this, and I won't do anything Grace doesn't want.

When her eyes blink open, the look she gives me sends my stomach to my toes. I could swear it's one of desire—as much as I'm harboring for her. And yet, when she blinks again, it's gone, and a placid smile hides whatever was there.

"Good job. Gruff was just behind you. He's twirled poor Janie away."

With a laugh, I tense my hands and arms around her in an odd semblance of a hug. "Good" is all I can say, because there's a not-small part of my brain and body that are both reliving the quick second of our kiss and rearranging everything in my life to make sure I can do it again.

Work? What work?

Promotion aspirations? Bah.

The only thing on my schedule for tonight and forever should be kissing Grace.

"So? Are you excited for Christmas with your family?"

she asks, as though nothing has happened between now and the last time she asked.

Okay, time to get back on track.

"It should be fun. I hope. And if you don't want to come—"

She's shaking her head before I can finish. "I'll be there. My parents will be on the cruise for a while. Your dad doesn't know about... everything, right?"

Dread injects into my gut at the thought of keeping something from my dad, a man who is the embodiment of honesty and honor. I know why we aren't telling him, though—he wouldn't understand. He'd think we're making a mockery of marriage when what we're doing is—it's more pragmatic than that.

My mother's fantasies come from romantic thoughts, and my father's come from honorable ones. I find I fall well between them, somewhere in the land of *this is reality, and here's how to handle it.* Granted, I'm not sure my life has all that much to show for it in terms of successful handling of the nature of reality since all my coping mechanisms thus far have centered on work—working more, working harder, promoting early and often and... well. Here we are.

Here I am with Grace Murphy, my wife.

"Right. But you still don't have to come. We can figure out an excuse."

She's insistent. "No. I'll be there. I love your parents and it'll be nice to spend the holiday with family." She swallows, a flicker of discomfort crossing her lovely face before she adds, "You know what I mean."

"Of course. And we'll only stay for two nights. I'm on Rear D for the duration of the holiday leave."

"Rear D?"

"Rear detachment—it means I'm in charge if anything

happens to anyone during the winter block leave period—the time when everyone goes home for the holidays. Someone has to be the point person, and since I have family close enough to be considered local, I'm only taking a few days, and I'll still be available by phone."

"Makes sense," she says, though there's an unidentifiable asterisk there in her gaze I can't quite pin down.

"And you? Do you have your work schedule for the shop?" I ask, because I don't want to seem like the kind of man who only cares about himself, even if all evidence would point to that very much being the case to date.

Without warning, she beams. "I only get it two weeks out. I'll make sure to let Andy know I'm free."

Not *free*, I want to say, though I can't. That's nonsense. I'll be working and I shouldn't expect her to take time off if I'm not doing the same. Why would I want that anyway? Her days off don't affect me.

But for what might be the first time in a long time, I wish I was taking more leave. I wish I'd planned for this—more time with her, more time to just... be with her. But there's no way to plan for something I never saw coming and which I don't have space for in my life.

Tension hooks its arms with ours as we say goodbye, each receiving cheek kisses from Megan and friendly hugs from James, curt nods from Gruff, and smiles from his unfortunate date or friend or whoever she is, Janie. She must be someone to him, because she's smiled and laughed though he has cracked nary a smile, so she isn't new to his sweet spirit.

It's there as we exit the ballroom and as I help Grace slip into her coat. It's there as we link fingers—in case anyone's watching, of course—and I open the door of the car service for her. It's there as we wait for the elevator, then take it to our floor. It's there as I open the apartment door and we step into the quiet, only the garland she's strung up with twinkle lights glowing dimly to greet us.

It is the mapping of new territory, a fertile, unexplored space we've now just begun to cross tonight. We've touched —hands, faces, *bodies*, even, and it has not felt awkward or laborious. It felt natural and right.

It has broken through my insistence that this is all for the agreement.

I have been mentally arguing with myself about why I shouldn't kiss her without an audience tonight. I've been considering whether I should ask her if she thinks we should practice, just to really sell it next time, or if that's even necessary. Maybe I can simply kiss her without preamble or excuse.

The door swings shut behind me, and I don't move to turn on the kitchen lights. She's in silhouette, the red hue of her dress visible as she removes her jacket. My fingers itch with the need to press against her skin, to grip her waist and guide her around a floor, or maybe just hold her close to me —as close as she'll let me.

I consider it, my heart climbing into my throat as I think about how to proceed in a way that is both respectful of what she may or may not want, but is clear about what I do. And I am no longer pretending I don't want Grace, even if that wasn't in the contract.

"Thank you for a lovely evening. I think we pulled it

off," she says, and she steps farther into the room, farther away from me.

"I think we did, too." *Probably because this isn't just for appearances anymore. At least not for me.*

The words are right there—right. There.

"Well, event number one can be checked off the list."

"It can, though I've realized something," I say, stepping toward where she's standing.

"Oh?"

It's maybe a little breathless, or perhaps it's just how I'm feeling as I near her and she lifts her chin. "We're going to need to practice."

Her lashes flutter. "Oh?"

A smile flashes across my lips—I can't help it. She charms me and I can see she's pleased she did with the way she bites her lip. My gaze drops to her white teeth on her plush lip, and I don't hesitate anymore.

"There'll be more mistletoe. We'll need to be ready."

Her lips part and she nods. "Of course."

Our eyes lock and if I was thinking more clearly, I might've thought better of this, but right now, all I see is her desire and consent mingling as her hands float to my lapels.

She's taller with her heels, so I only have to slide a hand to her back, her warm skin a delicious pleasure against my palm, and then I kiss her. It's soft—slight even, and her intake of breath tells me maybe she hadn't expected it. But then she leans into me, chasing after me until our lips meet again. She is sweet like the peppermint she had in the car, and she's soft and lush.

When she parts for me, allowing the kiss to deepen to something more, I go molten. And she must, too, because she slides her nails against the short hair at my neck again and makes a sound I will remember until my dying day. It's full of desire and need and matches my sentiments exactly. I urge her nearer, a satisfied rumble in my chest as our bodies slide close, and I mentally curse the fact that I'm still wearing my tux jacket and there's so much between us.

Then she freezes, like she belatedly realized what we're doing and she doesn't want this. I pull back instantly, because the only thing I want more than *her* is to make sure we're both in agreement here.

She smiles, but it's not relaxed or particularly joyful or even satisfied. It's an expression I haven't seen since the early days here. There's a forced quality to it I can see plain as day as she presses a finger to her lips, something that doesn't meet her eyes and that I can see even in the dim room.

"Well, that'll work just fine."

I realize then... she is not mapping new territory for further exploration. She is here redrawing the lines, doubling down on the very explicit requirements enumerated in our agreement amidst her handcrafted snowflakes.

I don't know why this detail sticks out at me, but it does. Maybe this discomfort is her recognizing that I am feeling more than she is, feeling too much, feeling anything beyond friendly and grateful. I took it too far, obviously, and I have to salvage this.

So I shut it down. I reach for the calm, the collected professional who has dominated every bit of me for so long, and I nod with a briskness I hope conveys everything is fine. "Of course. Well done. I appreciate your help."

She inhales and I could swear she holds her breath as she studies me, then nods, giving me that same smile.

"Have a good night, JJ."

I watch her disappear down the hallway and force myself to forget the discussion of what's under the dress or my ridiculous thoughts about wanting so much more than kissing her. I mentally demand that I do nothing, say nothing, until I hear her door click shut because this, after all, is just part of the job we've set out for ourselves. Part of the agreement.

"Good night, Grace."

CHAPTER TWENTY

Grace

Andy eyes me during the afternoon lull.

"Okay seriously, what is your deal?"

I shrug. "I'm wiping the counter... am I doing it wrong?"

She gives me as close to a glare as I imagine she can considering she has the most naturally cheery face I've ever seen—a mouth that turns up at the corners, smiling eyes and brows arching in a way that only contribute to them, and a generally sunshiny demeanor.

"No, silly. I just feel like you've disappeared inside your head a bit this last week or so."

I swallow, refusing to look at her. After all, wiping down a countertop is serious work, isn't it? "It's been weird lately, I guess. With Justin, I mean."

No one has come into the shop in the last ten minutes, and apparently, there isn't any hope of an interruption, so might as well be brave and face her. She's waiting for me, hip leaning against the space in front of the cash register, arms crossed. It's a little hard to take her seriously with the Santa hat perched jauntily between braided pigtails, though sincerity radiates from her.

"Any particular reason?"

Oh, nothing. Just the fact I think I like him, but I shut down an extremely hot kiss between us after the ball, and now he's vanished into thin air.

Honestly, what was I thinking, pulling away from the hottest kiss of my life? Like, here comes this gorgeous man who shed every nut and bolt of his robot persona for me, and he suggests we practice kissing, which we both knew was just an excuse to actually kiss, but I wanted that. And then he *does* kiss me, and any thought about him not having any desires or feelings flew right out the window because the man can kiss.

She narrows her eyes. "Just tell me. No judgment here, okay? You don't have to act or say or do anything you don't want to with me. I'll take you right as you come, terrible counter-wiping skills and all."

I send her a flat look even as her words alleviate an internal pressure I hadn't recognized. The last few years when I've shared almost anything with friends, I've faced judgment for it. Yes, it all mostly came in regard to work, though sometimes, it was other small things. The farther from those people I get and the closer to Andy I grow, the more I realize what shallow friendships those were.

I know I'll cry if I start thinking about it on the heels of a bad sleep and missing JJ, so instead I say, "Thank you so much. Not all of us went to counter-wiping school like you did."

She rolls her eyes and I roll mine right back, then I do tell her.

"We had a good time at the ball. We danced and—I told you about all of that. But then I kind of shut things down when we got home. We kissed, but he brought it up like it was practice. I felt like he... I don't know. I felt like maybe he wanted it to go further. I freaked out and made it all business. And I have hardly seen him since, save one work party thing I showed up to for an hour earlier this week."

Her face turns to stone. "What do you mean, he wanted to take it further—like sleep with you? In the apartment? Just the two of you? Alone?"

She is utterly indignant, and short of her fury at the way Gruff had behaved at the wedding *and* at the ball according to what I'd shared of him, I've never seen her this feisty.

"No, not like that. Like... continue what we'd started and were both enjoying. Keep doing things we clearly *both* wanted to do. I would've wanted to, but I flipped and backed way off and then he... took the note."

She sighs, her shoulders dropping in relief. "Okay, well. This we can work with."

I hum. "Yeah, I'm not sure. He's already a workaholic, and he's got it in his head it's his job to pick up the holiday slack so other people can leave early or do things they want to do. And obviously, he thinks I don't want him near me, so he's avoiding me. Hard core. Like, I'm pretty sure two days ago, he heard me bustling around in the kitchen. I thought I heard him coming down the hallway, then all of a sudden, he was back in his room and it was time for me to go."

"Aw. It's almost like he's scared of you. Or maybe, scared of himself with you?" She looks off into the quiet café and seems to be thinking about this possibility.

"I don't think he's scared so much as worried he did something wrong. He didn't exactly apologize for the ball, but he definitely keeps our texting interactions to a minimum, and I haven't set eyes on the man in four days."

Her eyes widen. "Wow. So is he just never home?"

I shake my head. "He's at the office or gym or whatever, and I think when I'm here on Saturdays, he makes a point to be home. I noticed a few things moved around after I got home on Saturday."

It's like living with a ghost.

But not an invasive ghost à la *The Christmas Carol*. I'm talking a ghost who only leaves trace evidence and isn't trying to teach me a lesson. Though trust, the ghost of Christmas past wouldn't need to visit me and show me how terribly I messed up the moment between us.

And present? Well, yeah. It's feeling a bit bleak, but what am I supposed to do now?

As for the future... *woof.* I shudder to think and therefore am happy to accept my own JJ ghost, even if it means I don't see him.

He's not your ghost, freaky.

Okay, even my brain is heckling me now... always a good sign.

Andy's back to studying me. "Do you *want* to see him? Or did you 'freak out' for a reason and it's actually better like this?"

Is it? I don't know. I toss the rag into the sink nearby.

No, I do know. "It's not better, not by any measure. We have this office Christmas party soon, and I think we're more strangers now than we were a month ago."

A month. Has it really already and only been a month since I dragged in from the UK and his mother proposed to me? I chuckle under my breath at the thought, but that's basically it, isn't it? *Ah, the romance.*

Maybe I'm feeling a little bitter—with myself, and with him. I pushed him away and he let me. But JJ isn't the kind of man who's going to insinuate himself into my space unless he knows I explicitly want it. And I made it pretty darn clear I didn't for fear *he* didn't, even though he'd made it clear he did.... *Ugh.* How have I created this soap opera for myself? Why didn't I just go for it, or at the very least, not shut the man down so thoroughly?

I just need to figure out a way to fix it, and I can't do that on text message.

Andy gasps, then starts dancing in place. She does this —a little salsa or two-step when she gets happy. Weirdo, but she's mine and I like it, her, our friendship, the me I am around her.

"What?"

"You're taking Saturday off. Trade Wendel for his Tuesday night because he's always moping about nights, and then you're going to ambush your husband. Maybe you even leave like you're coming to work, then you go back home and you corner him."

I start to shake my head and say no, but I don't want to. I need to see him, straighten things out and determine if we can find some kind of happy stasis before I'm faced with Colonel Gruff and anyone else who'll be looking closely. Because as much as I'm enjoying my mental vacation from the hospital and obligations therein, and as glad as I am to have a place to stay, if I'm not actually helping JJ, then all of this is moot. I can't stomach the idea it's just for me to have a house—we wouldn't have gotten married if that's all this is.

And if I'm still hung up on the kiss, that's my problem. Another one to add to the list, but hey, who's counting at this point? He clearly enjoyed it and then I freaked out. Maybe for him, it had stayed all business anyway and my overcorrecting made it more awkward. Whatever the case, I'm over this disappearing act.

"Let's do it."

Justin Jorgensen Justice? You better get ready to talk.

CHAPTER TWENTY-ONE

Justin

I've just settled on the couch to read through a document. Unfortunately, work is slowing down drastically, so staying at the office until after nine at night really isn't necessary. Gruff has commented on my curious need to stay at work while I'm a newlywed, to which I've responded that Grace is working a lot, too, and we're looking forward to a honeymoon in the new year.

Truth be told, though, even being her *fake* husband, I can't deny how foolish it feels to be missing time with her. I can only imagine how misguided it would be if all this were real.

And how truly awful it would be to sequester myself in a place where I have to experience *more* of Colonel Gruff in lieu of being with the gorgeous, alluring, completely-invading-my-brain woman who is my wife.

Longing spirals through me, but I smash it—better this

way—and sip my coffee as I space out staring at the little snowman perching on the mantle. I'd seen her only at the Christmas lunch event earlier this week and it'd been all very cold—smiling, my hand on her back, her piercing gaze sending my stomach to the earth's core every time she directed it my way—normal things. And then she left, off to work or to create more Christmas decorations for every inch of the living room, and I stayed at work. We said not a single word to each other outside of the event.

She redrew the line after the ball two weeks ago and I gave her as much space as possible, both for fear I'd made her uncomfortable and for fear I'd do it again. Not against her will, but just... behave in a way that's too familiar, too much like this is an actual relationship and not a formalized agreement I myself had drawn up the contract for.

Isn't this the whole reason to avoid romantic entanglements? This ridiculous distraction making every single thing I try to do more arduous, like my brain is walking through a giant vat of peanut butter, just to get basic work done? And in this case, the peanut butter is thoughts of Grace, all sticky and smooth and sweet and—

"Idiot," I grumble under my breath, just as the door swings open.

"Who's an idiot?" Grace's voice asks from the kitchen.

I freeze where I sit on the couch with a cheery little *ho ho ho* throw pillow under my lower back and a bright red, fuzzy blanket draped over my legs. I don't look because I haven't seen her since she walked away from me after the dismal work lunch and I'm not sure I'm ready to. I'm irritable and wistful, and I hadn't planned on leaving the apartment until later. I don't want to go to the office or the gym *again.* I want to stay here, on the couch in my sweats and T-shirt, until a little before I know she'd be getting off work.

"Uh, nothing. No one. Just... nothing." Me. I'm the idiot. Cue up T Swift, because *I'm the problem, it's me.* I have no particular affinity for Taylor Swift yet there's no ignoring that little refrain in this bumbling moment.

She's bustling in the kitchen. I can hear the fridge open and close. A cabinet and the scrape of a plate. A drawer. The *tink* of something against ceramic and finally, her footsteps. Every tiny disturbance in the air feels like a banging gavel, the verdict on this moment. Judge's ruling: awkwardness, ho!

Grace comes around the opposite side of the couch, the one a few feet from the fireplace, and apparently, she's going to sit at the other end next to my feet. I curl them up, instantly aware of the fact we've never sat on this couch and just talked. And if we do that, I'm going to mess everything up even more than I already have.

"Don't you have work?" I ask, trying not to feast on the sight of her as she bends to set a tray on the coffee table.

Her jeans fit her perfectly—worn and comfortable, and tracing the curves of her well enough that I shoot my eyes to the ceiling because ogling her very fine behind is not gentlemanly.

"I was on the schedule but ended up trading with someone so I could have the day. I just needed a little time at home this weekend." She hands me a small plate with some kind of pastry on it. "I got us pastries and coffees. If you want, of course. No pressure."

I should excuse myself and go work in my room or even go into the office. If I was a smart man, I wouldn't indulge in this time with her. I wouldn't sit here with this woman who is thoughtful and charming and insanely beautiful at eight on a Saturday morning in a space that feels more and more like *ours*.

But I've never claimed to be all that smart. I work hard, yes, but right now, even that can't save me. I accept the plate gratefully and notice the Christmassy mug full of what has to be something more than simple black coffee.

"That's very kind of you, thank you." And I mean it, even if I'm concerned about... everything.

She takes a sip of her coffee and hums, eyes closing. "Andy makes the absolute best peppermint mochas."

I hesitate, holding the plate, watching her lick foam from her lip, and then abandon my work, shoving my laptop and pile of folders to the far side of the table. But while my body shifts to settle in, my brain hasn't caught up with accepting that we're doing this. "So you... are here? Today?"

She pauses with her mug on the way to her full lips again and blinks, then continues the course, takes a sip, settles the warm drink in both her hands, and turns to me. "Unless you need me to go."

"Go? Where would you go?"

She laughs softly, though it's tinged with what might be disappointment.

Disappointment because... she wants to stay? She's frustrated I'm incapable of stringing together fully coherent thoughts? She's secretly wanting to spend the day with me and me continuing to be an obtuse idiot is bringing down the mood despite the delicious mochas and cheery Christmas décor?

"I'm not sure, but I can get out of your space if you need time here without... company."

"No. I wanted time at home after being gone so much lately, but I'm—" I swallow, because she'll see right through this. "I'm happy to have you here."

A grin flashes, then she banishes it with a small nod. "Perfect. Then I'll be here, and if it's okay with you, I'll be watching Christmas movies and making decorations, but if you need silence to work, just say the word and I can hang in my room."

Because I don't actually have to get anything done today, of course I agree to her version of things. The idea that I wouldn't want to spend time with her is ludicrous save the reality that I've done nothing but avoid her for well over a week, so I can't blame her for being unsure. I do pretend to work for a while, but after about a half hour, I set aside my computer again and lean back to simply enjoy the moment.

Until Grace came along, this isn't something I ever did. Occasionally, I sit on the couch and watch movies, though never on a Saturday morning. Then again, how often do I just *stop*—just take in a moment and be fully present? Do I ever slow down and feel the silly socks on my feet from my mother, the comfort of the couch under me, the scent of peppermint and coffee, and the sight...

The sight of Grace. Since I'm sitting sideways on the couch, *she* is my entertainment while the TV is hers. And despite trying not to focus on her, it's nearly impossible. She's selected *Christmas Vacation* as her movie and though it's one I always hated because the Griswolds give me anxiety almost as much as actual life does, seeing her laugh and cringe makes it something to enjoy. Her hands are busy stringing what looks like cranberries into a long line that will become yet another decoration.

She cues up a second movie, which I admit I've never seen.

"I've got to educate you in the ways of Christmas movie magic, JJ."

I don't object. No part of me wants our time here to be done, and if Grace is happy to be with me, then I'm happy.

If she's calling me JJ, it feels like an even better sign—it's familiar and warm and it feels right. She does know me—as well as almost anyone does. This probably means I'm bad at letting people in, but that's not news. That I want to let *her* in, more than I've ever let anyone in, *is*.

This is absolutely the reason for the peanut butter brain and the justification for every instance I've avoided getting entangled. What is happening to me now to make me so susceptible to her? It can't be the courthouse wedding and a legal agreement.

By the time the second movie wraps up, our stomachs are growling loudly enough to cause embarrassment, except we're *both* experiencing the hunger pangs, and we both laugh. It's not even that funny, though it hits us both as more hilarious than anything we've watched so far, and by the time we've sobered, I'm wiping tears from the corners of my eyes.

"Guess we should eat something," she says, her smile so wide and pretty it hurts.

"Guess so. Let's order in lunch, and then I need to get my run over with."

She swallows, the smile fading a touch. "Oh, sure."

Is it possible she wants more time with me? I don't mean to be the one breaking up the day—I've had more fun and relaxation today than I have the entire rest of the year combined. Not that I never have a weekend, but I usually spend them busy with other things—household stuff or visiting my parents since I'm stationed so nearby for once. Or punishingly long workouts and weekend to-do lists. When I travel to see friends, it's different. It's catching up, seeing their families, maybe a little sightseeing to facilitate it all. It's not just... resting.

This day has felt like a gift, and I certainly don't want it to end. "Then after I get cleaned up, will you continue my Christmas movie education?"

She squints and bites her lip like she's assessing me for some lofty position and not to couch surf with her. My gut clenches and it hits me just how much I want her to agree—to this suggestion, and so much more.

I want yes to the movies. Yes to more kisses. Yes to everything either one of us wants. It's getting harder to keep that under wraps, but I mentally tackle the desires that feel increasingly like needs and bury them under piles of snow.

"Okay, Justice. Let's do it. But first, we're going to get a tree."

CHAPTER TWENTY-TWO

Grace

It never occurred to me that buying a Christmas tree would be a stressful thing. I've always just chosen one from a little vendor in town and decorated it with a few cute items I've collected and voilà.

However, with JJ, I can tell this is so far from what he saw himself doing today as I snip the twine holding the boughs close to the trunk we've now nestled into the tree stand. The greenery spreads down with the pull of gravity and I urge them out farther. JJ eyes me, then brushes them down, too.

"Have you never had a real tree?" I ask, because it's the only thing I can think of that would make him so tentative.

We've got Christmas music playing, and we picked out the tree after a quick lunch. Overall, the logistics have gone just fine, except he's got this odd edge to him.

"Uh, no. I'm often traveling. Otherwise, I'm at my

parents' house." His brow furrows and he gently smooths a hand over the rough needles on his side. A collection falls to the ground and he glares. "Is it supposed to... shed?"

I stifle a laugh. "Well, it *is* an actual pine tree, and they do have needles that can fall. But I think it's just from all the movement. If we water it, it shouldn't drop too many more until it's dried out—probably after the new year since we're getting it fairly late."

He's already moved into the kitchen and taken out a broom and dustpan. Cue him flying his little neat freak flag. It's almost adorable as he sweeps around the bottom, accidentally knocking a few more needles to the ground. His jaw flexes and it's clear this is driving him nuts. I'm not sure whether to laugh or roll my eyes.

JJ is just himself, and I really like that. Through all of this, he hasn't tried to be more or less than who he is. And right now, he's a little intense with his need to police the natural effect of gravity on traumatized pine needles. Again, adorable.

"I promise, it'll be okay. I can vacuum up the needles every morning." I move to the bag of decorations I bought earlier this month when I gussied up the rest of the place and withdraw two sets of rainbow lights and a bright red felt garland. "You're just lucky I didn't get any tinsel."

His eyes flare and the look of horror crossing his face is priceless. I can see him sneering at every little plastic metallic thread that finds its way to the floor.

I laugh outright then. "Truly a nightmare for you, huh?"

"Not a *nightmare*. No."

Sure, sure, sure, Justin Jackson Justice. "Let's get some decorations on and then we'll sweep up whatever needs sweeping. Once it's done, it can just be pretty in a corner and you won't have to worry about it soiling your apartment."

The look he shoots me is downright ornery.

"I'm not that bad, am I?" He asks this with a decent amount of calm, but then he brushes his shoulder where a few needles have fallen and scowls. "Fine. I'm... not used to this."

"Not used to so much Christmas cheer?" I ask, determined to get him to enjoy this and not focus on the mess.

He just blinks, completely straight-faced, though there's a hint of humor in his tone. "Yes. It's all the cheer that's making it seem like I'm going to be finding pine needles on my floor for months to come."

I'm shaking my head as I plug in the lights to make sure they're all working. He's sassy JJ right now and I'm not mad at it because it's oddly endearing. And I'm not cowed yet. I'm still on a mission to break through the weirdness between us, and though we've had a great morning, I want more. I want to talk and get to know each other, and this is part of it all.

A wild hair prompts me to swing the garland above my head like a lasso in time to the verse of "Happy Holiday / The Holiday Season," by Andy Williams in hopes it'll finally crack him, but then one end catches and as I turn, unfortunately still attempting to twirl the thing, it yanks the tree, jolting it and sending another small spray of needles everywhere.

My gaze jumps to his unamused face. "I'm sorry. I really didn't mean to do that."

But there's no way I sound at all penitent because it's too funny.

Yes, JJ's a serious man, but this? This isn't stressful or hard. The man has been to actual war, so I know in the scheme of challenging life events, pine needles on his floor are not in the top hundred.

"You don't seem very sorry."

He narrows his eyes, but there's a twitch of his lips that tips me off.

"I solemnly swear I will clean up every needle." Hand over heart, I make the promise.

His aspect doesn't change, but I see the clench of his jaw.

I'm in too good of a mood to let him stay this way. He's missing it—this moment. And one thing I'm realizing about JJ is that I'm not sure he's great at being here now. He's always in his head, thinking about work and solving problems.

"Come here, Justice," I say, solemn enough to rival him.

He steps forward, eyes lightly wary—*smart man.*

I wrap the garland around him like a scarf, grinning at his stern expression. "My goodness, you are a Grinch. I never realized."

One of his brows arches. "I am not a Grinch for not wanting pine detritus on my floor."

This does it. I laugh instantly because, "Who uses the word *detritus* for pine needles? Oh, you are such a weirdo."

He rears back but loops the scarf over his shoulder, getting comfortable with his new accessory. "I have never disputed that I am a *weirdo.* I just hope you know you are, too."

I gasp in mock offense. "Me? Perfectly, completely normal me? How am I weird?"

He shakes his head, and a little amused smile peaks out as he takes one end of the lights and twists them into the tree. "You mouth the words to every line in every movie we've watched so far. You work at a coffee shop yet don't seem to really like coffee. And you still write in your journals—granted, I admire such consistency."

I can't decide whether to blush or laugh, but I have no choice, really, and end up doing both.

"Okay, fine. The mouthing words is because I'm trying not to disturb you, but I do deeply struggle not to quote along with the entire thing aloud. And I *do* like coffee, I just don't like prissy sweet seasonal creamer as much as *some* people do. And guilty as charged on the journals. I don't know how I feel about something until I write it in my journal." I shrug a shoulder, feeling oddly vulnerable having admitted this last bit.

"Better than never figuring it out, I suppose," he says, not looking at me.

I think I see something there, but don't want to pester him after grilling him on the pine needles. Frankly, I enjoy that he's neat and likes things clean. I'm not particular like that, but I can admire it, and I've done my best to keep my own tornado of stuff to my room and bathroom.

NSYNC sings "Merry Christmas, Happy Holidays" to us as we dress the tree for a while longer, joking about my angst for the boy band which, mortifyingly and yet also gratifyingly, JJ remembers.

"You used to blast this album from November first on. I remember Dayton Nelson laughing so hard at one of the songs..."

I roll my eyes because I can practically hear my rude neighbor snickering at me like he did everything I was interested in by my tween years, but I can't hold off a laugh. "That'd be 'Under My Tree.'"

Oh, how I loved the album. My little heart had fluttered endlessly, especially for JC. Weirdly, if I squinted, Justin shared some basic qualities with the boy band singer—dark hair, blue eyes... *I wonder if he can sing...*

No. *No.* If this man can sing on top of all of his other charms, I'm doomed.

He nods emphatically and grins. "Yes. *Yes.* What's the line? It's so creepy..."

And then, in the oddest moment of my adult life, Justin Justinius Justice and I say it together. "I wish that Santa could be here to see."

His eyes widen and he's shaking his head like it's the oddest thing, and I am holding my stomach because I'm verging on crying, I'm laughing so hard.

"I'll admit that reflecting on the lyrics with some adult context and retrospect is... illuminating. And I just..." I take a moment to catch my breath. "I just can't imagine wanting to spend the night under the Christmas tree with a lover and thinking I wished Santa could be watching."

He cracks up yet tucks the smile away instantly. "Well, Grace. Those boys might've been appealing, but I think what we all knew is that they were also deeply troubled individuals."

I shove his shoulder, and we finish the tree. It's amazing how natural and fun this has felt, even with his needle aversion and my heightened awareness of him. We haven't talked about the kiss. We *need* to talk about it.

But for now, we're just... together.

CHAPTER TWENTY-THREE

Grace

JJ and I part ways after we finish decorating. I decide I want to get in cozy clothes and respond to my parents' weekly e-mail, and he goes on a run. I'm a firm believer in working out for my mental health and guard my days off like a dragon, so today I get to relax in my bed while he's out doing his time.

I wonder if he ever has a true rest day. Has the man ever slept in and stayed in bed until, say, nine in the morning?

An image of JJ tangled up in sheets next to me as sunlight streams through a window flashes through my mind. And yep! It's time to get moving again or I'm in serious danger of dwelling on just how much I've enjoyed sitting next to him on the couch and laughing at stupid movies. We've hardly touched save a brush of fingers or besocked feet here or there, but I'm still all fluttery and wired from the time together after being apart for so long.

He's surprising and finicky but also not as fussy as I might've thought when I first walked into this den of gray. I've confirmed his sense of humor in spades and I've also admitted to myself I like him. Not that I'd really hidden this from myself, but more time with the man hasn't exactly turned me *off*.

Whether his persnickety feelings about pine needles or the surprisingly accurate memory of creepy boy band lyrics, it's all adding up to something too good.

Then I remember how I had to ambush him to get him to spend time with me and the fact that he seems outright addicted to his job, and I settle a bit. He's not *too good*. He's simply good—a good man and someone who's growing on me.

Ew, okay, no. Because that phraseology, as a medical professional, even one on a break, still icks me. Tumors grow on you. A person? A person can charm you, delight you, allure you...

That's better. JJ does those things.

He estimated he'll be back by three, so around two-forty-five, I wander into the kitchen to cue up our next movie—*Bridget Jones's Diary*—and make popcorn. I'm wearing my earbuds and listening to an audiobook while I putter around filling a water glass for me and an icy glass of red Fanta for him because the man's sweet tooth is real and though he views any such beverage as a treat, he doesn't restrict himself. He's got two kinds of soda and four kinds of flavored creamer in his fridge.

I'm chuckling to myself at this quirk when I hear something and turn, closing the fridge door, and collide with JJ.

But it's not just JJ. It's his naked torso *and* the glass of Fanta I just poured, which is now spilling all over him and me. He's reaching out to steady me, but I've stepped back, and the rug under my foot slips enough that I windmill my arms to stabilize myself. JJ somehow shoves the now-empty glass to the counter and reaches to hold me on either side of the waist. Sadly, I've overcorrected, the mat is still slippery as all get out, and we go down hard.

And by go down, I mean he falls backward, I fall forward directly on top of him, and we end up in a Fanta-coated heap on the kitchen floor.

"Grace, are you okay?" He's winded but still worried about me first.

"Are you kidding? I fell on top of you. Are you bleeding? Did you hit your head?"

I push up so I'm kneeling over him and search his body —no visible lacerations on his chest, no blood pooling on the floor behind his head. I gently press his forehead back and lean over to look at his pupils. I'll need a flashlight to be sure, but I can check in a minute.

"I'm okay. I didn't hit my head. Mostly just my back."

Fear spikes through me until I realize he's moved his legs and arms, so he's unlikely to have a spinal injury. Still, once a nurse...

"Let's get you up very slowly," I say, and grip his hand with mine, placing the other behind his shoulders and help him ease to sitting. "Good. You're okay. You're alright."

He's nodding, a perplexed smile on his face. "I really am. I'll probably be sore, maybe bruised, and definitely Fanta-coated, but it's nothing serious. I promise."

I don't know why I feel raw and relieved and like I might need to cry. The reaction is completely disproportionate, but it's there nonetheless. "Okay. I'm going to check your pupils, though."

His brow quirks, then he dips his chin. "Whatever you need."

It's then I realize I'm still kneeling over his legs, so I scramble back and help him get on his feet. I grab my phone and activate the flashlight, then check to make sure his pupils are responsive—yes. Shrinking up just like they should, then readjusting when I remove the light. *Whew.*

I'm rattled enough by the threat of him being hurt because of my clumsiness that I step up to him and wrap my arms around his shoulders. "I'm so sorry. I'm such a klutz."

I feel his laugh more than hear it.

"You're not a klutz. I startled you. And clearly, I need a different kitchen mat because that thing is a hazard."

Relief slips out in the form of a laugh as I pull back and agree. "Probably so. I'll find you something festive."

We're smiling at each other, arms around the other, and it's this moment I realize we're embracing and he's shirtless. I inspected him for injuries, and as a medical professional, I've seen countless bodies of all shapes, sizes, colors, ages, etc. But I've never had one that's supposed to be mine.

That by law, technically speaking, is actually for me.

But not really, right?

It doesn't matter that he's only legally mine, because by now, my body and mind have both fully registered the utter beauty of him. What used to be a rail-thin teen and then a wiry college student has developed into a solidly formed *man.* It shouldn't surprise me he has defined muscles everywhere muscles are, and yet I've not witnessed a man who looks like this in real life aside from the rare male patient, and I'm never looking at them like this.

I never have my arms around them, touching them. And they usually haven't just been doused in ice-cold strawberry soda.

"Grace," JJ says, his voice low and rough enough that it draws my eyes to his.

"Yeah?" It sounds like I'm the one who just ran five miles.

He leans closer, or maybe I do, and he drops his head so his face is close enough—we could kiss. Maybe we *should* kiss again, and this time with no pretext of practice. And if we do, it wouldn't be completely inappropriate for me to crush myself against this glorious torso of his, would it?

"Would you mind if I go get a shower?"

I freeze, the fantasies of pressing my mouth to the curve of his very well-formed deltoid or the jut of his clavicle evaporating.

"Of course," I nearly bark out and step away, turning before he can see the blaze lighting up my cheeks. "I'll get changed and do the popcorn and be ready! Take your time."

His hand on my shoulder makes me jump, though I don't end up causing a two-man pile-up in the kitchen again, so I take it as a win. I pull my earbuds and smile at him because he looks adorable and cozy and I really just want to hug him again, even if he has hidden away his majestic chest behind a soft-looking T-shirt that says *The Mountains Are Calling In Silver Ridge*. I've heard of the small ski town, but never been.

"Good shower?" I ask and then hope it doesn't seem like I'm being weird.

"Much needed. Sorry you ended up on top of me when I was all sweaty." He blinks.

I blink.

I crack up, and his smile flashes before he course-corrects. "You know what I mean."

I swallow because I have to admit the experience wasn't horrible and I will not not *not* imagine what any other version of that sentence would be like. *No.*

"Yes, of course. It was my fault so no apologies from you." I spin around, popcorn bowl heaping with freshly popped kernels. "Ready for more of our Christmas movie marathon?"

A look flickers across his face, but I'm not sure what it is. Before I can ask, he takes the bowl, his long fingers lightly brushing mine before he removes it from my hands.

"Let my Christmas education continue. Maybe by the end, my heart will grow three sizes."

It's a joke, yet I can't let it lie. "Your heart's just fine, JJ."

He frowns and those stunning eyes are locked on mine as we stand here in the kitchen with the popcorn between us.

"I'm not so sure."

I take the bowl from him and slide it onto the counter, needing his full focus on me and nothing between us. "I am. You like to frame yourself as this selfish workaholic, but I've seen through that and there's no going back."

He huffs and seems like he's going to reach out for me, but instead leans back while gripping the counter so his hands are pinned behind him.

"That's kind of you to say."

"I'm not just saying it. You've given me a place to stay when I had nowhere else to go. You're a good friend and a successful soldier. I know you're a good son."

He swallows hard, but something about my words has him launching from his spot and pacing around the kitchen island.

"I gave you a place to stay as part of an agreement. And if we're both honest, I'm clearly getting the better end of this arrangement. You get a place to stay, but I get a *wife*. I get a possible boost to my career, a companion for all of my season's social engagements, and to be around you. That's obviously an uneven contract, which is why I wanted you to have another lawyer look at it. I—"

"Being around me isn't a listed benefit unless I get to say the same. Being around *you*."

He shakes his head vehemently, like that can't be right.

"I've hardly been around." He runs a hand through his hair and, yes, I admire the way his biceps flex with the movement. "I'm trying to give you space."

Ah, so he's finally admitted he was staying away, and I can't let that slide without digging in. "Why? What did I do to make you feel like I needed space?"

He stops, his face blanking as he drops his hand at his side. "You didn't have to spell it out for me, Grace. I got the message."

I look around the kitchen like some formerly unseen person will assist me with him. Yes, I stopped the kiss, but had I sent some kind of covert sign, too? "What message? When did I send you a message?"

A frustrated sigh preempts his explanation. "After the ball. After the kiss. You made it pretty clear we were back to reality here. Back to the agreement."

I scrub my hand down my face, grateful I'm wearing super minimal makeup. "Ugh, I did, didn't I?"

He blinks like I've surprised him. "You did. And I understand. There is no need for anything more than what we agreed upon. We kissed to make things seem more realistic and make our lives easier in the future, and now that's done. I don't want you to feel pressured just because I clearly have feelings for you and you don't return them."

My mouth drops open, and I'm not sure this is real. Am I hallucinating this gorgeous human speaking those words? Is there a hidden camera somewhere nearby capturing my gullibility? "You have feelings for me?"

He looks down like his fuzzy ridiculous peppermint striped socks might have the answer and his jaw flexes—*oh, hello*—then he nods. "I do."

A delighted but shocked laugh bursts out of me because I did not see this coming and I especially didn't imagine hearing JJ say the words "I do" with such severity in reference to his feelings for me.

Whew. Give a girl a moment to recover because *that* is on my list of favorite things, thank you. I mean, I knew there was chemistry here, but there has been from early on. His evasion plan did the job of making me think we were far from on the same page. I'm borderline giddy, champagne veins and all, as my response wells up inside me and spills out. "Well—same."

His gaze snaps up to meet mine. "Same *what*?"

Heat flushes my cheeks in an instant and I'm here with a bright red ornament for a face. Perfectly matching the décor, I'd say. "I like you. *That* is the reality here, though I'm not sure what to do with it. *So*. Yeah."

There's a pause and the air practically shimmers with the traces of my words like they're little fireworks leaving a smoke trail.

And then, JJ is there. He paces toward me with the determined gait of a soldier with his target in his sights. He stands directly in front of me, not touching me, and pins me with a heated, urgent stare.

"You're saying you like me. In real life. Not as a part of the agreement for the sake of my job."

I nod because my *entire* body is fluttering with nerves and anticipation. "Yes."

"So you want to... date me?"

I grin. "Yeah, I guess I do."

He shakes his head once. "No guessing. If you're not fully confident in your response, there is no rush here."

With a roll of my eyes, I reach forward and grip the material of his T-shirt at his side. "I am sure. I'm just not sure what to call it. We're married for a contracted amount of time, living together, but... dating?"

His half smile threatens to murder me—it's so deadly sexy.

"Why not? And if it helps, we'll just call it research. We're researching how best to portray our marriage believably, satisfy the contract we both signed, and getting to know each other better during the process."

Hmm. That's an interesting take. Very logical, which fits for him, of course. I'll think about this more later, I'm certain. For now, I don't keep him waiting. "Sounds reasonable."

His smile widens. "Good. Then I think the first thing we need to do is mistletoe prep."

My pulse kicks. "Mistletoe prep?"

He crowds me, his hands settling on the counter on either side of my waist. "I'm sure there'll be more mistletoe at the party this week. Yes, we kissed before, but that was then. This is now, and a soldier needs to always be prepared."

I snicker even as a thrill streaks through me. "Isn't that the Boy Scout motto?"

By now, he's already dipping his head and sliding one

hand into my hair. It feels so good to have him just do this, just touch me because he wants to and I want the same. Then I'm tilting my chin up and he's leaning in and saying something about how he was a Boy Scout, too.

"JJ," I say, a little frustrated by the fact that his lips are still over there in his space and not on mine.

"Yes, Grace?" His eyes practically sparkle with amusement, like he knows how much I want him to close the distance between us.

And so, I don't play coy. Not this time.

"Kiss me."

CHAPTER TWENTY-FOUR

Justin

Grace's lips are soft and warm, and we sink into each other like we've done this before. I know I've kissed her in my dreams quite a few times since our last real encounter, but our short contact at the ball was nothing like this, and neither was our practice kiss. We didn't have the admission between us, the truth.

Her hands are on my chest, then sliding up around my neck; my fingers are in her hair, and I'm relieved to feel the silken strands against my skin. After one hot press together, we pull back and then dive in, flames in our eyes sparking right into blazing fire I have no desire to stop. She feels so good, so right, and she's just as alight as I am if the sound that escapes her is any indication. It's incredible to connect with her and instantly feel we fit without the rampant second-guessing of last time.

That's when it penetrates my thick and kiss-hazed brain

that this is our first real kiss. The last counted, yes, though the ensuing week of my disappearing act feels like we needed another chance. The first without the excuse of an audience, either physically present or potentially there in the future, to be sure. And it's been nothing sweet or exploratory. It's not an opening argument, it's a closing statement. And the verdict, to me, is clear. Yet it's only fair we ease off and give the jury, Grace, a chance to catch up.

That analogy really fell apart, but let's blame finally kissing Grace Murphy for the shortfall.

I pull back and take in the way her cheeks are flushed a pretty reddish pink, and her eyes look darker when they flutter open.

"Sorry. Got a little carried away," I say and smooth a lock of hair behind her ear. I draw my hand away slowly, the pads of my fingers sliding along the curve of her jaw.

Her intake of breath is quick, like this simple gesture has done more to her than the last minute of kissing. Maybe it has for me, too, oddly, because I'm watching my hand move slowly when she catches it with both of hers. She cups my hand in hers and presses a kiss to the center of my palm.

"Don't ever apologize for that," she says, and the soft smile reinforces her words.

Good grief, I like her so much it hurts. It's ludicrous she's my wife, and we're both blushing and overheated from a fairly simple, if passionate, kiss. I banish all thoughts of how this will progress, refusing to put a timeline on it or count down to the end of whatever this is becoming, and reach for the bowl of popcorn because I need a minute to recover.

I've only recently admitted to wanting her, and it's going to be a minute before I can accept I can have her, at least in some ways, and at least for a while. What it all means for us, for my work, for our agreement... I simply don't know.

She nods even though I haven't said a word, and we move the bowl, drinks, and ourselves over to the living room. This time, I sit closer to the middle, and though we've just shared a fire-hot kiss, nerves spark in my chest when I offer her my hand.

Pleasure snakes through me when she takes it, our palms sliding together and fingers lacing, and she sits right next to me. We watch Bridget fall for Mr. Darcy, and Grace adds color commentary on the parallels with *Pride and Prejudice* and all her favorite moments. She loves how Mr. Darcy loves the "hot mess" that is Bridget, as he puts it, "just as she is."

"Have people failed to love you as such? Just as you are?" I ask, my arm curved around her shoulders and her body leaning against me with delicious pressure I'll miss when it's gone, when all this is officially over.

She keeps watching the screen for a moment and I wonder if she'll ignore me entirely, though it wouldn't be like her. It isn't, and she proves me right.

"I think I'm feeling a little tender these days. Like who I've always envisioned myself to be is changing. I feel like I've been mourning that—like my time in London was supposed to rejuvenate my love of nursing and it ended up being a moment when I came to terms with what might be the end of it. I—"

I sit up and she straightens and swipes at her eyes. My heart sinks and I pause the movie. We don't need distraction during this.

"I'm sorry. You don't have to talk about it."

She smiles through shining eyes. "I want to, actually. I've talked a little to Andy, and I talked to my mom when I first got back. When I told my friends at the hospital I wasn't going to come back to work there, at least for a while, they couldn't fathom it. And I get it. I have all this education and experience. I have a life..." Her voice cracks.

I run a hand over her hair and down her back and wait for her to continue. It's a quiet, simple moment, but my chest is nearly glowing with the privilege of being the one to console her. She takes a sip of water and another deep breath.

"I thought I loved it. Maybe it's foolish of me to think I'd love my job my whole life, but it's not even that. The thought of stepping inside a hospital makes me go cold. It feels like dread has me by the neck just thinking of it."

I hate the way her voice is tight with emotion and the way her face is so downcast, like she's failed herself and everyone else she knows because she feels this way.

"It's not unreasonable to want a job you don't dread," I say, sliding my hand up and down her back.

She looks at me, her blue eyes so full of emotion, it makes my chest cave in.

"You don't dread your job? You don't hate it after working so many hours?"

This is a question deserving real reflection. I search my mind, wondering if I've somehow lied to myself about this, but no. "No. Aside from resenting it at times, and getting tired of being the go-to for extra duties, I love it. I genuinely do. It's why I want this promotion so much—not just so I can keep being a lawyer, but so I can do it for the Army."

She's blinking them back, yet more tears fall. "That's good. I'm glad you do. Especially since you basically lived there the last week."

I chuckle at the jab and pull her to me to press a kiss to her temple. She's so beautiful like this, vulnerable and real and still making me laugh. I can't think of anyone else who's this willing to be kind and generous to me about my work in the midst of her own professional crisis.

"Is it more you've lost your passion, or that you feel like you're letting someone down?" I ask.

She inhales, gaze cast across the room as she considers the question. "I'm sad I don't want to do the job. I spent the past year praying a switch would flip and I'd regain the ability to do the work without feeling completely spent, but it didn't come. That's one thing, but I do think I've mostly processed that. I'm working on what it means, and at what point I will really know I don't just need time, but I do need a complete change. What *else* I might want to do if I don't ever go back is a bit of a mystery, though I'm starting to get some ideas."

I nod, urging her on. I want to hear those ideas. I want to know everything.

"I think it's mostly that I had this life, this community in the hospital, and they're gone. They made it pretty clear they had no interest in trying to wade through the 'what's next?' question with me. They're busy and they've chosen to stay in medicine and fulfill their calling. I'm abandoning it."

"It's not abandoning it to take a break, or even to change course. There are so many applications for someone with your expertise, and I hate the idea of your old friends not recognizing that for some people, change is good. You're one of those people. I know it might not seem like it, but I am, too."

Her brow raises. "You are?"

I grin at the incredulity in her voice. "Yes. I like my routines and I can be a stodgy work drone, sure, but I move fairly frequently. I change units, jobs, houses, every few years. And at this point in my life, it works for me."

The feelings I have about what might change this desire, what might make me want roots, are for another day.

"I'm glad. It'd be hard to be in the Army and not find some sense of adventure in it."

She links our fingers and my heart squeezes.

I can't return to the movie and watch Daniel Cleaver acting a fool and serious Darcy winning the day until I've said one last thing.

"You need to know you are everything. Just you. Not based on what you do or how you perform. Not because of your ability to triage a person or save a life. Not because of any job you do or don't stay in for any amount of time."

She swallows and her lashes flutter, but the tears limning her blue gaze don't fall, and I continue.

"You, Grace Murphy, are worthy of every good thing purely because you are, just as you are. Period."

CHAPTER TWENTY-FIVE

Grace

I wake at midnight. I'm sleeping on top of a human furnace and my internal temperature has to be above a hundred degrees. JJ is literally *under* me, and though we hadn't been snuggled up quite like this during our last movie of the day, it's close.

After *Bridget Jones* and *Die Hard*, we grew so comfortable that we lay down together, him spooning me with his back to the cushion, and me resting against his arm as my pillow and his body as my heater. It felt wonderful, especially after our day together. We flirted. We *kissed*. And then, he let me get out some of the tangled mess of thoughts I had around work and identity. Not exactly light fare, except his response had been...

Well, it was perfect. I honestly never would've imagined someone so deeply work-driven would both seem to understand and empathize with me, yet also free me to do what I feel is right. There was no guilting, no suggesting I'm wrong for leaving a career in desperate need of bodies to fill jobs. There was nothing but support and love.

Of course, it's far too soon for romantic love. I know that. I do. But his gentleness, his words... they made me feel loved. I don't know how things will progress between us, especially when we have an end date, but I do know I'll always be grateful for this time.

JJ doesn't stir when I extract myself, so I cover him with a blanket and kiss his forehead goodnight. I have work early, but if I didn't, I'd stay tucked into him, relishing his closeness, all night.

Five days later, JJ and I have passed like busy little ships in the night, though this time, he hasn't been avoiding me. He's been working so he feels good about taking time off for Christmas—we do still have some progress to make on how much he works—and I've been loving the freedom of working and taking nothing home with me. I have no fear of what will wander into the ER the next day, no tears over unsolvable problems or incurable patients, no existential dread.

Also, I've been soaking up my time with Andy. I've realized that if I don't stay in the city when the first three months are up, I'll be moving away from JJ *and* her. And she has been as completely accepting and wonderful as JJ, if not more so because she's so effusively forthcoming in her support.

But Andy recently decided she's gearing up to make a

big professional move, and I'm hoping I can support her so when she's brainstorming or drafting business plans, I'm there to help as much as possible. I want to be around... indefinitely.

The work party goes well. There are no generals to impress, Gruff makes a few comments but is mostly just broody, and everyone else seems great. I'm happy to see Megan and James again, happy to meet a few more of JJ's colleagues. I do have to bite my tongue when someone cracks a joke about how sad they are to lose JJ to marriage because now they'll feel a little bad when he gets scheduled for every single TDY and crap job, but he just presses a kiss to my temple and I smile through it.

I'm smiling more than I ever remember doing, actually, all the way until we're loaded up in his car to head back to our small hometown to stay with his parents.

"So, I need to tell you something," he says, gripping the wheel as we make our way through DC traffic.

"Everything okay?" I ask.

In reality, I'm distracted by his hands. They're great hands, and having them parade around the steering wheel like that is just about killing me. He's got a Henley-style long-sleeved shirt on in a hunter green that makes his eyes look insanely vivid and fits his muscular chest and arms like a dream.

I've only seen him in suits, his uniform, and sweatpants plus T-shirt. When he walked out of his room in jeans and this mesmerizing shirt, I could hardly look away. Now he's sitting there flaunting his sexy forearms and hands like he knows it's making me fantasize about those hands on me.

We have kissed with abandon, but only kissed. We haven't had time to fall asleep on the couch together again, though I did manage it when we watched a movie together last night. Snuggled next to JJ, I feel so safe and cozy. He's like my own personal sleep aid, though not because he's snooze-worthy. He makes me feel so peaceful.

However, the forearm situation is *not* peaceful. The sure movement of his hands, the loose grip, the evidence of his health and hydration in the supple veins on the back of his hand that tell me he'd be an easy stick, and the smooth skin of his inner wrist... am I a vampire? This all feels a little vampy. Or maybe it's uniquely the thoughts of a nurse who's put in plenty of IVs. Whatever the case, I need to stop fantasizing about his rough palms cupping my face or—ahem, anything else—and listen.

He clears his throat and the nervous energy that has been picking at me all morning intensifies.

"As you may recall, my dad doesn't know about the agreement." He glances at me, then back to the road.

I must be a little slow because it's not clicking, though maybe we should blame it on the stubble grazing his jaw. I haven't seen him anything less than perfectly clean-shaven save the one movie marathon day when he didn't shave and it's so darn sexy. He can pull off a five-o'clock shadow like no one's business and I have no idea why this is doing it for me so thoroughly, but he is.

He's also trying to talk to me, and I've become an objectifying maniac. *Focus, Grace!* "Okay. That's not news, though. What's the problem?"

While he's concentrating on the road, I have the perfect view of his profile. It's just so handsome. He has a strong brow, those hazel eyes that look more brown with the offset of his green shirt, a strong nose and chin, the weirdly attractive and masculine laryngeal prominence, aka Adam's apple.

"It's not that he doesn't know about the agreement so

much as he doesn't know anything except that we eloped and got married." His eyes cut to me and then away. "So we will be maintaining the marital façade while we're there."

I'm not entirely unprepared for this, though it feels like it. I wondered what his father knew and how this time would go, though mostly, I'd relaxed into the idea that we'd hang out with his parents. Honestly, I hadn't actually thought about the details of this trip beyond looking forward to having uninterrupted, non-work time with JJ.

"Okay. But... your mom didn't tell him anything?"

His shoulders droop a bit. "My dad wouldn't like the situation. And because we're already pretending, my mom made me promise we'd keep it up at home so he isn't concerned."

"Won't he wonder why you didn't invite him to the wedding? Wouldn't he think it's odd you got married two hours from your hometown and didn't invite your own father?"

I'm borderline hysterically nervous at the thought of lying to JJ's dad. I didn't interact with him a ton growing up, yet even I know he has a reputation for being straight-laced, honest, and honorable. It's where his son gets it, to be sure.

Except maybe this whole fake marriage thing, which is tantamount to lying to everyone in your life who's not in on it. I haven't mentioned it to my parents because it won't be an issue. They're gone for a *year*. I'm hoping to fly out to meet them in the summer, and there's a very good chance all of this will be ancient history by then.

At least, that's what I've been telling myself. The thought came easier in the beginning. Now it feels wrong somehow. Like even if things come to an end here, which is what we said would happen and yet the whole dating thing certainly confuses the issue, JJ has changed me. Can I really move forward and not acknowledge this part of my life?

In my e-mails to them, they know I'm living in his apartment and while my mother was initially concerned at the unconventional setup—*if she only knew*—I've reassured her it's all very respectful and comfortable, which is completely true. I update her on my goings on and do mention JJ occasionally, though I don't give her details. She has no idea I'm technically dating my fake husband, for example.

JJ brings me back to the moment when he answers.

"He may, but he's also not a particularly sentimental person. I'm certain that to him, he'd rather see me happily married to someone who matters to me than bother with a big ceremony just for show." He swallows. "Anyway, I wanted to give you the heads-up because I know you were probably not expecting this dynamic. And I'll apologize in advance because I'm guessing my mother is going to be... a lot."

Through the tangle of nerves, I laugh at this. "I have no doubt Marcy Justice will be in rare form."

I just hope I can handle this. I don't want to mess anything up between JJ and his dad or even Marcy and her husband. I don't want to be so nervous that I can't enjoy JJ.

And I don't want to get so caught up in the pretending that I forget what's real.

CHAPTER TWENTY-SIX

Justin

Marcy Justice starts at a ten.

You know. The scale of one to ten? Where one is a low-key greeting where she's inside the house and she meets us with a smile when we walk in, and a five is she's pulling open the door and reaching for hugs. A ten is her waiting in the driveway *before* we've pulled in.

I can see her standing on the porch the instant we turn on the street. She's wearing a bright red Christmas sweater and a Rudolph antler headband with tinsel strung between each side. She's got on her Christmas lights necklace that is actually blinking in multicolors, her bright red Christmas bow earrings, and her Christmas Crocs. She is, as she is wont to do, the physical embodiment of Christmas cheer.

"My babies are here!"

She sets down a tray she's been holding on the railing of the porch and shuffles down the stairs before we've exited the car fully. She's wrapping her arms around me in a Hulk-hug that compresses my lungs, and her warm cinnamon-and-spice scent confirms what I already know. She's likely been up cooking since dawn.

"And my newest baby, come here!" She waves Grace into her arms and crushes her with a hug.

I laugh, relishing the brightness in Grace's cheeks and the way she hugs my mom back. What I don't anticipate is the twisting, achy feeling that cuts into my chest and wraps around my heart. It's like longing and loss combined—like "wouldn't it be nice?" and "what a shame this can't last" clasping hands.

With a shake of my head because I can't entertain the twin pulls of wanting something real with Grace and the reality that our arrangement and her time with me and even her desire not to work at the hospital are likely fleeting, I move to the trunk and grab our bags. Mom ushers us inside, and my dad is there to greet us with a more subdued and less overwhelming, yet still warm, greeting.

"Good to see you, son. Merry Christmas." He pats my back twice and releases me from the embrace.

"Good to be here, Dad. And Merry Christmas." I reach for Grace's hand and draw her close. "And you remember Grace..." My voice hitches but I press through and finish, "My wife."

My dad's smile is genuine as he reaches for Grace's outstretched hand. He presses hers between both of his and shakes twice.

"Delighted to see you again, Grace, and under such happy circumstances. Welcome to the family."

Grace's response is immediate. "I'm so glad to be here, Mr. Justice."

He tuts. "No, none of that. Call me Jonathon."

Grace nods and I wonder whether she avoids saying she's glad to be a part of the family because she isn't—not really. *Not yet*, my mind whispers like it's got plans. Yet I can't think like that, either, because as much as we seem to like each other, we're not here as spouses.

Okay, that's false. We are *technically* here as spouses. But if we're not planning on staying together indefinitely, then it's not the same.

And *indefinite* is just so... definite. It's more than either of us can offer the other, and I think we both know that. Deep down, we do, anyway.

Still, my dad's genuine greeting and Grace's response both make my chest feel a little tight again.

"Why don't you two get settled in your room. We'll do dinner around six."

Mom waves us off and I start up the stairs with the bags.

Entering my childhood space always feels like I've hopped into a time machine and it works, but it's missing a part or two. My room is forever in transition. Since I do come home to visit, particularly when I'm not stationed so nearby, my parents have maintained a room dedicated to *me* rather than turning my childhood space into something of a more generic guest room.

But...

Like her seasonal coffee creamer and her overabundance of holiday cheer, Marcy Justice has ideas about how her house should look any given time of the year. The spread on my full-sized bed is a red velvet color with a hand-sewn Christmas quilt at the end, holiday throw pillows finishing off the look. There are updated wooden side tables I haven't seen before that match the medium-brown paint on the bed frame and stylish lamps that appear to be charging docks as well.

And everywhere else is the untouched reality of my childhood.

Grace is taking in the same view as I am, and with no small amount of awe in her voice, she says, "So you were..."

"A huge nerd. Yeah."

She cracks up, her pretty smile lighting her up in a way that makes my stomach dip.

"But like, we have all kinds of fandoms going on here. There's no loyalty at all. It's just—*Star Wars*, Bam! *Star Trek*, Bam! *Lord of the Rings*, Bam!" Her eyes are wide as they jump around the room from various pieces of themed paraphernalia and books focused on each of these subjects.

"I am a man of many interests," I say with mock seriousness.

"I see that. It's... impressive." She's tucking her lips together to hide a smile.

I set up her suitcase on a low bench and mine on the top of the dresser. "It's true. Take a good look because everything you see here"—I sweep a hand grandly around the room—"is yours, too, now, wife."

She grins. "I just wish I'd known all this was waiting for me. If I'd known, I would've married you decades ago."

"Of course you would've. Who could pass up a collector's edition of the *Return of the Jedi* Luke figurine?"

She shakes her head, eyes wide. "Oh, certainly not me."

I chuckle low, savoring the lightness between us. We chatted on the drive here and listened to Christmas music between topics, though I've been worried she's upset with me for not clarifying about this trip. I don't think she had planned on having to pretend this whole weekend, and now we do.

"So, sharing a room," she says, sitting on the edge of the bed.

The bed. *The* bed.

The one bed.

Just the one.

"Uh, yeah. I didn't think ahead to this. I—I mean we're married. I'm sorry. We should've stayed at a hotel and then—"

She grabs my hand and pulls me to face her.

"It's okay. I'm not upset. I'm not freaking out. I'm just bringing it up now so we can figure out how we feel about it and we'll go from there."

She's so steady and genuinely calm. I tug on her hand and she stands.

She's in my arms in a heartbeat and relief courses through me. "Sorry. I—I'm not used to lying to my dad and I'm feeling a little bit like a teenager doing something wrong up here."

She chuckles and presses a kiss to my cheek, then pulls away to catch my eyes. "You sneak a lot of girls into your room or something?"

I laugh outright at this, a bit of the tension eking out. "Definitely no. You do recall what I looked like back then, right?"

Humor and something else spark in her gaze. "Well, yes. I admitted to my crush on you, didn't I?"

With a huff, I slump onto the bed and she joins me. "I was all elbows until I was like twenty-two. And obviously, the content of my conversation prowess would've been absolute catnip to the high school girls."

I glance around at the framed *Return of the Jedi* poster and a figurine of a wizard I recall taking particular pride in after saving up my lawn-mowing money to buy it.

Grace's fingers play with the short hair at the back of

my neck. "We're all nerds. In high school, in college... all the time. I was, too, in my own way."

I flop over onto my side next to her and prop my head up in one hand. This gives me the perfect vantage point to admire her. It's something I do a bit too much if I'm being honest, yet I can't seem to stop. I've felt more than a little enamored of her since the day I walked into the coffee shop and accidentally hit her in the stomach, and now that we've both admitted to being interested in each other...

The swoop of her nose and the silhouette of her lips are so pretty I want to draw them. She's looking up at the glow-in-the-dark stars still peppering the ceiling, and my eyes follow the path from her chin down the long line of her neck to the hollow of her throat, then further. The smooth, thin skin of her upper chest and down to the vee of her sweater.

I roll to my back and cover my eyes because this is not calming me down, and it's not helping me figure out what to do about sleeping in this bed with her. In fact, lying next to her in this bed and admiring how completely beautiful she is after we've just joked around is likely bad for my health.

Well, she is a professional. Maybe she should give you a checkup.

Gah. No. Stop.

Golf.

The sludge that leaks out of trash bags on pick-up day in the summer.

Poodles with ornate haircuts.

The feeling of Cap'n Crunch cereal tearing up the roof of my mouth.

I think of any unsexy thing that will come to mind until I can finally speak.

"I'll take the floor," I say through my hands.

"Uh, what?" she asks, rolling to her side and pulling at my wrist until I bring down my hands.

My heart stutters at the sight in front of me. She's leaning over me, inspecting me with her blue gaze and trying to figure me out. I know I'm all over the place, but can I be blamed when this gorgeous woman is sharing a bed with me?

No. No, I cannot be blamed.

I'd convince a jury of my innocence if they saw this snapshot, if they knew how her beauty is only surpassed by her goodness. I'd win the case—fully exonerated.

However, this is a confusing situation and we're in confusing territory. It's not the time to unleash all my feelings and desires, especially since that's not me. I've never been like this with anyone and the fact it's happening now is just... well, confusing.

"I'll take the floor tonight. I can grab blankets. My dad's not about to swing by and check on us, and my mom should know we'll need them as it is." I gesture to an open space on the floor between the bed and the wall. The room isn't huge, but I'll fit there just fine.

"Oh! Okay, yeah. That's great."

Is it my imagination, or does she sound disappointed?

No. I cannot think about that. If I'm going to make love to this woman, it is not about to be in my childhood bedroom surrounded by *Star Wars* and *Lord of the Rings* figurines, even if they are two of the greatest sagas of all time.

A knock sends me a foot in the air, my skeleton likely rising out of my body with the start.

"Knock, knock! Time for dinner, kids!"

M.O.M. NETWORK

M.O.M. Network Message board:

JusticeLVR: They're here! They're here!

CoolyKay: How do they seem?

SCLDG: Any progress?

JusticeLVR: Well, I've placed them in the same room so if there hasn't been *progress* yet, there should be soon.

Vic: You are shameless.

JusticeLVR: I'm a woman on a mission.

CoolyKay: She's a mother who knows what's best for her son.

SCLDG: She's focused. We don't try. We win.

Vic: Is this basketball? Are you about to coach us to the big game?

CoolyKay: What's wrong, @Vic?

SCLDG: She's just mad it's not her soldier home for Christmas. You'll get a turn yet, @Vic.

CoolyKay: Oh, honey. I'm sorry. It's hard when our chickens are in far flung places. It'll be okay.

JusticeLVR: I'm sorry @Vic. I don't mean to rub it in.

Vic: Don't apologize. I'm ornery. Ignore me. Tell us about the lovebirds.

JusticeLVR: Well, they're settling in upstairs. I knew I kept his old full-sized bed for a reason, ha! I'll let you know how the weekend goes. Merry Christmas, all.

SCLDG: Yes, do. Happy holidays.

CoolyKay: Can't wait! Merry Christmas!

Vic: Talk to you all soon.

CHAPTER TWENTY-SEVEN

Grace

JJ's hanging to the side of the ice rink with a death grip. He's doing the thing little kids do where they try to walk on the ice rather than glide. The idea was to have a little day date, do something Christmassy and fun, but it's gone south fast.

I'm not sure why I thought he'd be a confident skater. Maybe because I know he's a skier? They aren't the same, but both require some amount of eye-foot coordination. And this is a thing JJ apparently does *not* have when it comes to skates.

I'm by no means *good*, but I went skating often enough as a kid that I can move around fairly well.

"Having fun?" I ask as he finally comes even with me.

He exhales sharply. "Remind me never to ice-skate again."

I step in front of him and hold out my hands. "Will you trust me?"

He frowns deeply. "It's not that I don't trust you. I don't trust the math here—the surface area of the cheap, dull blade in borrowed shoes versus poorly maintained, slightly melted and refrozen ice... I'm already going to be bruised. Do you want me to break a hip?"

I can't hold in my laugh at his sourpuss rant. "Okay, wow. I didn't realize we were in danger of broken hips. How about I promise to keep you safe?"

I can't promise that, though I'm pretty sure I can keep him upright.

"You can't promise anything and you know it."

Busted. "Fine. Let me take you around the rink one time and then we'll check the box on Christmas Eve adventures and go sip hot chocolate. By then, I think my face will be frozen and ready to warm up."

With much ado, he sighs and extends one hand to me, yet keeps hold of the railing with his other. *Okay, so that's how we're doing this...* I give him a look, and with a flash of anxiety in his eyes, he reaches for me. We're both wearing gloves and it's one of those days where it's only a little below freezing, but the humidity is making it feel bitterly cold. For this reason, I'm glad we have the layer over our fingers, but I do wish I could feel his hands. I basically always want to hold them. He's so solid and warm, and there's no small thrill whenever we touch... though right now I'm primarily concerned with keeping him upright, so maybe it's for the best.

As I gingerly skate backward, checking behind me every few feet, JJ follows me with a *clop, clop, clop* of his blades against the ice. His cheeks are red from the cold and he's got twin lines between his eyebrows signaling his concentration.

This man is a decorated soldier, an accomplished lawyer, and a lieutenant colonel in the Army. He has deployed like eight times to three different countries and during four different conflicts. He's insanely intelligent.

Yet here he is getting bested by ice-skating at our town's dinky little ice rink, and I couldn't love him more.

I mean. *No.* Ha. Not *love* love him. I just love his effort. Love the part of him that has to work hard at everything, even if it's something totally insignificant.

I did love seeing him with his parents last night at dinner. He was so sweet, asking his mom about her crafting projects and her friends, peppering his dad with questions about his interests, and generally being an adorable son. I can see how much he loves his parents and how much they love him. As much as I miss seeing my parents, I'm so glad they're having the adventure of a lifetime they've worked hard for, and I'm glad I'm here. Even if seeing the house next door decorated for another family's Christmas did sting a little.

After dinner, we slipped into bed—separate beds with him in a sad little excuse for one on the floor. He'd made it clear earlier, which I was both grateful for and a little bummed about. I wouldn't mind snuggling up with him. In fact, the more time we spend here, in our hometown and away from the busyness of his schedule, the more of that closeness I want.

"You're doing great," I say, hoping I can encourage him as we round the midpoint and head for the exit.

He doesn't respond, just glances up at me for a minute before focusing back on his feet. Another little beat of tenderness pulses through me, right in time with the "Jingle Bell Rock" playing on the rink's speakers.

We're almost to the exit when he wobbles hard enough that he jerks my hands and in my effort to stabilize him, my skates go sliding in opposite directions. In seconds, he's on the ground and I'm thudding next to him.

"Didn't hit my head. I'm okay. I promise," he says, though he sounds like someone punched him in the gut.

I'm frantically checking to make sure he's right—he landed on his butt more than his back, and I'm sure he's going to have a terribly bruised backside. But the grumpy scowl on his face tells me it's not even his pride that's been wounded, it's his will. The same iron will that drives him to succeed and master any challenge has been severely injured.

It may make me a horrible person, but once I get a look at him and can tell he's not mortally wounded, I lose it. "You... look... so... mad."

He cuts me a storm-cloud look, and a grumble emerges. Too bad for him, this makes me laugh even harder. I roll to the side so I'm completely off him, very thankful I wore a pair of his old snow pants which cushioned my fall.

"I'm sorry. I'm so sorry, I shouldn't laugh." I pinch my lips together though to no avail.

There's a smile in his eyes as he shakes his head. "I blame you. You're just trying to get me on my back."

I blink, wondering if he hears it. Last time we fell together, he said something mildly scandalous then, too.

"I do look forward to someday getting you on your back in different circumstances." I waggle my brows. "Probably wouldn't want it to be here in the middle of town at the ice rink, though."

His eyes close slowly, and his head moves side to side

like he can't believe he just said that, or I did. "Forget I said that."

His blush turns him red and I take mercy on him, climbing to my feet and then helping him to his. In a few minutes, we're off the ice and he's shucking his rented black hockey skates like they tried to murder him, which makes sense since they kind of did.

"I hereby promise we never have to do this again."

His gaze snaps up and he looks genuinely troubled. "I thought you like skating?"

This response cracks me up. "Uh, I do, but not if the person I'm doing it with is miserable."

"I didn't mean to ruin it for you. I'm sorry."

It's a small thing, this apology, but I can tell he genuinely means it. And whether it's the way he approaches work or the way he treats his family, it's these small things that hint at what he might be like as a husband—a real husband. He would *try*. He would work at a relationship if it needed it, and he'd be dedicated.

"You didn't ruin it for me, JJ. I appreciate you going, but now I know. We need to find other activities that don't involve eye-foot coordination." I wink and nudge his shoulder with mine.

"How about something that isn't going to break my tailbone if I fall? I'd settle for that."

I loop my arm through his, and we walk toward a hot chocolate stand. "Oh, yeah. Broken coccyx is a rough one. I saw it quite a few times, and I will say snowboarding was the most common winter sport culprit."

He gives me a "there you go" gesture. "One more reason why I'm a skier."

I chuckle. "Well, skiing has a pretty high incidence of all kinds of broken things and head trauma, so be careful."

"I wear a helmet and I've given up skiing trees now that I'm older and don't bounce back like I did in my twenties. I was actually going to go on a ski trip this month, but my friend who planned it had to reschedule to February."

February. Where would we be... *what* would we be in February?

"Sounds fun. Where do you like to go?" I hope my voice hasn't betrayed me.

"His sister lives in a little town in Utah called Silverton, and they have this world-class ski resort, so we go there. I'd love to take you." His gaze finds mine.

My heart flutters at this mention of life after the agreement. Of a point in the future that seems so uncertain.

"I'd love to go with you." And wow, do I mean it with every bit of me.

It's becoming clear with every minute we spend together that I want to experience everything with this man. I want more Christmases with his family, and I want him to spend time with mine. I want to go on ski trips and get to know these Army friends he sees all over the world.

I want to have quiet evenings together on the couch and turn down the covers to a bed we share.

"We'll get it on the schedule, then," he says, though I think I hear a change in his tone, too.

We step up to the hot chocolate booth that springs up every year around the Christmas market and ice rink, and he orders two hot chocolates with extra whipped cream. We find a bench and watch the skaters swirling around the rink, the heat of the warm, chocolaty goodness bolstering me. I don't need to think so far ahead. I need to focus on right here, right now.

And that's why I turn and look right in his eyes from point-blank range. His brows pop like he didn't see me there, then he must register the energy, the need. His eyes drop to my lips, and then we both move. His gloved hand cups my jaw, and I wish it was his palm, though I'll take what I can get.

He tastes sweet and rich like the chocolate, his lips cool and his mouth deliciously warm. I'm just ramping up when a throat clears and we break apart.

"You may not be a town resident anymore, Grace Murphy, but I can still report back to your mother that I saw you snogging a man on the market bench." Rita Balmont huffs and her breath freezes in a white cloud before she halts and looks sharply at JJ. "And JJ Justice, you should know better."

With that, she bustles off and we're left to snicker into our hot chocolates like a pair of guilty teens.

"Hope we didn't upset her delicate sensibilities," I say, aware we might've gotten carried away if she hadn't interrupted us. At least I might've.

"It's for the children, Gracie." And though he's joking, I can't help the flip in my stomach at the nickname. I don't mind it one bit.

"It certainly is, Justin Jerusalem Justice."

CHAPTER TWENTY-EIGHT

Justin

My dad's study feels like an office, whereas my mom's crafting room feels like an entire craft store. The differences between them are stark. Dad's space houses giant vintage law books he's collected over the years, a globe at one corner of his regal cherrywood desk, and a leather-backed chair that is genuinely comfortable, especially after years of use. Bookshelves line the walls except for one window looking out onto the yard and street.

This has been his place as long as I can remember. If I was looking for my dad as a child, he'd be in his "office." He brought work home with him, and I remember sitting on the couch situated under the window and doing my homework so I could spend time with him.

In our modest home, this is the fanciest room, but it didn't start out this way. Things for this room were what he got for Christmas and birthdays for years. I remember the day we replaced the old, worn fabric sofa with this leather one my mom had bought from a rental agency who was going out of business.

"She's lovely, son." He enters the room behind me, setting a pile of books on the desk.

"She is." I sink into the old couch, taking a place that harkens back to so many important conversations in my life.

It's here I pled my case for going to camp or joining the track team. It's here I presented my argument for a raise in allowance or proposed a small business venture selling lemonade. It's here my dad broke the news to me about puberty. It's here he handed me the acceptance letter from West Point, and it's here he told me he had thyroid cancer and planned to retire.

There were highs and lows, truths shared and punishments meted out, all from this room. And never did he sit behind the desk and render the verdict or news. In these moments, he always came to sit next to me, a small signal that though he was a parent, he was also on my side, just like he does now.

"Why do I feel like I'm missing something here?"

His instincts, always impeccable as a district attorney for our county, are guiding him as usual.

I can't tell him the truth today. It makes me a coward, but I can't bring myself to admit any of it right now. "What do you think you're missing?"

Amusement flashes across his face. "Sounding like a public defender always tips me off." He crosses one leg and pins me down with his wizened gaze.

"No defending. Just trying to figure out what you mean." We'll call that diplomatic instead of evasive since it's more palatable.

He thinks for a moment, never hurried by pressure or

time. It's a quality I lack and one I admire, though one I've always found to be a torture device, too.

"You seem to genuinely care for her. I'm glad to see it. But there's something like longing between you that I'm working to figure out."

My throat tightens, his words a battering ram against a tenderness I haven't fully admitted to myself. I can't afford to. "I don't know what you mean."

He gives me time, seconds unspooling into threads of minutes, until we've sat there in silence for two, maybe three full minutes of silence. It's an unnaturally long pause, and it's done nothing to supply me with words for him, or for this situation.

"Is there anything I can do to help?" he asks, finally breaking through the quiet.

My heart squeezes and a list runs through my head. *Don't hate me when this all ends. Don't be disappointed that I haven't managed to find something real. Tell me how to be this new man who wants more. Tell me what to do to make it all work out.*

I run a hand through my hair, feeling about sixteen. "I don't think so. But I don't want you to worry. Grace and I..."

What can I say that's true? What can possibly explain this situation without blowing it all wide open and without lying to him any more than I have?

With a slow exhale, I try to make it make sense for both of us.

"We made the decision to be together for a reason." True. "I'm just finding the reality of the situation to be challenging."

It makes me sound like a jerk who doesn't want to be married to her instead of a man who desperately does with exponentially increasing intensity in relation to the number of minutes spent with her.

And yet, it's remarkably accurate. I have not ever lived my life in a way that factored someone else in. Yes, I've been a decent son and an okay friend. But I've never been… like this. I've never wanted to take time off to be with someone for no clear purpose other than to be with them. I've never considered rearranging my own life for someone else.

It might be the most self-centered thought I've ever admitted, but there it is. This is who I am and always will be… isn't it?

Dad's brow furrows low. "Marriage can be work, but I'll tell you what has made forty-six years of marriage far more good than bad."

"Please do."

"It's just what you said. 'We made the decision.' You, JJ, have a choice to make every morning. You choose to love—in action, even if the feeling doesn't show up first. It sounds simple but there are days when it isn't. It sounds ludicrous when everything's new and exciting, but when the realities of life roll in, when there's financial strain or, like you'll experience that your mother and I never have, military moves and changes of jobs. If you have kids, or if you don't—there are moments when it feels so painful, almost impossible to *feel* love."

Wow, he really thinks we're struggling. "I don't—that's not—"

"I'm not saying that's where you are. I wouldn't think it is, actually. It's almost like you're looking through a window at her and you can't quite reach. I don't know what's causing it, but I just want to give you this advice I would've given you on your wedding day."

Oof. Right through the heart. I nod, not sure I can manage words.

"You don't have to feel it. You have to choose it and then do the things that come along with the choice. You respect her. You respect yourself. You respect your marriage with appropriate boundaries and spend your time wisely."

He catches my eye now, and I can't look away.

"You don't let yourself put work above your family life. That's one I had to learn a few times over, and I wish it'd stuck sooner than it did."

He scratches the side of his head and gives me a look. Of course, it's not a surprise to me, though he was always a good dad. Always present, even if he still had work, though I'm realizing maybe it didn't feel like that for Mom.

"Point is, son, you get to choose. But you can only choose for *you*. She's got to meet you halfway with the same choices, the same values. If you'll both do that, I think you'll have a long, beautiful life together." He sets his big hand on my shoulder and squeezes like he has a hundred times before.

"Thank you. Really." I hope he can't hear the way my voice is strained or see emotion clouding my eyes.

"I love you, son. I want you to be happy." He clears his throat like maybe he's feeling all of this, too. "I know you'll do well."

This phrase has been a kind of catchphrase of my life. His unwavering faith in me, even when I fear I don't deserve it.

But as I wander slowly back to my room, taking time to stop and look at every picture on the wall and every knick-knack on every shelf to give Grace time to finish showering and getting dressed, I think about his words.

We chose to get married and had very clear guidelines

for our agreement, but the circumstances have changed. What if we *both* want something else? What if we aren't simply using each other for what we need, but would both choose to have the kind of relationship that is so much more?

I can feel the possibility between us. There's incredible physical chemistry, and I've laughed more with Grace in the last month than I have the whole last year. We've talked about real things, hard things, true things. She seems to be interested in military life, not scared away by it. She's amazing under pressure, and she already loves my parents.

She seems to accept how I'm driven by work and isn't put off by that trait.

Could she love me, though? And can I do right by her, loving her before all others, even my job? It sounds so false to even conceive of not prioritizing a *human* over my work, a job that could come to an end any day for any reason, and yet it's the path I've chosen. For over twenty years, I've chosen work first, work always.

Can I choose to change?

CHAPTER TWENTY-NINE

Grace

JJ and I sit on the couch in his parents' living room. The wood crackles in the fireplace and a piney scent drifts from the corner where their real tree squats, plump and bright and decorated with years of JJ's homemade ornaments and family memories.

Marcy relaxes in her overstuffed chair, humming along to the Christmas music playing just above mute as she flips through pages of a cookbook, and Jonathon has taken his seat in the easy chair where I assume he sits nightly. He's kicked back and already a few chapters into the crime novel we gave him.

JJ's reading a military history book while splayed on one end of the couch, and I'm laying with my head on a soft pillow in his lap, reading the book Marcy gifted me—a Christmas rom-com by one of her favorite authors. I'm not sure how she knows I read romance, but the choice is perfect and I'm loving it.

More than anything, I'm loving how the Justice family celebrates *Jolabokaflod*, the Icelandic tradition of gifting books on Christmas Eve and then reading them. I mean, literally, we ate a lovely Christmas evening dinner, we cleaned up, and then we opened books-only gifts from each other and are now sitting here, reading them. I've also consumed somewhere around eight snickerdoodles because Marcy makes the best ever and even as a child, they were my favorites.

"JJ, when is the promotion board happening?" Jonathon asks, peeking at his son from over the rim of his glasses.

All these toasty, cozy feelings shrivel, and a pit yawns in my stomach. I know what board he means. It is, at the heart of things, the reason I'm here. It's JJ's chance to progress into the next phase of his life, and even though I know the answer, the idea of rehashing the details makes my stomach knot.

"It convenes in early January. I'm unlikely to know results for several months after, but the decision will be finalized then."

His eyes flick down to meet mine. Is that him letting me know he doesn't expect me to stick around for so long? Is it... is there anything in his expression I can read? I can't disregard the dread I feel not knowing what's behind those eyes.

He traces the pad of his index finger along my hairline, his gaze following his progress, and it's such an odd, tender thing, my heart constricts.

"Any idea what your chances are? Anything you can do to make it a sure thing?"

Marcy's sip of hot chocolate chokes her and some dribbles onto her Rudolph sweater.

"Oh, dear," she says, eyes shooting to me.

Maybe because she's embarrassed, though I doubt it. More likely because *I* am the thing JJ has done to help his promotion. Or, it's one of the things. He doesn't say so, but he does launch into a few tasks and trips and *enter military and law jargon I cannot yet follow*, so I sit up.

I can't sit here and listen to him talk about his future— one I want to be a part of but won't be. Or... will I? I can't tell anymore and hearing about boards and promotions just drills home the agreement we made and how unplanned any of this real connection is. Maybe this holiday really has been just a vacation from reality...

I'm going to metaphorically plug my ears and sing *fa la la la la!* by drinking more hot chocolate and soaking in the good feelings and stoutly ignoring the conversation between JJ and Jonathon.

"Let me help you," I say, hustling over to take the dripping mug from Marcy and we move to the kitchen.

I rinse the mug and put it in the dishwasher while she swipes at the sweater with a clean, damp cloth.

After a moment, she gives me a look and says, "Be right back. Would you freshen up everyone's mugs?"

I'm grateful to have a job to do that lets me step away from the ticking clock presented by the conversation between JJ and his dad, and Marcy has made an elaborate hot chocolate buffet to accompany our "book flood" evening so we might as well revel in it. There's a spread of various flavored marshmallows in different shapes and colors, several kinds of chocolate chips to intensify the chocolate, and even powdered sugar or chocolate or cinnamon and small stencils to top off the drinks however we want.

In a minute, I've loaded up a small tray with mugs and

fixings. Marcy grins as she comes back in and gives me a little squeeze by the shoulders as she steps behind me.

I turn and smile back at her, wanting her to know I appreciate her. But then her gaze sharpens, and I have the sense she's a shark and I'm nothing short of chum.

"You're doing very well, you two."

I swear her pupils have gone black. Is she about to murder me?

"I think so, too," I say, because I really don't know what she wants.

One of her brows raises, and I've totally seen this look on JJ before. "One might even be led to conclude it's not just for appearances."

Ah. There we go. I can hear the hope in her words. "We are enjoying our time together."

Her smile beams and the sight of it halts me, but I press on because I don't want her to have a broken heart, too.

So much for ignoring all this.

"But as you heard, the board meets in January. So once we're in the clear, I won't be acting as his wife anymore. We'll evaluate things but he doesn't seem like he wants to extend the contract."

Whenever it's come up recently, he seems so certain we won't renew it. The original terms were through February first which would give him the clearance to stay fully, legally married through the month the board would meet just to make sure nothing odd happened, and then we'd go our separate ways. Which gives me time after the holidays to find a new place to live, and to finally decide...

In truth, I've already decided. As much as I have loved being back in my hometown for Christmas after missing it last year, I haven't missed the holiday schedule, the jockeying for time off and bartering for who would cover which holiday shifts.

I don't miss my job. I miss being a woman who knows what she wants and who had a plan. And though I don't know exactly what I'll do, Andy has given me a lot to think about, and so has JJ. I've looked at apartments here in town and in Alexandria. Nothing sits right, but I've tried to keep my options open so I'm not painted into a corner like I was these last few months. That's progress, I say—looking at the fire's pattern rather than letting it catch me unawares and burning me to a crisp.

"Can I tell you a secret about men with the last name Justice?" Marcy's expression has softened, no more predatory mother in sight.

"Please do."

She glances toward the living room, though we can't quite see into the space where the men are seated, still chatting based on the low hum of their voices.

"Those two are peas in a pod. They're both driven by work on a fundamental level."

A breathy laugh escapes. "You don't say?"

She gives me a fakely perturbed look. "Yes. And your *husband* is just like his father."

I absorb that and try to understand what she's saying, though all I can come up with is, "Sounds like there might have been some challenges on that subject over the years."

Her eyes widen. "Ya think?"

We chuckle together, and she continues. "JJ's father is a DA, as you know. He was always typically overworked, underpaid, and underappreciated. Short-staffed, unrested, a little too thin from being so busy he didn't stop to eat lunch. And then one time, JJ didn't invite him to his soccer game. This was when JJ was about seven, I think. And Jonathon found out about the game and was so shocked JJ didn't say a word to him about it. When we got home, JJ told his dad about the game—he'd scored a goal for the first time ever. And when Jonathon asked why JJ didn't invite him, do you know what he said?"

I wait, knowing it's coming.

"He said, 'I thought you'd be at work.'" She lets the point hang for a moment before going on. "He didn't mean it ugly, didn't mean to hurt his dad. And JJ wasn't upset, even. He just wished his dad had made it to the game, though never expected he would. But Jonathon... I'm not sure I'd seen the man cry since JJ was born, and that night, I found him in a heap on his couch, tears down his cheeks. He gave me this look like..." She shakes her head, and her eyes cast around the kitchen.

I reach out and set a hand on hers, an impulse telling me this is painful for her, even though it must've improved.

"He told me how sorry he was, how this was a wakeup call, and he hadn't realized how absent he'd been. And he changed. Was it overnight? No. But you can bet your butt he didn't miss another soccer game. He didn't work Saturday mornings, and he only worked after JJ was in bed in the evenings. He made it home for dinner more and more. And of course, we got the office gussied up for him so it'd feel like a place he could focus and get the job done, yet still be here with us at least part of the time."

"I'm so glad he had that moment when JJ was relatively young."

She dips a ladle into her crock pot o' hot chocolate and spoons a bit more of the molten sweetness into the mugs I made to give them a warm-up. "It didn't happen overnight, and it wasn't without ups and downs. I had some resentment stored up that took time to work through, and he struggled with boundaries on and off for years." She pins me with a look. "I had my own culpability. I hadn't communicated well. I didn't have my own boundaries or share my expectations. I had my own work to do, too."

I nod, fully getting the message there.

"JJ's just like his daddy. I can vouch for the fact that a man with that kind of work ethic will not let you down if he gets his priorities right."

My chest felt tight and fluttery at the same time. Here she goes again, ladling fairy dust on this beautiful, maddening, unlikely fantasy of us being together for real. "I can imagine."

She dips her chin and one brow raises. "And let me tell you, that *work ethic* will pay off in innumerable ways."

It doesn't hit me until she winks.

She winked. And *holy Christmas nightmare,* Marcy Justice just gave me so much more intimate information than I ever wanted from my fake husband's mother. No, no, no, no.

"You might be blushing to high heaven now, my sweet, but once you two figure things out and make this thing happen for real, I'm just going to guess it's going to be great." She waves her hands around as though to clear the air of the wildly inappropriate innuendo. "And I mean in a foundational way. The way he will love you will be singular and devoted, and if you were to have kids, well."

The soft smile on her face effectively banishes the lingering horror. I clear my throat, my emotions barely hidden under the surface.

"I've already had that thought. But this... we don't have that kind of relationship. I can't speak to his work-life balance. I can't force him to change and we—we aren't a family." My words are just above a whisper, and I'm grateful for the low hum of the Christmas music for covering my words in case JJ has started listening.

Marcy shakes her head, eyes closed and chin raised. "You may not believe it, but I can see it between you. There's tenderness, honey, and I think there could be a lot more. We just need him to see it's worth the risk."

"You two okay in here? Need any help?"

JJ wanders in and the sight of him with his scruff and his red plaid pants and T-shirt is enough to send my heart racing.

Marcy hands him the tray of hot chocolate. "We're just fine, but you can carry this so we can all have another hit of our drinks. We'll never meet our chocolate quota for the night if we don't keep at it."

JJ gives her a wry smile and then winks at me. "No slacking, got it."

He wanders out and Marcy wraps an arm around me and ushers me with her, whispering one last thought as we go.

"Promise you, it's worth it."

CHAPTER THIRTY

Justin

It's nearly midnight by the time we bid my parents goodnight. They've become late-nighters and though Grace and I are both early risers thanks to our work schedules, we slept in this morning and we will again tomorrow. My mom has a strict policy on lazy Christmas mornings. Sounds counterintuitive but after the years of my early childhood shuffling me back and forth to both sets of grandparents, she put her foot down. Wherever I find myself in the world, I keep to this same tradition if at all possible.

I'm looking forward to a good night's sleep, yet when Grace returns from changing in the bathroom, I'm unprepared.

Granted, feeling *unprepared* for Grace applies to everything about the woman, from our first meeting to the tiny peppermint red and white striped pajamas she's wearing.

The miles of smooth skin between her bare feet—toes

tipped with red nail polish, of course—and the hem of her shorts practically calls to me. It reaches out and says, *"Look at how gorgeous your wife is, JJ! What an idiot you are for marrying a woman who is the most beautiful person you've ever seen! Wouldn't you love to slide your hand up this lovely stretch of pale, uncovered leg?"*

And that's about enough of listening to the snarky voice in my head because it's doing nothing to calm me down. I'm a simple enough man that the sight of this completely appealing woman in her pajamas has my mouth run dry and my eyes cast down to my hands, which are now clasped together tightly in front of me. They're a new focal point and one I will not remove my gaze from until she's safely tucked under the velvety bedding my mom put on the bed.

Grace is doing something by her suitcase, probably tucking her clothes from earlier in there and… and I have no idea what else because the things that complete synaptic circuits in my head have been temporarily broken by this situation.

My avoidance of this sight last night had been strategic and has now been fully justified. She insisted I brush my teeth and get ready first, so I used the bathroom, then changed in the room while she took the bathroom. And I did have some semblance of a self-preservation instinct because I made a pact with myself not to look at Grace in her pajamas.

What I hadn't realized is that these are not winter pajamas. Bad enough to imagine her in some cute flannel set with Christmas bears on them or something, but this? Really, Grace, this?

"Did you fall asleep sitting there?" she asks, her voice quiet in the room.

Before I can answer while still inspecting my hands

with every ounce of my focus, she's there. *Right there.* And despite my determination to *not* feast on the glorious sight of her, she steps in front of me and her bare thighs brush my hands in the same instant her hands sift into my hair.

My stomach drops through the floor and splatters somewhere on the kitchen tiles below. My heart rate becomes jagged, a wild, messy thing, and my body responds instantly.

She has no idea what she's doing to me. No idea. I can't summon the image of a poodle for all the money in the world.

She's saying, "Are you okay?" but my hands are at her hips.

"I'm good," I scrape out, but that's the biggest lie I've ever told. Bigger than when I *did* put the frog in Ms. Grossman's desk in second grade. Bigger than when a friend down the street and I never did own up to scraping Mr. Murphy's car bumper when we were seventeen. I'd tucked two hundred dollars—all my savings at the time plus extra yard work around town for weeks—in an envelope a month later and slipped it in his mailbox, though I never did admit it.

It's a bigger lie than when I'd fooled myself at the beginning of all of this and convinced myself this would be nothing. That I could pretend to be close to this woman, to be in love with her, and to get to know her, and I wouldn't fall.

That said, all evidence to this moment in my life pointed to it being possible. The problem is, she's different. She's the variable, the element on which all of this hinges, and I'm confronted by the reality that it *has*. *I* have.

"Look at me," she almost whispers, both hands in my hair.

So, unable to do anything else, I do.

When our eyes lock, a few things click into place. First, I've worried her—the furrow between her brows tells me this. She doesn't realize I've been sitting over here agonizing over how to keep my hands to myself. She thinks something is *wrong*.

Second, I have never wanted anyone like I want Grace Murphy. Some part of me admits this has been true from the second I saw her, from the minute I entered that coffee shop and we started talking.

And third, I love her. I love her with a heartbreaking intensity I never anticipated. I love her in a way that steals my words and has me shaking my head, scrambling for a way to ease her mind and not upset her by throwing these way-too-soon feelings all over her. We don't know where we're going, let alone have a destination in mind.

"I'm good. Promise. Just... tired."

Someone record this speech for history. It can go down as the stupidest thing a man has ever said after realizing he's in love with someone.

Not just someone.

His wife.

Her blue eyes at this close range are stunning. This is not news, yet I have to stop myself from telling her how beautiful they are. I don't want it to sound like a line and it would. In this moment, when she's standing between my legs where I sit on the edge of the bed, in her short little candy cane shorts and a tank top, when my hands are on her hips and thumbs are somehow resting on the warm skin of her stomach and she's inching closer to me, it would.

Her gaze searches my face, and one hand drops down to slide along my jaw. There's a soft rasp of her fingers against the bristly stubble there, and her touch feels so good I could cry. I won't cry, though, because too many other things are happening.

Namely, she's saying, "JJ," with those big blue eyes blinking back at me, and I finally hear it. She's not *just* saying my name, and she's not asking a question. She's... she's inviting me. She's maybe even pleading, and I know this for certain only when she steps fully between my legs and tilts my face up, up, up to hers while she leans down and our kiss detonates.

In an instant, we're not just kissing. We are devouring each other. The slow slide of some of our other kisses feels like another universe compared to the primal hunger and need wrapped up in this. A kiss is simple, I've always thought. A kiss is one gesture among many to express feelings, but it's mostly a step in a direction. It's a part of the path to a more intimate joining.

Kissing Grace is the destination. Yes, I want more, but right here, with her moving closer, straddling me so she's not having to bend down, and now deepening the kiss, dizzying my mind, is perfection.

"I feel like we're getting farther apart," she says between presses of her perfect lips, her hands tracing up my back.

I don't know what she means. We've spent the last two days together—we've had more time in the last forty-eight hours than we ever have before. I'm reeling from how much more time I want from her, with her, of her. And yet, there's an echo of truth in her words. There's a ticking clock on this agreement, and I don't think either of us knows how to move forward. We don't know how to be fake married and falling in love. We don't know what happens after or how to talk about it.

Shouldn't I be better at this than... this? Shouldn't I have words to spill out, to make sense of all of these feelings and desires? All of these dreams cropping up that take me far beyond a promotion board and a short-term ruse to accomplish a professional goal?

Because that's what it was about. What it still *is* about. We—Grace, me, us—were never part of the deal. It's not in the contract we signed. It's not our arrangement.

And yet...

So I do what I can to reassure her. I tighten my hold and pull back, pinning her with my gaze and willing her to understand something I'm not sure I could verbalize even if I tried. "I'm right here. I'm right here with you."

She holds the eye contact and, again, I cannot imagine wanting to be this close to anyone else. I can't imagine wanting anyone else, *period*.

"Sleep in the bed tonight."

My mouth opens and I want to scream *"Absolutely!"* and *"I don't have that kind of self-control"* but she grins at what must be my stunned expression and lets me off the hook.

"Just sleep, JJ. If we're going to be together like that, it's not going to be in your childhood bedroom while your parents sleep down the hallway."

The wry grin on her perfect mouth compels to me to kiss her again—just one short, hot stolen moment. I ignore what my internal response does to the very open door of *if* like it might happen. We both know it's not happening tonight, and I'm not sure it should happen... not while we're mixed up in confusion of real and fake, now and future, push and pull.

Ignoring all of this, I say something pure and true.

"In that case, it'd be my pleasure."

CHAPTER THIRTY-ONE

Grace

The trees are dissipating and we're approaching the city. Even on Christmas Day, there's traffic. This isn't a shock, but I'm realizing I've never been in DC on Christmas Day. Odd.

"I wish we didn't have to come back yet," I say aloud, more than a little wistful.

I feel it—a longing for more of this time. I've fallen for this man and there's no going back. We're leaving the place where we both grew up and after this holiday, where I've recognized what my heart wants—him. We're inching back toward DC, and I can't help but feel like everything's going to change in ways I'm not ready for.

It's been nothing shy of magical, and I don't want this laid-back, accessible version of JJ to retreat back into work.

That won't happen though, will it? Not now. Not after sharing time with his family and reading books on

Christmas Eve nestled together on his mother's couch. Not after the kissing and cuddling and very clear desire we both have for so much more.

The days at his parents' house have been lovely. Waking up next to JJ was more than lovely. And our little Christmas celebration complete with Marcy's homemade cinnamon rolls and later an afternoon feast that still has my pants feeling too tight were also perfect.

I can't actually remember a more pleasant Christmas Day. Of course, I've missed my parents, but we managed to do a video call. I'd so wanted to have JJ join me and let them meet him as an adult. They'd get such a kick out of seeing him again, and in this context... if it was real.

As much as I wanted that, I stopped short of hauling him up to the room with me. He stayed downstairs and chatted with his dad while I worked on packing up and got caught up on all things Murphy. It's been great to hear how much fun they're having. They seemed relieved I'd spent the night at a friend's house and I know they could tell I'm feeling relaxed and happy instead of harried or working through the holidays like I have many, many years before.

But the closer we get to returning to the city and re-entering our more normal lives, the quieter and more distant JJ seems. I can't tell if he's just mulling something over, or if there's anything actually wrong. It's these moments I wish I knew him better, and then I feel foolish for how out of control my feelings are. How can I feel so much for a man I can't even read?

"We both have work tomorrow." JJ's response comes after what feels like minutes of silence.

"True enough. Though I'm not convinced you should be going back already. Don't you have leave saved up? Can you take the day off and relax?"

It seems silly how all of this lush holiday downtime should be shuffled to the side so instantly. I hate the thought that he's going to snap back into the workhorse he defaults to, and I can't get his mom's words out of my head.

"A man with that kind of work ethic will not let you down if he gets his priorities right." Does JJ have his priorities right? How will I know?

He shoots me a look I can't decipher—what's new?

"You're working, too, so I might as well."

I shake my head. "It's not the same, though. You're working a job that's difficult and often requires you to come home with more work to be done. I'm doing basic customer service and wishing people Happy New Year when I serve them their peppermint mocha or gingerbread latte."

He doesn't respond, and it's *this* that is driving me insane. I shift in my seat and bite down on the ever-growing impulse to just yell "What are you thinking about?!!" repeatedly until he answers.

That'd get a great response, right? Right. Foolproof plan.

But if he won't give me more, how do I know where this is going—where *we're* heading? How can I help him figure out his priorities, or get him to see *us* as one, if he won't use his dang words?

He speaks then. "It shouldn't be all that busy. Most people haven't been working over the holidays except our forward-deployed elements, and they know everyone's out of office. I'll mostly be doing catch up."

I bite the side of my cheek and try my best to keep the words in, but my stubborn side has its way. "Couldn't you just do that the day after, then? Why do you need to be there tomorrow?"

"I'll remind you, you're going in tomorrow, too."

I huff because it's not the same thing. "It's shift work, though. I'm not a salaried employee. I have nothing to catch up on, and if I truly wanted to reschedule, I probably could've. I took it because you'd already said you needed to be back."

He glances at me and adjusts his hands on the wheel as we decelerate into a completely nonsensical traffic slow-down. "This is an important time for me. In any other industry or firm, I'd be working nonstop at this level, too. I don't expect it to be easier just because I'm in the military, nor do I expect to be able to ease off now that I know I've done everything I can for the board. I won't do anything less than my best."

This grates on something raw in me—maybe the part that still feels like we're operating on different planes. But I've accepted the changes I'm making—I'm embracing them to a degree I never imagined. So I don't need to feel bad if JJ's standard for work-life balance is life at zero and work at a thousand.

And because of that, I'm not going to leave him unchallenged.

"Is this really your best, though? Obviously, I have no idea what the quality of your work is, but is your *best* feeling like you have to work all the time? Having weak or no boundaries at all for a job that will never appreciate you the way you should be valued?"

His jaw flexes and I know I've gone too far. I've started now, though, and it feels a little like my heart is bleeding as we inch along the highway toward the apartment where we live together in a legal marriage arranged specifically to facilitate and further his career. That's reductive, but it's also true.

Traffic clears and he accelerates, whisking us off the

interstate and into downtown. We're minutes from the apartment complex now and I know we both need the space.

"The military asks a lot of its people. Demands it, even. And if I intend to continue in this career, which I do, then this is what it takes."

This is so, so stupid, but my hackles are up, and I can't seem to stop myself even if I *know* this isn't the time to pick a fight. I'm frustrated and a little upset about how big my feelings are for him and how much it feels like he might return them. Why am I poking at him so much?

Maybe you're a self-sabotaging lunatic?

Even with such a helpful thought flitting through my head, I don't hold my tongue like I know I should. "Is it worth it? Working so hard and so much you hardly have a life?"

He's focusing ahead of him, and my eyes are welling with tears. I've crossed the line and I know it, but I can't haul the words back into my mouth. Something desperate and wild feels backed into a corner with these feelings, and I don't know how to handle them. I *can't* handle them, and it's clearly what has me lashing out.

I didn't have a life when I was a nurse. The parallels between us aren't lost on me. If I'd kept at it, I would've lost myself. JJ will, too. One day—someday. And I don't want that for him. Not for this man I love with all I've got now. He cannot be made to feel an ounce of the despair I felt in my life, yet it's also not my decision to make. It's his choice.

I work through how to apologize, wondering if maybe he'll just ignore I said it. Maybe we'll just forget about this whole mess and snuggle on the couch watching one last Christmas movie when we get home.

The talk with Marcy has thrown me. I don't know why

I've expected him to seem like he's changed his priorities in the span of a few weeks with me, or a few days off over the holiday. I don't know why every second in this car feels loaded, like packing peanuts are going to burst from the seams when we open the doors.

I can't figure out why it feels like his answer right now is the answer I've been working toward—the thing that will explain whether there's room in his life for me or not. It doesn't make sense for all the reasons he's already mentioned—I'm working, too. We haven't talked about *us* at all. And yet...

And yet here it is, and he's made it clear I don't get it. Even after all the events I've gone to and the conversations we've had. The time together, the shared space, the new memories. Even after pouring out pieces of myself and collecting those he's given me.

JJ glides into his parking spot and turns off the car. He steadies himself for a moment, and I resist the urge to run away by exiting before he can say whatever it is he plans to say.

"Not everyone understands what this life asks. I don't expect you to."

My mouth drops open, and I feel the punch to my stomach before he shakes his head and exhales sharply, then continues.

"I know you understand dedication and demand. I don't want to sound like I think you don't. I *know* you do. And I'm glad you're taking a break from nursing. But what I want and what you want from our careers are two different things. I—" He clears his throat and glances away, out his window and notably away from me.

When he looks back, our eyes meet. As usual, I can't magically read everything he means on his face, though I see one thing very clearly, and it's regret. He drives this point home when he finally finishes the thought.

"I've been like this all my life, Grace. I'm not about to change now."

Oh.

Oh.

This is what a broken heart feels like.

CHAPTER THIRTY-TWO

Justin

Gruff's gaze is heavy.

He's picked the wrong day to mess with me. I haven't slept more than a few hours at a time since Christmas Eve. Nor have I had a real conversation with Grace in five days, not since I bungled every single word I said aloud and ruined everything.

"What's eating you, Justice? Things off with the happy couple?"

Gruff leans back at his desk and I hate him. I'm not sure I've ever hated someone like this, but in this moment, I could happily put a fist to his thick skull and feel utter bliss.

Alas, I am deeply nonviolent and would never do such a thing, though the fantasy is great. There's snow falling peacefully behind him and a little sleigh jingle sound effect to accompany the punching sound.

Weirdly vivid, and yet so satisfying.

"My marriage is none of your business," I say and then regret rising to the bait.

He smirks, because of course he does. "Your marriage is exactly my business for two reasons. First, because I was the lucky man who got to witness your blissful nuptials, and second, because I put in a word with General Cooley about said marriage."

It's four o'clock on Friday, December thirtieth. I want to go home. I want to see Grace and apologize and tell her how much I know I screwed up. I want to change everything about how I have handled our relationship, this fake marriage, and even my professional life.

Because it's *this* moment I realize it's all just crap. Every ounce of this jockeying and hustle has been for a chance for other men like Gruff to judge me based on a sheet of paper. Most of my accomplishments don't even make the board file. Many of the things I'm most proud of don't either because they aren't about the military milestones.

Yes, I'm proud of the rank I've earned, the education, the successes. But if I look back on it, the most valuable things have been the people I've helped. Whether it was Rae Jackson dealing with her harasser or my friend Nate as he navigated battalion command or the guys at EMU figuring out whether their mission sets passed legal snuff, *those* are the things I take home with me at the end of the day.

And pretty soon, if I'm not careful, I'll go back to taking them home to an empty house.

I never realized how empty and bland my apartment was before Grace, but now that she's filled it up with color and life and even a few quirky Christmas mugs, I don't want it to end. I don't want to go back.

I want to return to the woman who's been brave enough

to forge her own path. The woman who got a job at a coffee shop and was utterly lit from within from the joy of doing something simple and satisfying and good. I want that goodness with me every day of my life whether I climb the next rung of this ever-more-narrow ladder or not.

"You know, sir, I think we both know you want to say something about me and Grace, so go ahead."

He crosses his arms and his expression shifts from that self-satisfied smile to an alarmingly serious look. "Don't say a word, Justice."

I narrow my eyes, trying to make sense of him. "What do you—"

"I'm saying I don't have a problem with you and Grace other than you're here at nearly five o'clock on Friday, and I assume you have a woman waiting on you at home. What are you doing?"

Hate recedes and pure confusion hits. "Are you kidding? You demanded I be here. That I 'man the office since no one else will.'"

With one flat look, I feel like a child. He doesn't stop there.

"I know you have a backbone. I've seen you employ it. If you're going to succeed as full-bird, you'll need to have boundaries. I've been waiting for you to push back, and I thought maybe, even if this coincidentally timed wedding seems rushed, you might finally have a reason to."

I am... astounded.

And furious.

But also embarrassed.

"Now, now, Justice. Don't hate me or yourself. I can see you self-flagellating already. The point here is, go home. Be with your wife. Consider consummating your marriage if you haven't yet."

I shoot out of my chair, and he starts laughing his low, rough laugh that sounds entirely unnatural.

"You're... something else." It's probably the first time I've ever failed to properly address him with a sir.

"You too, Justice. Now, git."

His casual dismissal hits me harder than any other reprimand could've, like he's been waiting for this to click and it finally, fully does. He doesn't need to say another word, nor do I.

I turn on my heel and I'm gone. I'm racing out of the building, out of the parking lot, out of the gates, a wild mix of relief and disbelief and anticipation hitting me. And more than anything else, clarity.

I want to go home to Grace.

I've worried about finding someone and being distracted by them. But I've been distracted by Grace since our first meeting. It's actually why I had so much crap work to catch up on before the end of year close out. And I've thought of this as a weakness.

When I attempted before, I was too focused on work and everything about the relationship ended up feeling like an imposition. No wonder my ex could sense that too.

I thought having a companion, a partner, a person who you came home to and who might steal your focus at times during the day would be a disruption and nothing more. There would be no reward great enough to merit the deviation from fully focused productivity.

Yet, haven't I seen the pay off? Haven't I witnessed the joy and beauty that comes from opening one's heart to another? I've seen it with Rae and Gabriel, with Nate and Ariel, with friends and even my parents over the years. I've borne witness, and I've now experienced it. But fool me ran from that truth, too scared of the risk to what I've always done.

Gruff's suggestion that I now have a reason to make boundaries and ask for more from my life... it's not wrong. And while it's not *only* about Grace's presence in my life, it also absolutely is. Because she's jarred everything loose I'd glued down so tightly, refusing to let the natural course of falling for someone influence me. But it has.

She completely has.

A laugh trips out in my silent car, and I hit the gas pedal, racing toward Grace and our little apartment and hoping against all hope I can find a way to rectify the mess I've made.

I made her feel like she wasn't enough to pull me away from work—that the next job, the next promotion, and my military life was the most important thing to me. In the past, it has been. It's why that's my default setting. I came out of the box this way.

That said, I've been out of the box for forty years, and it's not an excuse anymore. I can't blame Gruff or the Army or anyone else for my misguided super-focus on work. I simply can't. It's on me.

And the truth is, Grace is so much more than a distraction or a problem I have to solve on the way to a promotion. She's not to be used or reserved for days off. She is... she's everything.

We didn't say we were talking about *us* in the car on Christmas Day, but we both knew that's what all of the talk about priorities and work and not having a life was leading to. I knew it, and the heartbreak on her face told me she did, too.

She's ghosted me and I stayed at work long hours the first day to give her space, only to come to find she'd hardly been home. I only knew she'd stopped by because I found one of her socks in the dryer after one of my loads.

She's been staying away, letting me have what I thought I wanted—the time and space to focus completely on a career that has functioned as a spouse for far too long.

Not anymore.

There's someone I want more than focus, more than advancement, more than anything I've ever wanted before—a warm, intelligent, wonderful woman who has already shown me she's faithful, loving, kind, and so beautiful it makes me ache.

And now, I can only pray she'll let me explain and give me a second chance.

CHAPTER THIRTY-THREE

Grace

I've managed to stay in my room or be gone from the house more in the last five days than I ever have since moving in.

I hate this accomplishment. Frankly, I hate giving JJ space and feeling sorry for myself, especially since it's not simply feeling sorry. It's a soul-deep wound now. I'm going to carry this around for the foreseeable future, and I don't know how to get on top of these feelings.

Everything about the fight we had and everything about the way the last few days have gone feels utterly upside down. I've used up nearly every last page in my journal, and I'm sick of my own thoughts *and* handwriting by now as I've worked to process all of this. Much good that did me, still feeling like I'm walking in an utter white-out where I don't know my north from the floor.

It's a little after eight when I hear the soft knock.

Problem is, I've hallucinated him coming to me before, so this might be a reunion fantasy, and I don't have the heart for another one. I've spent the last two days fending those off because anytime I have one, I feel so much worse when it's over and I realize he's not going to come to me and try to resolve... everything.

My pulse jumps when I hear it again and yes, sneaky sad brain, I really did hear it. I slip out of bed and pad to the door, my heart pounding so hard I'm almost lightheaded. When I open the door, there he is.

He's still in his everyday uniform. He's got the barest hint of stubble, and he's run his hands through his hair so it's far wilder than he'd normally tolerate. He looks exhausted, but there's a wiry energy to him as he stands in front of me nearly bouncing on his toes.

I refuse to cry at the sight of him. What a stupid response, right? And yet, that's what my heart is trying to engineer here. I grab hold of the door frame both to steady myself and to remind me he's stayed away. He not only made very clear his work would always come first, he's also backed it up by disappearing, as though the last few weeks together have meant nothing to him.

So instead of smiling at him or letting these feelings leak out of my eyes, I pull my shoulders back, lengthen my spine, and ask, "Can I help you?"

He opens his mouth, but nothing comes out. His gaze searches my face, and then he just shakes his head, and his hands shoots into his hair for a second before he seems to straighten himself out and start talking.

"I'm sorry. I'm so freaking sorry. I messed everything up last weekend and I hate it."

He stops, waiting to see if... what? I'll slam the door in his face?

I want to. I want to shut him out the way he's done me—first with his words, and then with literally disappearing again.

Honestly, the man should take up a residency in Vegas for his disappearing acts. It's downright *magic*. But I'm also too lovelorn to want him hurt or even punished, as sad as I am.

"I do, too," I say, then hug my arms around myself because I can feel the draw to him and sorry doesn't fix everything. Sorry doesn't change how in the end, we are at odds. It's not a misunderstanding. It's not an untruth. It's a fundamental difference in how we want to live.

"I've lived my entire adult life driven by the need to keep working hard. It's become a hamster wheel I can't get off, and until recently, I didn't really want to. I've caught glimpses of it when I visit friends who have families and a clear purpose outside of work—I know what it looks like for those people. But I've never had such motivation for myself, and it's been a long time since I tried to find it."

We'd talked about past relationships over the last few weeks, neither of us having all that much to tell. A few long-term relationships that feel like ancient history, and one for each of us we'd thought might be something special yet turned out to be nothing. We had just enough experience with trying at love to know we hadn't found it.

Maybe that's how I know I have.

I came into this looking at it with as much pragmatism as I own and here I stand, flooded with the reality that I love JJ more than I could've ever imagined loving someone. It's imperfect and it's been a little messy, yet it's real. Even when I've been frustrated, I'm still alive with hope and anticipation. Even when I'm unsure, I'm ultimately certain of myself.

He lifts his hand like he might touch my cheek or shoulder, then it drops to the side and he shakes his head just once like he's promised himself he wouldn't touch me. I'm so jumbled, wanting to throw myself at him yet needing him to say so much more before anything feels resolved.

I need him to know I love him, but I have to make sure he understands and doesn't think I'll go along with being what amounts to a side hustle in his life.

"You've had this huge change in your life over the last year—you've realized what you don't want, which is huge, and are beginning to see what you do. I envy the way you've been honest with yourself even when it's been painful and hard. I'm in awe of how you're reinventing yourself and embracing what's best for you. I'm trying to learn from that, Grace, and I'm hoping you'll be patient with me."

My throat is tight and I can't think of a single useful word, but I dip my chin to show I'm listening. That I hear him, even if I'm not sure what it means.

"It's too much pressure on you to say *you* are the reason I want to change how I do things. I won't put it on you because it's not fair, but I want you to know..."

He reaches for my hand and I give it to him.

His warm, dry hand enveloping mine feels so right, I have to gulp in air to make up for the way I've been holding my breath.

"I want you to know that you are amazing. You are a compassionate, thoughtful woman who gives so much to the people around her. I am in awe of you. I'm sorry if anything I said the other day made you feel anything less—I was scared and could feel myself changing, but as you may have noticed, change isn't exactly my forte. And I hope you believe that you are the person who has made me realize I want to change—you've shifted something in me, and I don't ever want it to go back."

I swallow, barely keeping it together. Emotion is hot on my cheeks and tight in my throat. I'm pretty sure my breathing is erratic, and I probably have a wicked case of sparkly eyes.

He plows on, still giving me more.

"This whole situation is a mess, and I never should've let it get this far. We never should've gotten married, and yet I can't pretend like I'm not grateful we've been forced to get to know each other. The thought of missing out on this..." He shakes his head like it's a thought he simply cannot bear. "I am so deeply humbled to have spent this time getting to know you and I will never be able to thank you enough for letting me into your life, let alone helping me to become more of myself. I know it's a lot to ask after this week, but I'm hoping you'll think about going to the new year's reception with me tomorrow."

I open my mouth to say yes, but he squeezes my hand. My chest is alight with so much feeling it's like I'm filled with helium and might float away. My pulse is cranking and I might actually be a little dizzy from his confession—from his implications. It's not crystal clear—I don't know what's coming next. But I know I want to give him the chance to spell it out.

"Please don't answer yet. Think about it. I'll check in with you tomorrow, and you can tell me then, okay?"

A laugh tumbles out, and I'm grateful it's that and not tears. "Yes, Colonel Justice. It's okay."

He grins and the sight sends butterflies through me.

"Alright then. I'll see you in the morning." He leans in and presses a soft, slow kiss to my cheek. "Sleep well, Grace."

Amazingly, I do sleep well. I feel more rested than I have since Christmas morning, but as this day dawns, the last in a year full of personal progress and unbelievable change and growth, I am more full of hope and anticipation than I have been in so, so long.

We have a lot more to discuss. I have no idea what all of this means for our relationship in real life or legal terms. I don't even know what this means to JJ—he wants to try officially dating? He wants to... I don't know. I just honestly don't, and we need to talk. But I know with certainty I forgive him for being absent, and I don't think I *need* to forgive him for the fact that change is hard and his way of thinking is shifting.

I'm working this morning until noon, so I tiptoe out into the living room to find him sitting on the couch reading a book.

My heart flips.

He's got his feet kicked up on the coffee table, and he's wearing the same pajama pants he wore at his parents' house. His gray T-shirt will be the one with the Millennium Falcon wearing a Santa hat, and it's so nerdy and festive it makes me want to hug him even before I've seen it.

"No work for you today?" I ask as I round the couch to sit across from him on the low table.

His slow, pleased smile has sugar plums bursting in my chest.

"Good morning, Grace. Happy last day of the year," he says, then sits up and removes his feet from the table. "And no, no work today. I have better things to do."

This, for some entirely inexplicable reason, makes me nervous. "You do?"

"I hope, anyway. Depends on you and whether you can forgive me, but yes. If you do, then I have a date tonight."

Cue Champagne veins. I press my lips together to try and seem calm and collected and not wildly happy with this response, though it's no use. I grin at him and get to the point as I move closer to him.

"I do forgive you. And at the same time, I'm not sure it's really a matter of forgiveness. I think I understand better now, and I also do agree it's going to be a process. It's not an instantaneous thing to adjust course after doing things one way for most of your life. *Ask me how I know.*"

He takes my hands in his and that smiley version fades into something earnest. "I'll do my best, but you'll need to be patient with me."

"I can do that."

He reaches up and tucks some hair behind my ear, then a half smile pops on his handsome face as he inspects me. "Why am I not convinced?"

Nerves swarm me like a storm because I didn't intend to bring this up before work. "Uh, well. The way you're talking, it sounds like..."

I can't say it. I didn't think through how to approach this.

Though maybe JJ did because he scoots to the edge of the couch so our knees are threaded together and he's holding tight to my hands.

"It sounds like I want a future with you? Like I'm planning on you needing to be patient with me while I figure out how to find some balance?"

I nod, so hopeful, so full, I can't possibly speak. It's

impossible there are *more* sugarplums in there, but if there are, they're about to explode all over the place.

He's instant in his response. "Good. Because that's exactly what I want."

Then he smiles again and honestly, who is this smiley, bright man? Even over Christmas he wasn't borderline *cheery* like he is now.

Then he pulls me to my feet and stands at the same time, heat entering his gaze as continues. "I want a lot more than that, actually, but you've got to get to work, right?"

"Yes. Just 'til noon."

"Perfect. I'll have everything ready for tonight once you're off."

Then he leans toward me as he slides one hand into my hair and takes my mouth in a wildly possessive, hot kiss.

It's there, consuming me, and then it's done, and I'm standing in the same spot, barely resisting melting onto the floor like a marshmallow in hot chocolate.

Wow, the man can kiss. And he can apologize. And he can... whatever this is this morning.

"See you later, Grace."

I flutter my fingers and say something genius like, "Yep" or "You too" or some other brilliant combination of syllables, and I leave. I'm in a daze but all I can think is that if he wants a future with me—if he's talking about me being patient with him, it's not just until the end of our contract. It's more than that. And if he feels even a fraction of what I do then this... this really might work.

CHAPTER THIRTY-FOUR

Grace

By the time I wrap my apron around me and tie the knot at the café downstairs, Andy has already eyed me and asked me what's going on twice. We lightly chat between customers, and though it's New Year's Eve and a Saturday, people are still guzzling the caffeine like they're about to nine-to-five it.

I've avoided answering with anything meaty, but now that we have a lull, instead of putting her off or keeping it to myself, I want her to know. I want *everyone* to know. So I tell her.

"JJ apologized and I think he wants... I'm pretty sure he wants to be together. Like, indefinitely."

Just saying the words aloud that I've been thinking since he kissed me and I left the apartment earlier has little angel wings flapping around inside me.

Or, maybe not, that sounds disturbing, so we'll stick with butterflies.

She makes no attempt to hide her smile. "JJ, huh? I'm assuming the apology was appropriate and convincing?"

I nod. *Boy, was it.* Maybe even a bridge too far considering he didn't need to apologize for who he is, only for shutting me out.

She returns the gesture, a short approving movement. "Good. About time."

I chuckle under my breath and then exhale to calm myself. I probably shouldn't have had any coffee today, let alone a flat white, even if it was half caf. I'm jittery and it's adrenaline and joy and anticipation and yes, caffeine, all making me feeling like I should go jog around the block and get some energy out.

Just then, to the tune of NSYNC's classic "Merry Christmas, Happy Holidays," JJ walks in the door. The line is three people deep, and I've halted all progress on the drink I'm making because he's pinned me with those hazel eyes I love. Yes, love.

I love him so much and it's absolute nonsense, though I'm starting to think maybe I don't care. Maybe, in the same way I've been honest about my need to change careers—a reality that has been clinched by this holiday season feeling less stressful and replete with dread than any other in my adult life—I can be honest with myself about this. I love and am in love with Justin Justice, he of the alliterative names, and even though it feels fast, in some ways it doesn't. We've known each other our entire lives. We grew up together. Though I still have things to learn about him, I do know him.

"Earth to Grace. Do your job and then you can take a break, woman!"

Andy says this not so quietly over her shoulder, and I jolt into action, drawing my eyes away from the gorgeous man at the end of the line and focusing on pulling espresso and doing the stuff of making the list of drinks piling up.

Five minutes later, JJ's order comes through. I grin but try to keep a leash on the thing when I see it because I don't need to see the name to know it's his. Peppermint Mocha with whip and sprinkles. I've kept my eyes on the espresso machine this entire time, but now I get to hand over the drink.

Why does his sweet tooth with both coffee and cocktails make me like him even more? I don't know, but it does!

"Peppermint Mocha for JJ," I say, even though he's standing *right there*.

"Thank you, ma'am."

Ooh, his voice sounds rich and deep and a little like a sip of the very drink he's taking from my hand, brushing my fingers with his when he does. I normally just set the drinks down but for this particular patron? Hand-to-hand delivery is a must.

"Anytime." And then I can't pretend I'm not elated to see him, so I say, "Glad to see you."

I take stock of his black wool coat, red-and-green plaid scarf, jeans, and some kind of stylish shoe I don't quite have a good view of. He's ridiculously handsome, and I suddenly wish I wasn't covered in chocolate syrup and espresso grinds.

"I couldn't seem to keep myself locked up there in the apartment when I knew you were down here."

Sugarplum fairies and little Christmas elves throw a party. Yep. Still creepy, but there we have it. I'm all aflutter.

"Well, that's very... I don't know what it is."

Of course this is what I say because my ability to form

coherent thoughts around him ceased somewhere around eight fifteen last night and has very clearly not resumed.

He smiles, though it's not wide or wild. It's soft and almost secret, like he knows he's having this effect on me and he likes it. In true JJ style, he doesn't draw attention to it, thankfully. Instead, he leans close, and I'm compelled to do the same.

"I can't wait to spend the evening with you, Grace."

And then he gives me a bigger smile and walks out, leaving me to stare after him like a starstruck fangirl instead of a woman who has been living in the same apartment for six weeks now.

"Man the counter!" Andy says, bolting out the door and jogging past the windows to stop JJ.

I can see them talking, but sadly, my nursing degree didn't supply me with the ability to read lips. She hands him a small paper and I am so very curious. Next, she gives him a very awkward pat on the side of his shoulder and he nods, seeming... pleased? Charmed? Something good, I think, and likely proving she didn't just threaten him on this small scrap of paper.

She hustles back in, the jingle bells replacing the regular single bell giving us a loud announcement of her return. Thankfully, I've just poured a black coffee refill for a regular and there's no line.

"What did you just do?"

She shrugs a shoulder and goes about wiping down a counter and tossing an empty milk jug.

"Okay, no. What did you just do?" I insist.

She turns to me, a smug little smirk on her face. "I helped him out. Just a little. And you'll be glad I did. Now get back to work," she says, and snaps the towel at me.

I glance back out at the sidewalk but of course JJ's long

gone. He's not working, though he seems like he has something to do. I have three more hours of work and it feels interminable, so I decide to make her distract me with future plans.

"Okay, then while we're working, I'm going to need you to tell me all about how the cat café plan is coming along."

CHAPTER THIRTY-FIVE

Justin

The calm I've often prided myself on is nowhere to be found tonight.

I'm pacing a figure eight from the kitchen, through the living room, and back. I'm trying not to bemoan the fact that I'm wearing my dress blues and have been in my uniforms during evening hours far too many times this month, while at the same time eagerly anticipating when Grace will come out.

The woman at the little boutique Andy referred me to was begrudgingly willing to let me buy something, and just as Andy said, she knew Grace's size. At least, she said she did. She also seemed to know a dress Grace had been eying for the previous ball that'd looked wonderful on her, but that she ultimately couldn't wear since it wasn't available for rent.

So I bought it. As though she wasn't making a fairly nice

sale, the woman eyed me like she was suspicious of me instead of a man buying his wife a dress.

I walked home second-guessing everything. Should I have taken Grace with me? Was this overboard? Would she like it? Did the woman really remember the dress? Would she even want to go out after working early this morning? Would she want to show up to this event we'd previously planned on attending but now that things have changed, don't have to? She said yes before, but maybe the shift at the coffee shop wore her out.

I suppose one issue is that we haven't determined how we're moving forward in terms of the marriage and our relationship. I tuck a hand into my pocket and feel for the small velvet box there—still safe.

I know how I want the evening to go, and how I want our future to look. I just hope and pray I'm not too far off what Grace wants.

Her door opens down the hallway, and I brace myself with one hand on the back of the couch. Thank goodness I did because Grace is an absolute vision.

She's fiddling with the clasp on a small purse so she doesn't see me until she enters the living room and looks up.

"Oh, hey. Sorry to keep you waiting. I need your help, if you don't mind." She turns around and I see the last four inches of her dress aren't zipped. The good news is, she accepted the dress. She wore it instead of tossing it out the window.

I didn't actually think she'd do that, but when you've been an idiot repeatedly and over time, you can't exactly bank on a smart woman like Grace *not* refusing you. Thank goodness she's smart *and* merciful.

She's also walking and talking like this is any other day and not the first of the rest of our lives—or so I hope.

"You're so beautiful," I say, then obediently slide the zipper up the last few inches.

Her shoulders and arms are bare, and the deep silvery gray material is something the couture owner called *brocade*, and the bodice fits tightly against her with subtle folds across the front, then flares out in an A-line—also only a word I know thanks to the snippy woman who clearly got the size just right.

Her hair is smooth and pulled back from her face and pinned up so the glorious expanses of her uncovered skin are on full display. She wears sparkly earrings and no other jewelry.

"You look very handsome. This is another iteration of the blues. I'm surprised I haven't seen this one yet." She runs her hand over the placket of large brass buttons that run down the front of the jacket.

"No mess dress required, so I'm happy to wear this one tonight." I haven't stopped feasting my eyes on her, everything from the soft, pale inside of her wrist to the curve of her shoulder. She's simply magnificent.

I take her hand in mine, cradling the back of hers with my palm, and slowly raise her arm so I can kiss the thin skin of her pulse point.

"JJ, should we go?"

It's soft and breathy, and she doesn't move. Her eyes are glued to my lips as I kiss an inch farther up her wrist.

With herculean effort, I pull away from the mesmerizing feeling of my lips against her skin and realize two things. First, I have no desire to go socialize with work people, let alone leave this house, and second, there's no way I can wait until after the party to do this—at least part of it.

"Not just yet." I cross the room and grab the small package. "I neglected to give you your Christmas gift earlier this week, and I wanted to make sure you have it. I have one more small thing, but that's for later."

And while it is literally small, the significance is huge. But I want to start here.

She sets her purse on the back of the couch and looks at me askance while slowly untying the bow. "I thought we said we weren't doing gifts?"

True. We'd said no gifts.

"We'll call this a happy new year gift. Or a congratulations gift, if you prefer."

I nod to the present, urging her to open it. I am certain there will be more nerves as the day wears on but for some reason, my heart is galloping in my chest as she slides a finger between the folds of the paper and finally opens it.

Her bottom lip drops a bit, like she expected a book and instead, finds the journal.

"It's beautiful." She opens it and bites her lip in an expression I know is pleasure, which she confirms when she beams at me. "It's lay-flat."

I return her grin because it's infectious. "I saw you wrestling with yours at the table a while back. Thought this might be a way to remedy that."

She flips through a few more pages and rubs the paper between two fingers. "It's such nice, thick paper without being stiff. I can't wait to write in it."

I forbid myself from letting anything on my face other than a placid smile because otherwise, the excited little boy jumping up and down inside my head will say something to completely spoil the rest of my plans.

"I thought maybe it would be nice to start fresh with the new year. Or if you like to finish each one to the last page, maybe this could be a place you brainstorm ideas for what's next—not to say that being a barista can't simply be what you do. I don't mean to disparage that."

She steps right into my space and wraps her arms around my neck. "I know you don't. And I think it's a great idea. I've tried to figure it out a bit, but I've been... preoccupied with other thoughts lately, and I do enjoy working at the shop."

"You make a mean peppermint mocha." I press a featherlight kiss to her cheek, then just in front of her ear, then the soft spot just behind it.

"If you have any desire to go to this ball, you should really..."

Her words fade as I kiss down her neck one, two, three times. I've reached the stretch of her shoulder, now the hollow of her throat.

"Seriously, JJ. If you want to leave this apartment, you have to stop."

The urgency in her voice stops me, and I straighten so I can see her face. She's shaking her head with a little curve to her lips that makes me want to taste them. But she's also wearing vibrant lipstick, and I hate the thought of upsetting her by messing it up.

"If you keep seducing me, we won't make it out of here, and I'll never get to wear this gorgeous gown before it has to go back to the store."

"It's yours, Grace. It's never going back." I can't express what the gleam in her eyes is doing to me.

"Oh, well then..."

She steps back and smooths her hands over the material. *Winter weight* was something the owner bandied about, but all I know is it's a different texture than her red dress or her wedding dress. I like touching it, though nothing will ever appeal as much as her skin.

"Why wouldn't you get to wear the dress? You're wearing it now, aren't you?" I say, a tone to my voice clearly indicating I'm being deliberately obtuse.

She rolls her eyes, then something wicked enters her expression. She leans forward and her lips coast along my jawline until she's speaking softly into my ear. "Because I'd want you to take it off me, JJ. I'd want you to keep kissing me everywhere."

I know that's what she meant, but I didn't take it seriously and I also never really thought about the power her lips saying those kinds of words might have over me. Turns out, the power is nearly absolute.

"Come on, Justice. Let's move."

She's by the door somehow, and I'm still standing where she left me. She has her jacket and I realize I've been frozen in place by the sheer blizzard-level storm of wanting.

I shake it off as I lurch toward the door, neglecting the overcoat authorized with this suit because I'm overheating so thoroughly, I know I won't need anything but Grace to keep me warm tonight.

CHAPTER THIRTY-SIX

Grace

We've been at this event for an hour before I realize the fancy older woman and her husband who welcomed us are a retired US senator and his wife. It took another ten minutes to realize *that's* where I'd heard the name Gruff before I met Colonel Gruff.

The man himself is standing like he's attending a funeral, nodding crisply at anyone who passes. He does spare me and JJ what I think is his version of a smile. JJ tells me about their conversation yesterday, which helped him connect the dots to a realization that has been rapidly approaching—or so he says.

This gathering is on a smaller scale than the ball weeks ago. We're in the Gruff mansion, which sits on a glamorous DC street in a wealthy neighborhood and seems historic. I wonder if they've purchased it recently or if it's possible the colonel was once a child. That's nearly impossible to imagine on several fronts.

"He may be lightening up? Yesterday certainly felt out of character, but we'll see how he takes it when I refuse the many *opportunities* for overtime he'll undoubtedly still attempt to give me."

His breath whispers against my skin, and I wish we could slip out of here and head home. The food tuxedoed waiters are passing around is fantastic, and I've gotten to see Megan and James, both of whom gave us large smiles like they can tell we're closer than we were last time we saw them.

"I hope so," I say, because I'm having a hard time concentrating. There's a string quartet playing Christmas music, and everyone is eking out the last of the holiday spirit before the clock strikes midnight.

JJ has his hands at my waist and... yep. That's it. I need a minute of fresh air before we circle back and hobnob more. Maybe it's the dress, which is gorgeous and quite comfortable, though really very heavy, or maybe it's the glass of champagne I drank when we first arrived. It could be that Mrs. Gruff has it fairly warm inside since there are doors open leading to the balconies on the second floor and people entering and exiting keep sending gusts of freezing winter air through the entryway downstairs.

"Can we step outside?"

JJ searches my face for signs of distress but doesn't say anything. He simply links our fingers and draws me with him to the nearest exit. The sharp, cold air hits me and I nearly groan with relief.

"Are you okay? Should we leave?" he asks, all concern and sweetness.

"No. I just overheated. I'll be fine in a minute." I spot a

bench toward the edge of the balcony and decide sitting for a minute might be nice. The passed hors d'oeuvres and drinks have been lovely, yet with no seated dinner, we haven't sat down since we arrived.

JJ lingers by the door a moment, and just when I'm going to ask him if he wants to come sit with me, he slides into the space next to me on the bench.

"Any better?"

I take a deep breath and exhale it, pushing a little white cloud into the chill night with my warm breath. "Yes, much."

He's quiet again, looking out at the view of green space and glittering lights, and a little ways off we can spot the Capitol and probably more monuments. A tiny white speck appears on the dark blue sleeve of his unform, and we both look up to see thousands of little snowflakes spiraling down.

JJ pins me with that gaze of his, and even in the dark, I can tell what comes next is going to be important.

"Living with you for the last few months has been some of the best moments of my life," he starts, his voice a little rough.

"Mine too."

"At the same time, they've been some of the hardest. I've realized so much about myself and what I need to change."

I squeeze his hands. "No. Please don't think you need to—"

"I do need to change. But it's not because you're demanding it, and I know it. It's amazing to me that, unless I'm reading this all very wrong, you've cared for me even before I finally committed to finding more balance."

"You're not wrong," I say, my voice a little watery and my heart absolutely exploding.

"I've learned so much, but the most important thing I know now that I didn't when all of this started is that I love you, Grace. I never imagined I could love someone this much but here I am and I now cannot imagine what it would be like not to."

I immediately reassure him because I'm not about to play games or act coy. We've come way too far for that, and I don't want there to be a sliver of doubt. "I love you, too. It's just... so wild how fast this happened. But I do. And I definitely loved you before yesterday, for the record, though I am also so proud of you for planning to adjust a bit."

He gazes at me with something like wonder, then pulls me in for a gentle kiss. I haven't had nearly enough by the time he pulls back.

His eyes hook into mine, and I think he's going to stand and lead us inside so we can toast to our newfound love or something, but instead, he shifts and sinks to one knee. His other hand is slipping into his pocket, and then the whole picture comes into view as my blood rushes to my head.

JJ is kneeling. And the little box he just flipped open holds a gorgeous diamond ring.

"Grace Maryanne Murphy, I know it's fast, but I love you. This first shot at marriage has taught me a lot and I know there is so much more to go, and I want to travel that distance with you. I want everything with you. Will you marry me indefinitely?"

It's so perfect, the way he's put it. No timing or schedule involved. No term limit.

I launch myself into his arms and hug him first, then kiss him with every ounce of love I have in my heart, and after, I pull back, laughing and crying at the same time because this is insane, but it's also exactly right.

Just like I thought earlier, it *is* right. So I tell him that.

“Yes, Justin John Justice, I will marry you indefinitely.”

He laughs outright, his face beaming with delight, then shakes his head and presses his forehead to mine. “I’m really going to have to teach you my middle name.”

I kiss him again, lean back. “Oh, Justin Jonathon Justice, I love you.”

“I love you, Gracie.”

EPILOGUE

One Year Later
Justin

As mid-November approaches, so does our first, first anniversary. And yes, we'll have a second first anniversary—that'll be the anniversary of our real wedding. We never annulled the first one, because why? We'd already committed to each other, and it seemed superfluous. We did get married in the eyes of God and make vows in front of all our families and friends this past summer.

It's remarkable to think how different the two ceremonies were, yet also how different our experiences of both events were. We'd entered our first marriage as an agreement with all the contractual goodness I could supply in the document we now have framed on the wall of our blissfully shared bedroom. Our second ceremony and the party that followed was like the culmination of something.

I won't say marrying Grace was an inevitability because

I've never felt that way about anything. I've always assumed we have choices to make and we either make them or we avoid them and in doing so, we make a different kind of choice anyway. I saw the choice to marry Grace last November as a mildly foolish but somewhat convenient (for me) and very generous (for her) exercise in meeting needs in creative ways—her need for housing, my need for a legal partner without the mess of obligation or emotional attachment.

If I have ever believed in fate or soul mates, it's now. It's after finding a woman who loves me as is, and also loves me as I grow and change. Just as I am, even as that morphs with time.

And maybe, I believe in the power of the M.O.M.s network—yes. Mom finally came clean, and though I'm not altogether shocked, I am surprised her little plot worked.

Surprised except that her choice of woman was right. So maybe the surprise comes in the fact that Grace has been willing to put up with me.

"Happy anniversary."

Her voice reaches me where I sit with feet propped on the coffee table, then she slides her hand down my chest and kisses my cheek from over the back of the couch.

I hook an arm around her head and turn mine so I can capture her mouth, and despite the awkward angle, I'm always happy to steal a kiss.

"Happy anniversary, wife."

She grins and gives me another peck, then shuffles into the kitchen. She packed her lunch last night and just needs to fill up coffee, so we've only got a few minutes left together. I launch off the couch and follow her, loving the sight of her bouncing energy.

"You still thinking you can get off an hour early today?" I ask.

In a true reversal, I was able to take the day off, but Grace couldn't. She's taken a position as a school nurse at an elementary nearby and loves it. Last spring, she dipped her toes in by subbing in the school district after a colleague who'd made the switch from working in a hospital to the school system recommended it. By the end of the first two weeks, she'd applied for the permanent position. By the end of the school year, she'd been hired on for a full-time job for this year.

I couldn't have been prouder of her, or more relieved she'd truly found a way to use her vast experience without continuing burnout. If she'd been satisfied with working at the coffee shop, it would've been just fine with me, but not long after the new year, she started getting restless and asking around, and that's when the idea of subbing as a school nurse popped up.

She shoots me a look. "I have it all planned. I'll meet you at the courthouse at three. I'll only miss the last half hour."

"Good. Then go help some little kids, and I'll see you in a few hours." I kiss her again—one more for the road.

Something anxious flickers across her face, but she nods. "See you then."

Grace

I'm rushing. It's silly, but I hate being late because JJ is so freakishly prompt. It's something I admire about him, yet promptness for me is still aspirational. I'm on time to work by a hair but inevitably, I'm a few minutes late leaving, and therefore a few minutes late jumping into my rideshare car and then a few minutes late meeting JJ.

It's only when I see him standing on the courthouse steps in his service uniform that I *feel* the significance of today. I've been looking forward to this, though it gets me, like everything does lately, right in the heart.

I swipe at a tear as I approach, and he's shaking his head with this perplexed little smile that makes me want to kiss his face off. He reaches for me and tucks me close.

"Why are you crying, Grace?"

He whispers this low in my ear, and it feels so good to be near him, sheltered from the brisk November wind and knowing he's mine. For good.

"I had this crazy-strong visceral memory of how it felt a year ago. How nervous I was and the doubt I had. I've thought about it a hundred times since, but being right here where we dove in... it's just making me so glad we figured out we actually belong together."

He's holding my head in those hands I love, and he swipes his thumbs under each eye to banish my tears.

"Me too, my love. Me too."

His gaze is so steady and clear. He's solid and gentle and persistent and more wonderful than I could've hoped for.

I hadn't lost hope of finding love but coming off my years in the UK and feeling like I'd lost my career, I wasn't focusing on romance. Yes, I'd always had a crush on JJ, but that didn't seem like a factor when Marcy approached me. Honestly, simply having someone tell me what to do, or at least give me a really clear, if kooky, path had been a godsend.

And then JJ.

He turned out to be not taciturn or withholding, but warm and generous. Instead of quiet and stern, he was loving and had the most ridiculous giggle I've ever heard. He's grumpy when he doesn't get his work done and even worse when he realizes he should've had better boundaries with work, though he's trying. It did pay off—he did get that coveted early promotion—but the wisdom gained hasn't been wasted. He's working hard to pave the way forward for himself, and for us. For our family.

And it's this thought that moves me to speak now instead of at lunch in just a few minutes. Why not here?

"I love you so much, JJ. You've been the best husband—fake *and* real—I could ever ask for."

He smiles, all white teeth and gorgeous, sparkly hazel eyes. "I feel the same about you. I've never been more grateful for a meddling mother."

"I can't disagree with you."

We chuckle at that, as we have many times. And trust that Marcy Justice has taken many a victory lap. When we decided to have an actual engagement and plan a wedding reception, JJ sat down with his dad and told him what had happened. To no one's surprise, Jonathon hadn't been altogether in the dark, and had said JJ would come to him when he was ready. Now that's a smart man.

My parents were utterly shocked to learn I'd married JJ, though honestly, they were very quick to get on board once we said we were staying together and going to recite vows and celebrate in the summer. My mom launched into wedding-planning mode, and they are still elated.

"What is it?" JJ prompts, evidently seeing my train of thought wandering around.

And I know I can't hold it in another second. "I have been feeling a little different lately."

His brow furrows and he cups my shoulders. "Are you okay? You have seemed tired. Should you go to the doctor? I know you're a very capable nurse, but sometimes, we're too close to the problem to—"

"I'm pregnant."

His lashes flutter and he stops, blinks again, and then I only see a flash of his smile before he's enveloped me in a bear hug.

"I know you wouldn't joke about this, so I won't ask if you're serious, but this is... this is..." He laughs out a loud, disbelieving sound and pulls back to look me in the eye. "This is amazing, Grace. You've made me happier than I ever dreamed possible. I never imagined having so many good things all at once. "

He kisses me quickly, then studies my face. I swipe at more tears because his response is so enthusiastic and perfect. I wasn't scared he'd be upset or stressed, though I know some stress is definitely on the horizon. It's just his complete joy, and it's the knowledge I've brought him even a small bit of that.

I cup his face in my cool hands, his smooth-shaven cheeks warm and soft in my palms. "You always deserved it all, JJ. Remember? Because of who you are."

He swallows hard and kisses me without another word. After a while, we walk hand in hand down the courthouse steps, retracing the whirlwind of the last year, hearts so full we can hardly stand it, and yet we both greedily embrace it.

Later that night, after JJ has expressed just exactly how happy he is about our growing family and our first anniversary, his phone buzzes for the tenth time.

"Who keeps texting? Your mom and dad had a date night, right?"

We have plans to see them this weekend, so I don't think it would be them unless something has happened.

JJ reluctantly rouses himself from the couch and goes to check his phone. He's gotten in the habit of leaving his phone out of reach quite a while ago. This helped him detach from all the different messaging chats and work-related activities, though it also meant that when he's home, he can be hard to reach.

His brow furrows, and eventually he rears back, then his gaze shoots to me. "It's Gruff. He's freaking out."

My eyes widen. Colonel Gruff has become a good friend to JJ, ironically, and it all started after they had their tête à tête before the new year. I wouldn't have known they were friends until JJ told me because Gruff still acts like he's in physical pain whenever he interacts with other humans.

He even took part in our real wedding last summer, and I don't think he'd ever been grumpier, but then he approached JJ and gave him a big hug and a *giant* gift we're about to take advantage of when we fly first class out to Silverton to meet up with some of his friends and ski at Silver Ridge Resort. Well, I won't be skiing, but I never was going to. I'm a hot chocolate and a book in the lodge kind of gal.

"I can't really picture Gruff freaking out unless it's just him getting more and more silent and irritable."

JJ's rounding the couch, still slowly scrolling through his messages. I feel the first trickle of unease, but then he starts laughing. He's laughing and laughing, and I finally snatch his phone out of his hand to figure out what is so funny.

Oh.

I start laughing, too, because on the screen, the last message he's sent says it all:

Long story short, I need you to be a witness at my wedding. Courthouse. Tomorrow at noon. Bring Grace if you can.

I only stop laughing when I get a text and see it's from Andy. And when I read it, I can't believe it—cannot even begin to believe it. Hers is even more unexpected than Gruff's if possible. It reads:

So, remember that crazy thing I lightly but vaguely mentioned a while back? Well. Um. I know you work but can you meet me at the courthouse at noon tomorrow? I may or may not be entering into an arrangement not unlike the one you did last year...

M.O.M. NETWORK

M.O.M. Network Message board:

SCLDG: Well, ladies. My turn.

Vic: Oh, good grief. Isn't it always your turn?

CoolyKay: Be nice, @Vic. What's happening @SCLDG?

JusticeLVR: I can't say it's unwise. Obviously, it's turned out beautifully for me!

Vic: Yes, yes. We're all so happy and proud etc. etc.

CoolyKay: What's happening, @SCLDG?

SCLDG: It's my son. I've found him a wife. We've all been working on it, and I've lined everything up. Didn't say anything until now, but the wedding's tomorrow. More soon.

Thanks so much for reading I'll Be Married For Christmas! If you're curious about Gabriel and Rae Jackson's story, you can catch it in Don't Stop Now. And if you're curious to see how things play out between Gruff and Andy? Well... stay tuned for their story in Have Yourself a Married Little Christmas ;) Sign up for Claire's newsletter so you don't miss a thing.

ALSO BY CLAIRE CAIN

Veterans of Silver Ridge Series

Small Town Veteran Romance

Love Undercover

Romantic suspense light

Back to Silver Ridge Series

Almost Perfect, Book 1

Almost Real, Book 2

Almost Sure, Book 3

Almost Home, Book 4

Almost True, Book 5

Almost Ready, Book 6

The Silver Ridge Resort Series

Unexpected Love at Silver Ridge, Book 1

Second Chance at Silver Ridge, Book 2

Patrolling for Love at Silver Ridge, Book 3

Fire and Ice at Silver Ridge, Book 4

Soldiers Overseas Romances

Sweet Military Romance

The Rambler Battalion Series

Sweet Military Romance

AUTHOR'S NOTE AND ACKNOWLEDGMENTS

I know my fellow military spouses might've rolled their eyes when they read that JJ was looking to increase his chances of early promotion to Colonel. Getting married is unlikely to be beneficial at that stage of the game, true. So why did I include that little tidbit?

Well, because we've actually heard this at several different points in my husband's career from different superior officers. Nothing official, of course, but an encouraging word to him as a lieutenant about how married lieutenants aren't as wild as the single ones, or as a captain in command and how that meant he could understand and better care for the families in his company since he had a family of his own.

(And then, there's observing the single soldiers taking the brunt of seasonal travel because they don't have partners and kids who'll miss them (oof, this one kills me). This is a very real thing, and while many of the single soldiers kindly volunteer, it's a problem.)

Is this all nonsense? Kind of. Maybe? There are certain circles where not being married might be a disadvantage. But for our purposes, it's just a fun way to force JJ and Grace together courtesy of crotchety Colonel Gruff.

What's that guy's deal anyway? ;)

Thanks for reading and rolling with the silliness. I hope you enjoyed.

Now, onto the thank yous...

Thanks to Genny Carrick, for reading early and helping me think through how to make this what it needed to be. Thanks to Amanda Krieger for being honest and patient with her beta reading thoughts, and thanks to Ashley Bullock for all her support and for reading an early version of the book. Thanks to my amazing neighbor, B. R. Goodwin, for letting me whine about writing and motherhood and all the things.

Huge and endless thanks to my editor, Zee Monodee, for working with me as I quite angstily worked on developing this book into something a little more like a romcom than it had been. Thanks to Amanda Cuff for clean-sweeping this baby, and to Jamie McGillen for catching every little thing and doing it in style from coastal Italia this time!

Thanks to my husband, who has been cheering me on and supporting me in my various career angst and reboots since we first became friends over twenty three years ago. You are the tops, love.

Huge thank you to the ARC readers, bookstagrammers, newsletter subscribers, and facebook group members who have supported my releases this year, especially Suzan, Moni, Brittny, Elise, Angeline, Rebecca, Judith, Rachel, Deb, Joanna, Madeline, Hannah, Becky, Cathi, Abby, and many, many more. You have been amazing and I cannot tell you what your support and excitement for my books means to me!

Thank you to *you* for picking up this book and spending time with JJ and Grace. You're awesome.

ABOUT THE AUTHOR

Claire Cain lives to eat and drink her way around the globe with her traveling soldier and three kids, but is perhaps even happier hunkered down at home in a pair of sweatpants and slippers using any free moment she has to read and cook. Or talk—she really likes to talk. She has become an expert at packing too many dishes in too few cabinets and making houses into homes from Utah to Germany and many places in between. She's a proud Army wife and is frankly just really happy to be here.

You can also join Claire's facebook reader group for exclusive content and fun: https://www.facebook.com/groups/clairecain/

Website: http://www.clairecainwriter.com

E-mail: Claire@ClaireCainWriter.com

Newsletter sign-up for new releases, exclusives, and freebies, including a free book:

http://www.clairecainwriter.com/newsletter

amazon.com/author/clairecain
bookbub.com/authors/claire-cain
instagram.com/clairecainwriter
facebook.com/clairecainwriter
goodreads.com/clairecainwriter
pinterest.com/clairecainwriter

Made in United States
Troutdale, OR
12/02/2023